UNMISTAKEN

A SECOND CHANCE ROMANCE BOOK

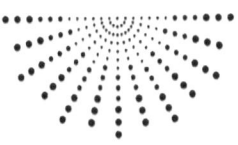

LYZ KELLEY

Belvitri
Services

A SPECIAL GIFT JUST FOR YOU.

I have a present for you…

…your very own ebook exclusive when you
sign up for my newsletter.

Newsletter Sign Up:
https://geni.us/LyzKelleyFreeBook

CHAPTER ONE

Nothing could be worse than the feel of your car's tires spinning and sliding when you hit the brakes. Noelle Conroy eased off the accelerator and waited for the tires to grab on the snow and ice.

I got this.

She turned the wheel into the slide by a few degrees, and away from the sloping bank to the river.

Come on. Turn!

The brakes pulsed under her foot again and again. The car slid around the corner.

With the mountain on her right and a drop-off on the left, she had very little wiggle room. The car picked up speed on the downward slope.

Turn, darn it.

Panic rippled in waves. Snow streaked like bullets through the headlights toward the car. Seeing a mound of snow ahead, she again tried to turn.

No. No. No!!!

The car bounced and jiggled and came to a final rest on top of a pile of snow.

Her orange tabby, Cheddar, who was curled in a tight ball on the passenger seat, stared at her wide-eyed.

"Don't you dare glare at me like this is my fault. You try to drive on black ice and see how well you do." The snow swirled in the beams of her headlights. "I'll back up, and we'll be on our way." The perky positivity in her voice didn't sound convincing, even to her.

Putting the car in reverse, she rotated the

wheels left and right to clear the snow away from the tire path, then straightened the wheels and pressed on the accelerator. The whirl of wheels caused her stomach to churn.

Stinking-singing-monkeys-on-a-stinking-pogo-stick.

She closed her eyes and continued her colorful cursing.

Her prior all-wheel drive stick shift would have come in handy about now. She pumped the accelerator slowly, and rocked her body along with the car, as if by some miracle the extra bit of oomph from her body would help her little car roll itself off the pile of snow.

Nope. Totally stuck. She rested her head on the steering wheel. A breath she didn't even know she was holding whooshed from her lungs.

She peeked at her cell phone.

No signal.

Just perfect.

Stuck in a snowstorm. Late at night. On an icy, rarely traveled road.

"I'll dig the car out. That's what I'll do." She added a heaping load of positive energy to convince herself the idea wasn't entirely insane.

Her orange-striped tabby nuzzled further into the quilted throw but maintained his pointed stare.

"Okay, so maybe surprising Mom for Christmas was a bad idea, but I know she'll be happy to have me home for the holidays. No one else will be there." Thank goodness. She could only take so much of her siblings' whiny negativity. "It'll be great. You'll have a place by the fire. Mom and I will set up the tree, and we'll do singing and baking. You'll love Mom. She'll give you treats. You'll see."

She grabbed her winter jacket out of the back seat of her happy blue Yaris, then paused to tuck the edges of the blanket around Cheddar. Her teeth chattered as fast as a woodpecker pounding on a dead tree.

She stared into the moonless sky. The mountain ridges towered above the car like black skyscrapers, and made her feel small.

What was it she read about being stranded? Should she walk for help? Stay put? And what was she supposed to do if someone offered help? The rules were changing so often, she couldn't keep track of them anymore.

She should never have read C. J. Box's novel about two girls who vanished on a remote stretch of highway. Every time a semi truck passed her during the long drive from Nashville, she wondered if the driver was a serial killer. Just thinking about the book gave her the heebie-jeebies.

"I don't have to worry. I'm going to get this car unstuck and be on my way in a few minutes—

"What?" She glared at Cheddar, trying to guilt the cat into changing the are-you-kidding-me expression on his fuzzy face. "I will, too. Just you watch."

She was reaching for the car manual in her glove box when headlights lit the interior of her car. The possibility of help spawned a relief-terror tug-of-war.

Stay calm.

But what if he's a murderer?

The driver had to be a he. Who else would stop in this kind of weather? Couldn't he just slide on by?

Maybe I should hide.

Find a weapon. Yeah, that's it!

She wrapped her fingers around a plastic fork, pointy end up, then discarded the flimsy object, then checked to make sure the doors were locked.

In the side mirror she watched the tall man's slow approach along the icy road. The blinking of his amber SUV's hazard lights spelled caution in more ways than one. Her hands tightened on the door handle. Her fingers shook with a shot of adrenaline.

When he knocked on the window, a sharp panic wedged in her throat.

"Ma'am, is everything okay?" He bent to shine a flashlight inside the car.

Blinded for an instant, she sputtered, "I'm all right."

"What?" He turned his head to listen.

The stranger's face cast in shadow seemed for a moment to match a menacing serial killer's profile. Dread scraped a pathway up her spine and expanded across her chest. She rolled the window down a quarter of an inch.

"I said I'm fine. Just a little stuck, and I can't get a phone signal." She held up her cell phone.

He tucked his chin in his jacket to ward off the cold, revealing a nice-looking, regular guy. "Yeah," he said. "This is a dead zone."

She wished he hadn't used the word dead, and she wished she hadn't told him her phone wasn't working. Totally a dumb move.

Fear jammed in the back of her throat, and played havoc with her can-do attitude.

He straightened and scanned the area. "We need to get you off the highway. That black ice is nasty, and we might get hit by the next car coming through."

At least you didn't hit me.

His exhaled breath wisped away like a

ghost into the night. "I'll get my shovel and a bag of Ice Melt. We'll see if we can't get you going again."

His confidence allowed her to take a full breath, one she hadn't been able to take since the snow started to fall in an impenetrable sheet of white. "Thank you."

"I'll be right back."

The beam from his flashlight bounced on the black sheen of ice as he made his way back to his car. She zipped up her jacket, got out of the car, and studied the snow packed around the front tire. She dug in a heel and pulled a heavy wad of slush away from the tire.

"Let me help." The nearness of his voice made her jump. "Front wheel drive, right?" She took a step back and studied the bag he'd thrust in her direction.

"You know your cars."

"Mostly," he nodded. "I'll shovel while you toss down the snowmelt."

She yanked her gloves out of her coat pocket, jammed her fingers in, and accepted the small bag while she observed the man.

He seemed nice enough.

And he was trying to help. Not that she was good at accepting help. Never had been. Independent was how she was raised.

"I'm Noelle, Noelle Conroy."

"Conroy?" He studied her for the first time, seeing her, not a stranded driver on the side of the road. "As in Maggie Conroy?"

"She's my mother. Do you know her?"

He leaned back and murmured something she couldn't hear. Then he said, so she could hear, "Everyone within a hundred miles of this place knows Maggie. Those who don't aren't worth much." He blew hot air into his hands and rubbed his fingers together and then extended his arm. "Ethan Brennan."

Brennan? She shook his hand. The name sounded familiar. Her mind tumbled back in time. "There's a doctor in Elkridge with the last name Brennan." *And you're not him.*

Ethan puffed out a hey-neighbor kind of chuckle. "Tom Brennan. He's my uncle."

"Small world."

"Yes it is. Now let's see if we can get you on your way. The road is narrow here, and those snow plows might not see us in time to stop." He shoved the short shovel under the front of the car and pulled away a massive heap of snow.

She'd known Doc B for years. He always carried a supply of cherry lollipops in his pocket, and had treated her strep throat and stitched up her arm when she fell off her bike. She'd never met her biological father, but she wished he would be just like the kind, rural doctor who knew everyone in the county, and took his job seriously.

Ethan reminded her of Doc B, at least physically. He was a little over six feet tall, definitely on the cross-fit side, with a face that, if aged thirty years, would look a lot like her favorite, lollipop-dispensing Doctor B.

For the next five minutes, he dug while she tossed, trying to keep ahead of the snow pelting down.

"Why don't you get behind the wheel? Time to find out whether we can get you unstuck." He jammed the shovel into a two-feet-deep pile of snow, the black handle now barely visible.

She set the half-empty bag beside the shovel, then put a hand on the car's frame to maneuver around to the driver's side safely.

"I think we're good, Cheddar," she said, then closed the driver's side door and rubbed a circle on the windshield so she could see out. "We're going to get unstuck. Just you wait and see."

A face with intense features appeared in the windshield circle. "Straighten your wheels." Ethan placed his hands on the hood of the car and settled his feet into a better pushing position. "That's it. Take it slow."

As if she didn't know how to get a car out of the snow.

Resentment welled up, but she swatted the negativity back down. He didn't know her, and he was just being a guy. Besides, she wasn't going to get stuck in the muck of skepticism like her brother and sister. Nope, life was full of the good stuff, and she would cherish the moments filled with cat snuggles and bubble baths.

As for digging out during snowstorms, she had done it often enough living in the mountain town. Preparing for winter was part of life, especially since Elkridge was so isolated from the populated ski resorts and larger towns in the area.

She pressed on the accelerator, then let the car rock. When the tires caught, she increased the pressure slightly, backing out onto the highway. When she was in a good position, she pulled forward and out of the way of oncoming traffic and flipped on her hazards.

Ethan was already on his way back to his car, as if helping a stranded driver was an everyday occurrence. It wasn't for her. Accepting help was hard, and she was grateful for his no-fuss kindness. "Hey, Ethan?"

He glanced over his shoulder, then turned

to face her as she walked his direction. "Is there a problem?"

"You could say that."

She liked the way he took a ready stance, preparing to help with whatever she needed. "If I get to my mom's place and she finds out I didn't invite you by for some hot soup or a piece of pie as a way of saying thank-you, I'm going to hear about it."

"I'm good." His shoulders dropped and his stance relaxed. "I've got protein drinks in my car."

Her tongue curled just thinking about seaweed and soy and sandy grit rolled into a single swallow. *Yuck.* "Please tell me you don't prefer a cold protein drink to homemade chicken noodle soup with rich, buttery broth and tender, white pieces of chicken breast."

She chuckled when he licked his lips.

"Since you put it that way."

"Great." She walked backward with a little more pep in her step. "I'll meet you at the café?"

"Lead the way," he said, with a slow cadence that reminded her she wasn't in a big city anymore.

The sudden urge to swing her arms and skip came out of nowhere. She didn't, of course. Landing on her butt in front of a stranger would make her look like a dork.

She made it back to her car in time to see him roll up behind her, keeping enough distance to be safe in icy, low-visibility conditions. She adjusted the rearview mirror. Sure enough, there he sat, waiting for her like a gentleman.

It had been a long while since she'd run into his type. She usually fell for the gregarious kind. The life of the party, flashy neon, party-hat type of guy. Ethan didn't appear to be a partier. Much too serious. However, he didn't quite fit any one checkbox. There was something about his guarded way that intrigued her. He was different. Strong, and quietly confident.

Cheddar cried to get her attention. "Yes, I

know." She glanced at the rearview mirror again. "It's your dinnertime, and you probably need to use the litter box." The orange furball stretched a paw in her direction. "Hang in there. Just a few more minutes and I'll get you out of the car. Here, eat these." She dumped out a few treats from the plastic dispenser by Cheddar. He sniffed at the treats, then turned and curled in the opposite direction.

"Suit yourself."

Noelle put the car in gear and skidded her way toward home.

Elkridge sat nestled in the valley between two ridges, and reminded her of an old-fashioned Christmas card, untouched by time. Random lights sparkled across the hillsides, and the cluster of lights in the center warmed her soul.

I'm home, whispered her heart, but she wasn't staying. She still had a dream to fulfill.

She pulled up in front of the café, parked, then popped her trunk. Ethan drove into the space next to her.

"Can I help with something?"

Her breath hitched. In the beam of the café's lights, she saw what she couldn't see before. Below his knit cap was a sculpted face as stunning as any artist could sketch. She loved his chin dimple. His high cheekbones and strong jawline completed the Mountaineer Magazine cover model look.

"I need to get Cheddar."

He tossed the backpack she had in her hand over his shoulder. "I'm sure you can get some cheese or whatever else you want to eat inside."

"Cheddar is my cat."

He pointed an accusing finger at her car. "You drove here with a cat out of its kennel? That's not safe."

"It's not safe to have a scared and pissed off cat, either. How would you like to be locked in a cage for thirteen hours with no way to go to the bathroom or get a drink of water?"

"Good point." As she lifted the cat carrier

out of the back of the car, he took it and said, "I'll wait while you get your cat."

Noelle held onto the side of her car and maneuvered to the passenger door. "Come on, Cheddar. Let's get you inside where it's warm," she said, loudly enough for Mr. Self-Assured to hear.

Keys in hand, she slipped her purse over her arm, gathered Cheddar and his bed, and cuddled the cat to her chest. She beeped the car locked, then shuffled-slid her way to the café's front door.

"Not many people would have stopped on a night like this. Thank you again, Ethan."

"You're welcome." For the first time, he smiled. Not the passive kind people gave while offering a generic greeting, but the real deal. He shifted her backpack on his shoulder. "How long will you be in town?"

"Not long. I'm just stopping through on my way to LA. I'm headed there after the New Year."

He held open the café's door, and she walked into the place where she'd spent more time than anywhere else she'd ever been. An inner lever released the tension holding her body hostage, and she stretched stiff muscles as the rich smells of home-cooked meals and fresh-baked bread soothed her weary body and soul.

"I hope you like LA better than I did," Ethan interrupted her reverie. "The smog is bad. The traffic is worse. The hospital I was working at wasn't a good fit. I was looking for something else when Tom offered me a position. It also helped that he found me a place to stay."

"Elkridge sure isn't LA. Nothing happens here."

"I used to think I needed to be in a metropolis so I could find a cure for malaria, cancer, AIDS—or any major disease. Some way to make a difference."

"And now?"

"Tom's convinced me I only need to help one person at a time."

The look he gave her could melt all the ice on the ridge.

Cheddar struggled to escape her hold, and she pulled him closer, thankful for the distraction. She didn't need to get involved with some doctor. In fact, she didn't need to get attached to anyone. She had plans and dreams to pursue. "Helping one person at a time. That sounds like Doc B."

"How long have you been away from Elkridge? I noticed the Tennessee license plates."

"Eight...no, almost nine years." She brushed a hand down Cheddar's back. "After I graduated from high school, I got restless. There was nothing to do but work in the café. My boyfriend at the time was heading to Nashville, so I hopped a ride, accepted the first job I could find, and started auditioning. The boyfriend thing fell apart pretty quickly once I discovered singing was the only real thing we had in common."

"You're a singer."

He sounded so intrigued, she hurried to correct his mistaken impression that she might be someone famous. "I like to write songs. The singing part I'm still working on. I'm in between gigs at the moment," *because my leech and liar of a manager/boyfriend didn't keep his promises.*

Ethan let the conversation end as the door to the kitchen swung open.

"Sorry, we're about to close...Noelle?" the familiar boom of her mother's voice came from the doorway. "Honey, what are you doing here?" Maggie came rushing forward with a half-smile. "Is everything okay?"

"Hi, Mom. I thought I'd surprise you for Christmas." She shifted the bundle in her arms as her mother wrapped her in an embrace.

"Where's Jon? I thought you were spending the holidays with him."

"That sleazebag." She squirmed under her mother's scrutiny. "You warned me, and I didn't listen. I did my research. He looked legit. Introduced me to a few good industry people. Got me some gigs. Then all of a sudden he needed fee money to secure me slots in some upcoming shows. Then needed money for marketing. I can't believe I trusted that jerk."

Maggie brushed Noelle's long, shaggy bangs out of her eyes. "Oh, honey. I'm sorry."

"Well? Aren't you going to say I told you so?"

"Now why would I do a thing like that when you need room to make some mistakes of your own? You never listened to me when you were young. Now you're all grown up, it's up to you what choices you make."

"I listened." Her voice dwindled into a contrite tone. "I just didn't always agree." But she should have listened. Besides being the best home-style cook in the county, Maggie had a sixth sense that was usually right—about everything.

"Let's be honest, hon." Maggie gave her a direct stare. "If I said something was blue, you'd insist it was green." Her mother's gaze softened. "But, let's not argue. I'm glad to see you. You must be cold. Com'on let's get you some hot soup." Maggie glanced over her shoulder. "Hi, Ethan. What are you doing with that kennel?"

"Your daughter can answer that question."

Noelle looked at her mom. "I skidded on black ice and slid into a snowbank. Ethan helped get me out, and I promised him something to eat as a thank-you."

"Of course. He can have anything on the menu." Maggie pulled back the edge of the blanket. "What a beautiful kitty."

Noelle's mellow boy blinked up at her mother. "Mom, meet Cheddar."

The cheery greeting in Maggie's expression fluctuated and turned murky. "I take it you're not home for a visit."

"I'm meeting a friend in LA. We're trying out for a girl band together. You might remember me talking about Jade. "

"Jade. Wasn't she one of your roommates?"

"No. She's another creative like me." Jade Green towered above six feet. Neon green covered her nails and the tips of her black hair, and cat-eye-like contacts enhanced her don't-mess-with-me attitude.

Jade made everyone take a second look, but no one would dare mess with her. Why she had taken a liking to her, Noelle didn't have a clue. They were as opposite as sociable and aloof. In fact, Noelle wasn't even sure Jade Green was the woman's real name.

"She plays the base guitar in a couple of bands," Noelle added while she checked on Cheddar, to avoid meeting her mother's intense stare. "We met a couple of years ago. She knows the organizer of the group, so there's a good chance of getting the gig. I'll be heading out the first of January." *If I can make enough money to get there.*

The lines of Maggie's face deepened as she scanned her daughter's face. Seconds passed before Noelle's mom put an arm around her shoulders, and guided her to a booth. "Sit. I'll get you something to eat." Maggie gestured to the doctor to sit anywhere. "Turkey club with sweet potato fries?"

He nodded with a grin. "And a Coke."

"Coming right up. Ted?" Maggie's voice blasted through the restaurant like a microphone on steroids. "Turkey stacked with sweets."

"Got it." Ted leaned through the kitchen window and winked. The big, burly man dressed in all black with a white apron could have starred in films as a prison inmate. His scarred face and the snake tattoo circling around his thick neck could make a woman pee her pants if she discovered him next to her in a dark alley. But Noelle had known Ted most of her life. He was a lot like his barbeque sauce—sweet, with a spicy-hot kick. His dark brown eyes softened. "Mighty glad to see you, Miss Noelle."

"Hi, Ted." Feeling a pang of regret for not keeping in touch, she smiled at him and asked, "Are you going to make your famous elk meatballs for Christmas?"

"You know I will."

Maggie continued to roll through the café like a tricked-out Harley—loud and in command of her space. She disappeared through the swinging metal doorway.

The doctor took a seat at the counter and

pushed the napkin-wrapped silverware aside and propped his elbows on the laminated top to thumb through his email messages. Now he'd taken off his coat, she could confirm her previous impression. The doc was one chiseled man—broad shoulders, narrow waist, long, lean legs. She bet he'd look good on one of those marathon running posters.

But she couldn't let herself be distracted. She had plans.

Noelle settled Cheddar and his blanket on the vinyl seat beside her, then gazed past her reflection in the window. "Did you see the look on Mom's face?" she asked her fuzzy orange companion. "I don't think she's happy about me going to LA."

Nine years hadn't diminished her insecurities about never being able to please her mother. She hated being compared to her father—the man who left her mom pregnant and penniless. What kind of upstanding guy does that?—*a jerk.*

She plastered a smile on her face, the one she often practiced in front of a mirror, then glanced back at the manly hunk sitting at the counter doing his best to ignore her, although he wasn't doing a very good job.

"Here you go." Her mother set a steaming cup of chicken noodle soup on the table, along with a wheat roll with real, creamery butter, then slid into the booth across from Noelle. Steam from the rich, fragrant broth swirled into the air before dissipating. "Eat up."

"I was hoping to make it here before dark, but I got stuck on I-70 behind a big accident. Where is everyone?"

"We closed a little while ago. I kicked the locals out to make sure everyone gets home safely. The snow is starting to stick." Maggie pushed a napkin in Noelle's direction. "We're going to need to find you a place to stay for the night."

"What do you mean?" The rejection stung. "I thought you'd let me stay at the house."

"I'm not even staying at the house. Since all you kids said you had other plans for Christmas, I decided it was time to get my floors re-sanded and my kitchen remodeled. I'll be out of the house until the middle of January, and I'm staying in one of the rental cabins out back. All the hotels and rentals have been booked for months, since the usual hordes of vacationers have arrived to ski for the holiday."

"Maybe I can stay with you tonight, then look for a place in the morning."

"You know how small those cabins are. There's little enough room for me, much less you and a cat." She glanced out the window. "Is that your car? It looks so small."

Noelle shifted in the booth and glanced toward the counter, once again distracted for a second or two by a pair of nice, broad shoulders. "It gets good mileage."

"I'm sure it does, but it's not going to get you around safely in this snow. It's expected to snow all week."

Wow. Good thing she wasn't planning to drive straight to California. She'd never make it over the pass with no snow chains for her car and a tank running on fumes.

Maggie's eyes narrowed. Did she spot Noelle's dried hair ends that hadn't been cut in over six months, or her tired eyes, or her coffee-stained T-shirt. She hoped none of the above. She stirred her soup, watching golden broth swirl in a circle so she could avoid looking at her mom.

"Harold has that old trailer, but it's no good in the wintertime. It's got no heat." Her mother spoke the words aloud while her concern lines deepened.

"It's okay, Mom," Noelle reached over and squeezed her mother's hands. "I'll think of something."

"No, *we'll* think of something." The stern words were so comforting. "If I had known you were coming home, I wouldn't have started on those repairs." She drummed her fingers on the table. "I have an idea." She shifted in the booth. "Hey, Ethan. Are you still looking for a roommate?"

Ethan slowly rotated on his stool, looking at her mother over his shoulder. His eyes narrowed, but he didn't respond.

"I overheard you saying you needed to find a roommate, someone to help look after Trapper during the day while you work."

"Well, I…"

Maggie slapped the table. "It's a perfect solution. No one will be looking for a long-term lease this time of year, and I'm sure Noelle wouldn't mind taking care of Trapper while you're at work. It sounds like it will only be a couple of weeks."

Ethan flashed a glance at Noelle as if she'd sprouted antlers.

"Don't look at me," she said. "It wasn't my idea." Noelle tugged on her mom's arm to get her attention. "Mom, this isn't a good idea."

"Why is that?"

"I'm not very good at taking care of people. I can barely take care of myself. You of all people know that." She opened her eyes wider, hoping her mom would get the hint that she didn't want to stay with this guy.

"Hon, that's not true. Everyone you meet loves you."

Everyone except music producers.

"Trapper is a dog." Ethan chimed in.

"Oh...a dog." Noelle's leg bounced under the table, outpacing her thoughts. "Cheddar has never been around a dog—or another cat, for that matter. He might not get along with another animal."

"It will have to work for tonight," Maggie announced, putting the kibosh on further debate.

"Wait a minute." The doctor's eyes clouded. "She can't stay with me." He pointed to Noelle.

Maggie spun around and looked at Ethan. "Why not?"

"Yeah, why not?" Noelle crossed her arms.

"You're okay with this? Letting your daughter stay with some random guy?"

"Oh, hush. You bet I trust the guy who's poked around at my doo-dads."

"You've touched my mom's boobs?" Her head swung back and forth between the doctor and her mom like a Newton's cradle. Her jaw dropped. Eyes narrowed.

He pointed an accusing finger in her

mother's direction. "She had a lump. I sent her for X-rays."

Now Noelle glared at her mom. "Lump? What lump?"

Maggie glared at Ethan and shoved up from the booth. "Isn't there something about doctor-patient privilege?" She adjusted her black apron back into place.

"What lump?" Noelle looked at Ethan for answers.

"Ask your mom."

My mother never tells me anything—especially about her health. What was up with her? Was she sick? Dying? A numbing daze crept over Noelle.

Ethan studied her with a stone-blank expression.

Frustration curled her fingers into a ball. *Obviously I'm not going to get any answers from you.*

First things first. A place to stay.

Mr. Self-Assured couldn't be happy about the prospect of having a female and cat invade his space. Then again, she wasn't quite sure how he felt. He sat motionless, so calm his expression was almost blank.

Unlike her. She wore every thought plastered to her forehead like a billboard display saying, "read my mind here."

The current sign read: Danger. Slippery road. Proceed with caution.

CHAPTER TWO

What the hell just happened? Ethan rubbed his tired eyes, doing his best to stay vertical after his twelve-hour shift. *I can't believe I just agreed to let a woman stay at my house.*

But telling Maggie Conroy to find another option was like telling a herd of deer to stop pooping in his yard or eating his bushes. He'd lived in Elkridge long enough to know once the café's owner made up her mind, not much could change it.

"Is my mom going to be all right?" Noelle touched his arm as he set the kennel in the back of his car.

"You need to have that conversation with your mother."

"My mom never tells us kids anything. You must know what she's like."

When those troubled green eyes looked up at him, he donned his shield of impartiality. "I do. Your mother is like a cabinet filled with medications. She's always there to help ease the pain, but she doesn't come with instructions, and she might have some unexpected side effects."

The little twitch at the corner of her mouth eased the tension tightening across his shoulders.

"Exactly."

Noelle's eyes sparkled with a kinship he didn't want to feel.

She pushed her fingers through the kennel's metal grate to reassure Cheddar and give him a little scratch. "Is she going to die?"

His gut muscles clenched with regret. He hadn't meant to cause unnecessary worry, but he had, and that was on him. He closed the hatchback of his car slowly, then turned to look at her directly. "Someday, but not any time soon."

"Good. That's good." She crossed her arms and drew a circle in the snow with her foot. "You don't have to do this." Noelle's thoughtful yet worried face tugged at his hardened heart. "I have bedding in my car."

"Sleeping in that thing would be like using one of the sleepers at an urgent care clinic, only worse. There's no way to stretch out." He sighed and opened the passenger side door. "Besides, you must remember what it's like to live in small-town USA. Everyone knows everything. If you sleep in your car, my uncle will find out, and then your mom will refuse to make me my favorite sourdough blueberry pancakes."

She thought he was serious, but a speck of humor tickled his throat.

"Believe me, I know how tiny this town can be, but what will people say about us staying under the same roof?"

"Your mom doesn't care." And since he wasn't planning to get within twenty feet of her, he wasn't worried about the short-term situation. "I'm tired, and I can't put energy into what others think. I can handle it if you can."

"It's not like I'm shacking up with a loser."

"A loser?" He swallowed back his annoyance.

"I meant—"

He waved off whatever she was about to say. "Well, at least you don't think I'm a rapist attacking lone women on the side of the road."

Her face lost a bit of her cherry color. "I would never think that."

He leaned in. "Right. When I first arrived, you looked at me like some prison escapee. Doctors are telepathic and know when people are lying."

A curious glaze covered her eyes. "Do doctors take classes or something?"

"No. We watch *Lie to Me.* You might not have seen the television show. The crime drama only ran for three seasons, but we watch the reruns. It was a fascinating show about microexpressions and body language. I was bummed when it got cancelled."

"Too bad I didn't watch a couple of episodes. My judgment is poor when it comes to men, and I'm always the one who's on the losing end. But, I've recently established a no-jerk rule."

"No-jerk rule?" he choked out.

"Jerks are no longer permitted to impact my life."

Ethan scanned her good-natured eyes framed by blond curls peeking out from under her hand-knitted cap, but right now teeming with turbulence and...hurt. She looked adorable, and Ethan could see how some guys might take advantage of her cheery and vulnerable nature, but he wouldn't be one of them.

"I'd better get you in bed."

"Excuse me?"

Her eyes and lips bulged like one of the squeeze toys he kept on his desk to relieve tension. The exaggerated expression seemed adorably funny, especially to his overtired mind. A pebble of joy skipped across the surface of his mind, disturbing the guilt plaguing him for the past three years. His heart pounded a bit faster and flickered to life.

"Look, I didn't mean that the way it sounded. I'm sure you've had a long drive and are tired." He walked around to the other side of his car before he said something else inappropriate. Maybe if she didn't remind him of a cinnamon roll—all sugary sweet, with vanilla cream frosting—he'd be able to think straight. Sure enough, when she closed the passenger door, she smelled even sweeter. Her scent wafted and concentrated inside the car. He cracked his window to freeze his over-imaginative brain, which had decided to take him places he shouldn't go.

"Are you sure I can't make it to your place in my car?"

She wanted to have her car with her, a way to escape, and he didn't blame her. He glanced in the rearview mirror at the pile of stacked luggage, guitar case, and litter box. How she'd managed to fit all that stuff in her compact car, he wasn't quite sure. "Positive." He shoved his car in gear and backed out of the parking spot.

At the edge of town, the fidgety Noelle returned.

"I thought you lived in Elkridge." She leaned forward, looking left and right.

"I do. I live on the ridge." He pointed, "over there. I like the peace and quiet."

She didn't comment when he turned off the main road.

The gravel road steepened and snaked up the side of the hill to his place. When his tires slipped on the ice, he stopped to adjust the traction settings. The vehicle's tires spun, then caught, and began slogging up the hill.

While he bounced from rut to pothole, she peered over her shoulder to check on the orange cat.

"We're almost there, Cheddar."

Noelle's amiable nature was almost too much to handle. She reminded him of his wife. Brigitte put everyone else first, which was why he never felt he deserved her. She took her time with each person, and effortlessly made every individual feel special. The outside world disappeared when she took your hand. He never could put a finger on the pulse of why she loved him, but she did. But if she hadn't been so giving, she wouldn't be dead.

Guilt gripped him, as black and hard as the ice beneath his tires.

Noelle grabbed the door handle while the car rocked back and forth.

"We're almost there."

"I'm good. Maybe you can drive around for a while. Bouncing around like this might make my fitness tracker stop squawking at me to exercise."

The corners of her mouth curled up in tight little swoops. When she got older, those little smiles would bracket her mouth with marionette lines—proof she'd lived her life fully and well.

Back in his twenties, he would have considered her smile cute—and maybe not just her smile. She had an appealing face, with pillowy lips, soft and smooth as a lake in winter. If he were younger, he might consider taking a glide across her amenable mouth, circling to cover every surface. But his older, more conservative self knew the dangers of indulging.

His wife had encouraged him to explore life. Push to the edge. Take risks. She was a balloon filled with helium, and he was the string who kept her grounded. Finding that type of uplifting bliss had been a blessing, one he treasured, if only for a short while. Brigitte was gone now, and nothing could bring her back.

He parked in his regular spot and shut off the engine. "The front door is open. I'll get your things if you want to take your cat inside. Be careful, though. It's probably a bit slippery. I haven't sanded the steps, and Trapper most likely will greet you at the door. I'm not sure how he is around cats."

"You don't lock your doors?"

"There isn't anything in there worth stealing."

Because Brigitte and Callie aren't here.

With kennel in hand, she made her way up the slippery path toward the door, pausing to set the kennel on the wooden porch. Turning the handle, she pushed the door open an inch or two until the fat head of a Rhodesian ridgeback nudged the door open and pushed through the open crack.

"Oh. You're adorable. Look at you." She knelt and let the old guy lick her face. "Yes, I know. I kept your daddy away too long. I bet you need to go potty." She set the kennel inside, and unhooked the leash from its place on the wall by the door.

"He doesn't let other..." *people walk him.*

Trapper trotted after her like he had a new lease on life. Not once did he look back. *How odd.* Just yesterday he could barely get down the stairs.

Desperate to ignore Noelle Conroy's disturbing presence, he concentrated on carting her luggage inside and up the stairs to the second bedroom.

Getting involved with another free spirit, especially one who would be here only a short time, wasn't smart. Well, at least the temporary bit didn't figure into the equation. He had a medical practice and patients to focus on. He was just getting established in the town, and he wanted to keep his feet firmly headed in the same direction.

On his last trip inside, she reappeared. "All done. He's a good boy. He went number one and two, so he should be done for the night."

One and two? He closed his eyes, remembering Callie with Trapper as a puppy. They went everywhere together. His daughter would have said something similar. Callie found humor in the slightest things. A butterfly. An anthill. A weird-shaped rock. She was his energy. His cloud of joy. His light—a light that no longer shed its warm rays on his heart.

He struggled to swallow back the picture book of memories so he could breathe.

"I've put your things in a room upstairs. The sheets are clean, and there's another blanket in the hall closet if you get cold."

"You're being kind, but believe me, I'm just grateful I don't have to sleep in my car. Do you have somewhere I can put Cheddar's litter box?"

"By the back door is a laundry room. You can put it in there."

When he handed her the box, his hand touched hers. The ordinary exchange shouldn't have meant anything, but his hand and arm tingled anyway.

"I want you to know how much I appreciate your help." She took a step closer, then tipped her head to see out the front door. "It's a full moon tonight. It must be my lucky day."

Ethan tilted his head back. "It is a full moon. In some cultures, a full moon is a symbol of transition from life to death— neither good or bad."

Noelle stared at him for a long, silent

moment. "You didn't have to let me stay here, you know."

"Where else would you stay? Your mom is right. All the rentals and hotels are full for the season. And besides, it's only temporary, since you're off to LA with the New Year, right?"

Yeah, keep reminding yourself of that, Ethan. She'll be gone in a couple of weeks. He wasn't interested in another flighty woman who loved to travel and dream and be where the action was instead of being surrounded with friends and family in a safe, stable environment.

"I am. But still."

Her eyes searched his face as if studying a map, trying to find the best route to take. After a few seconds, she shook her head and sighed. "I have friends here. I'll try to find somewhere else to stay tomorrow."

Relief surged and eased the tension knotting his shoulders. Not having Miss happy-happy-joy-joy around would make his life easier. He might just coast his way through Christmas and New Year's if he didn't have to deal with this perky blonde.

Twelve more days. He could make it through the end of the year if he just kept putting one foot in front of the other.

People, whether they realized it or not, had expectations. Like having a conversation, or showing an interest in something trivial. He didn't do trivial. He'd forget important things like birthdays and anniversaries and social commitments. His mother used to tease him that when he was born the only thing left to hand out was smarts, that benevolence and grace were out of stock.

His mother never figured out that he withdrew into his mind because the outside world presented requirements and demands he could never live up to. He was eight when he overheard his parents arguing about how he wasn't trying hard enough—that he wasn't living up to his potential. After that he retreated and focused on his studies, hoping one day he could please his parents with academic success and prove he was lovable.

He bet Noelle had no concept of being socially awkward. She was the brightest light in the room. Just like Brigitte had been.

"You don't have to worry about anything until tomorrow. Feel free to make yourself at home. The kitchen is at the end of the hall. There's only one bathroom, though, but I'll consolidate my stuff before I go to bed. Extra towels are in the hall closet."

Ethan expected her to flee upstairs with her cat, but she seemed content, or maybe undecided about which way to turn.

Did she need directions? "I put your stuff in the second bedroom. It's the third door on the right at the end of the hall."

"Thank you." She scanned his sparse living space. What did she see? A couch. A fireplace. No television. No pictures. No life.

She shrugged out of her ski jacket, draped the hood on the coat hook, then opened the kennel door to watch Cheddar stretch, then make his way into the hall, sniffing each surface as he went. "Do you have any hot chocolate?"

"Hot chocolate?" He did a quick mental inventory of his sparse staples. "No, but I think I might be able to find a tea bag if you would like."

"That would be great. I'll get Cheddar settled."

"The water can be heated in the microwave. I'll leave the tea and mug on the counter."

"I thought maybe you could join me."

"For tea?" Oh, that would be a bad—a very bad—idea. Keeping conversations to a minimum created distance and allowed him to remain disinterested. "I don't do tea. Only beer, and a whiskey once in a while."

"Don't doctors usually warn patients about drinking alcohol before bed?"

Not everyone's seen the horrors I have. "Do you believe everything you read on the Internet?"

Color blotched her cheeks.

"Sorry. That was rude." He massaged his neck. "I should seriously shut up now."

Her mouth curled like she was doing her best not to smile.

The tender expression on her face seemed out of sync with her stated no-jerk rule. He was being a jerk, and there was no reason she should be so polite.

Noelle must be the type of person people smile back at for no reason—a sparkling little snowflake who brought joy to everyone around her.

He couldn't be around a person like that.

Not today.

Not tomorrow, either.

She was just too…too extraordinary, and he couldn't handle being around someone so completely disorganized. Spending even one day around someone who disrupted his stable, predictable life was taxing. Two weeks might just trigger heart failure.

Then again, a social butterfly determined to break into the entertainment business wouldn't want to settle down with a small-town doctor in a place she obviously wanted to escape. He was safe.

"Help yourself to whatever you like in the kitchen. The tea and cups are in the cabinet to the left of the sink." He took a step back, then another. "I need to hit the sack. You probably won't see me in the morning, since my shift starts early."

"I'll make you breakfast. It's the least I can do."

"I don't eat breakfast."

"Let me guess. You drink protein shakes." One brow slid in a questioning arc. "No eggs? Toast? Orange juice?"

He shook his head.

"Why not? Breakfast is the most important meal of the day."

Her attempts to lighten his mood didn't go unnoticed. Having Noelle in his life for a few days might restore a childlike quality to his life, a cherished essential missing for far too long. She might remind him what fun was like. She might take him on an adventure. Fill his life with blueberry pancakes, raspberry waffles, or huevos rancheros. She would naturally want to fill his life with sugar and spice, and everything would be so blissful and nice, because she was that type of woman.

Yes, Noelle Conroy would make him feel something good, even hopeful, and he just couldn't go there. Once in his life he felt fulfilled and blissfully happy. His life had been perfect. Only to be snatched away.

Allowing Noelle to tempt him with her soft smile, warm heart, and sensual curves could create memories, new memories.

"I'll pass on breakfast and say good night."

Without waiting for a response, he made his way to the staircase while he whistled for Trapper. The dog's nails click-click-clicked across the hardwood floor, finally pausing his lumbering gait at the bottom stair. Trapper looked up with a soulful whine.

"I know, buddy. Those hind legs don't work as well as they used to. I'll help you up the stairs." Ethan lifted the dog, and Trapper laid his head on Ethan's shoulder, no doubt watching his newly-discovered friend disappear with every step taken toward the second floor.

Ethan didn't look back.

Just twelve more days.

He just needed to stay numb for twelve more days. Then it would be a new year, and he could start counting the days all over again.

CHAPTER THREE

A pure, emotional song floated up from the kitchen.

Was the radio playing?

There was no band, or accompanying instruments. Ethan stilled so he could listen for a few more minutes, then headed for the stairs. It had to be Noelle.

How had she managed to infiltrate his life in only a few hours?

He hadn't slept. He could hear her talking to her cat. Smell her in the bathroom. The cheery, full-of-sunshine personality he couldn't tolerate.

Ethan ambled into the kitchen. "What time did you get up? Or did you even sleep?"

"I couldn't sleep. So I made coffee." She pointed at the back door. "I found Trapper in the kitchen this morning. I'm not sure how he got down those stairs, but he kept nudging the doorknob with his nose, so I assumed he wanted out. I hope it's okay."

"Trapper won't go far," he mumbled, working to grind out every word.

Morning communication was akin to talking with a wired jaw. Nothing came out clearly. He expected her still to be in bed so he could conveniently slip out the door—avoid any interaction—but no, she was in his kitchen, serving coffee, making breakfast, and letting his dog out. The whole scene was way too domestic.

The circa-1980 clock radio on the window ledge was silent. "It was you singing."

"Did I wake you?" Her blush matched her fuzzy pink shirt and bunny slippers. She pulled an elastic band off her hair, then bundled, twisted, and efficiently wrapped it in a practiced motion. She glanced at him, then back at the skillet. "I like to sing. It's a song I've been working on, and sometimes I get lost in the melody and carried away."

"As in one you wrote?"

She glanced at him. "Song writing is my therapy. Some people do yoga. Some meditate. Some journal. I write songs."

"What are your songs about?" he asked, before considering whether the question would lead to a barrage of information.

"Pretty much everything."

He cringed. That mystical grin of hers, the one that demanded a response, twisted him in knots each time she aimed it at him.

"Love songs, I bet."

"Some. But lately I've been exploring some deeper topics. Life isn't all puppies and flowers, you know. Love is hard —complicated."

Love *was* hard. Too damn hard. His heart shriveled a bit more, and he pushed out a breath. "What topics are you exploring?"

She shrugged. "I'm working on a song

about what it would have been like to meet my father. He died in a motorcycle crash before I was born, and I've always wished I could have met him, at least once. The refrain goes like… 'Would he be my daddy? Would he be the person I hoped he'd be?'"

Her rich, alto tones reminded him of his mother's sweet and savory whiskey steak sauce. She might be brown sugar sweet, but her voice had a certain tang that drew him in and forced him to pay attention.

The notes floated and expanded and transported him to another place. The passion behind the melody was raw—perfect.

She didn't move, just let the music emerge and do its magic all on its own. The song oozed into every nook and cranny of the kitchen, until there was nowhere else for the song to go. When the song ended, she looked at him. He didn't breathe.

The song was captivating.

So was she.

When he didn't say anything, she picked

up a sponge to clean the sink, and the moment shattered into a million tiny shards.

"You didn't have much in the way of food." She chattered on as if the last few minutes hadn't touched his heart. She cleaned, but his brain only translated the melodic chirping of a bird, twittering her morning greeting, full of spirit and enthusiasm. He could hear about every other word, and had to decipher the conversation. Just like the swallow outside his window, he didn't get what she was saying, but he liked the way she filled the silence with beautiful sounds.

He slid onto a stool at the kitchen island and took a large gulp of coffee, desperate for the caffeine to work its magic.

Noelle held a plate in front of her. An expectant look was the only clue she'd given him.

"You want me to eat that?" He pointed at the plate of fluffy eggs, squinting against the morning sun streaming through the normally closed blinds. Maybe if he just kept quiet she would give up and he could get back to the business of being numb.

"You need to eat something." She plopped the plate on the counter in front of him.

He propped his head up with his fist, the curiosity seeping in again. "Why do you care if I eat solids?"

"Everyone needs to eat, especially if you're going to be taking care of other people."

"My protein drinks are full of essential vitamins and minerals."

"And, if it tastes anything like my friend's wheat germ drink, it tastes like sawdust. She has to add yogurt and fruit so she can gag it down."

Her scrunched-up, just-ate-a-lemon face was adorable. Too adorable. "You get used to the taste after a while." He stabbed at the eggs with his fork. "Didn't you say you wanted to look for another place to stay? I do live out of the way if you're here to see friends."

"I would like to be closer to town, so I talked to my mom this morning. She's looking."

Hope made him look up. Noelle was like a moth and he the flame. The sooner he could get her away from the heat the better.

"Did she find anything?"

"She's calling around, but, as expected, so far the places are booked solid."

Bummer. Ethan stuffed a wad of eggs in his mouth, then paused to let the savory bliss of fresh bell peppers, mushrooms, and onions combine with just the right amount of salt and pepper. "Wow. This is good."

Noelle walked to the back door and opened it, automatically grabbing a towel to wipe Trapper's paws. When she leaned over, he closed his eyes to avoid seeing the wonderland of delectable curves and her flawless, sculpted bottom.

"What did you expect?" Noelle folded the towel on the counter. "Maggie had us kids working in the restaurant as soon as we could see above the countertop."

"No. I mean like orgasmically good." The praise rolled off his tongue lickety-split, before his brain fully engaged.

The smile on her face was like watching a kid spoon fresh whipped cream off the top of hot chocolate.

"Orgasmically good? It's just an omelet. I would hate to guess what your sex life's been like if you think that's equal to an orgasm. I could make you my grandmother's flourless cake. Now that chocolate butteriness is truly orgasmic."

If only he could stuff all her cuteness in a paper bag and take it to the urgent care clinic to hand out to the nurses. Those ladies needed an extra dose of smiles and appreciation.

"You're right. Bad word choice," he mumbled, hoping the words came out sounding like an apology.

"Orgasmic is an utterly sexy choice."

He groaned inwardly. Figures she wouldn't let the slip drop.

Sex was technically a bodily function term.

Not something spicy or savory.

Being in the company of a woman who

used "sex" and "orgasm" as non-clinical terms was a turn-on, and proved he'd been surrounded by doctors, nurses, and technicians way too long.

"I need to get to work. I'm sure there are some runny noses and coughs I need to be treating."

He wasn't about to spend the rest of the morning exploring the nonclinical definition of orgasm with a cute blonde. Ms. Perky was sure to come with a set of emotional expectations. She wasn't the type to use sex as a tension reliever. He hadn't been raised that way either, but in Africa he'd changed, adapted. Something about being surrounded by a culture that saw the human body and its urges as sacred, to be honored and celebrated, reworked the way he viewed things. Sex was as natural as the sun rising, and a fun way to relieve tension.

His daughter, Callie, was conceived during one of those steam-blowing-off sessions. He and Brigitte had dated on and off for several months, and eventually she moved into his small apartment, a short bus ride from the hospital. Neither had considered marriage since both their careers were ramping up. But a positive pregnancy test made him reconsider. And when he held Callie in his arms for the first time, his life changed forever. When his precious baby wrapped her small fingers around his, he was irreparably smitten. He swore to protect her—and yet he failed.

He pushed back from the counter.

"Do you mind if I take Trapper for a walk today?" She grabbed a rag and wiped down the kitchen counter. "His back legs seem a bit stiff this morning."

"He's old, but does need his exercise."

"I know he's old. His face has more gray hair than Santa Claus, but I think he'd like to get out, read the newspaper."

"Read the what?"

"Check out who's been in the neighborhood. Dogs like to sniff around, smell what's been going on lately."

I need to get away from this woman. She's too

sweet. Or is it savory? He took another step back. "I usually take Trapper into the office on the days my schedule is light."

"Oh, okay. Then do you mind if I make some cookies and brittle?"

"Weren't you the one lecturing me about diet?"

"Yes, but I always make my grandma's recipes at Christmas. I was hoping you would let me borrow your kitchen since my mom is staying in a cabin that only has a microwave and hotplate."

The remembered, mouthwatering smell of his favorite cookies and treats in the oven made his mouth water. "What about fudge?"

"I make the best peanut butter fudge."

His nose closed in, and his taste buds retracted. "Peanut butter. That's almost sacrilege."

"Maybe you should shake up your life once in a while. It doesn't hurt to try something new. You'll love my peanut butter fudge. I guarantee it."

"If you say so."

A smile lit up her face like a stupid Christmas tree. "I'll make chocolate fudge just for you."

Before he could respond, her orange cat announced his presence, walked two steps, stretched, then waddled his way over to Trapper's bed. The chubby feline licked the dog's head, then nested in between his forelegs for a catnap.

The whole Norman Rockwell scene destroyed his determination to stay numb.

"Feel free to do whatever you would like."

The gratitude in those soft green eyes kicked him in the man parts, and he felt an ache all the way to his toes.

He might have just met the one person on the planet who might give his Brigitte a run for the woman of the year award. His wife had been perfect in every way, and why she loved him, he never understood. She was his rainbow in the storm clouds.

Guilt pressed in as he flicked away the comparison. "Sing. Bake. Makes no difference to me. I'll be working anyway."

"Right. You'll be taking care of those runny noses and coughs." The teasing laughter dancing across her face set off a disturbance in his chest.

"You know," he leaned in close, "it is flu season. You should be careful teasing the only doctor in town."

"You're not the only doctor. Besides, your uncle loves me. He's given me my shots and physicals since I was born."

Another reminder that his uncle had been part of the town forever. Tom was like one of the statues in the town center. Permanent. Strong. Rooted in the community. Ethan wanted to be that person, but somehow he always ended up stranded on the edge watching everyone else. Story of his life. "Come, Trapper. Let's go to the office. I'll shower there."

He took, one, two, three steps before pausing, missing the noise of the dog scrambling to his feet and brushing past him to get to the front door. "Aren't you coming?"

Trapper lifted his head, and nestled his

muzzle on top of Cheddar's stomach, then settled again. Ethan looked from Trapper to Noelle.

"What did you do to my dog?"

She looked at him with more patience than he felt. "Don't blame me. He seems to have taken a liking to my cat. Cheddar's easygoing, and gets along with everyone."

Just like his owner. He studied the two animals curled together on the round fleece pillow in the corner of the kitchen.

Callie and Trapper had been inseparable. Where there was one, the other was never far away. It had never occurred to him to wonder if Trapper might need a companion. Lord knows, he was never there for the dog. Sure, he fed him, took him for walks, brushed him, took him to work on slow days, but he was never really *there*. Trapper reminded him of Callie, and the memories were too close to the surface some days.

Noelle checked the dog's nose and lifted his ears. "There's no heat. He's not sick. He can stay with me today. I don't mind."

Traitor. "Fine, as long as you don't give him any sugar. He gets the farts if he eats sweets."

"Dog farts are the worst."

When she scrunched her nose, she looked so cute the only thought in his morning brain was—*rruuunnnn!*

When he was halfway up the stairs, the singing began again. The pure tone eased a hidden ache inside. He slumped down on the step to listen.

Brigitte was more of a classic rock kind of lady. Everything she did was with big, bold strokes. She lived loud. She crossed boundaries. He'd loved her the best he could, but he never felt like it was enough.

The last time he saw her she'd been restless, fidgety, as if the thousand-square-foot apartment had become too small. Late that morning she decided to take Callie for some last-minute Christmas shopping and begged him to come along. On the way out the door, the hospital called.

He had to go. They needed him. The brilliant Dr. Brennan.

He scoffed at his own importance.

Later, he wondered time and again if he even said goodbye. Why hadn't he gone with them? Why had he chosen his work over his wife and child?

He closed his eyes to see those last few seconds. The picture played over and over and over in his mind, but the rich alto voice from below kept the image from forming. He grabbed the railing to stand.

An ever-present, ever-faithful guilt cut like a scalpel across his vein.

He needed Noelle out of his house.

Actually, he needed to leave. This place wasn't his home. He'd never have a home again, not without Brigitte and Callie.

CHAPTER FOUR

After a shower and a couple of hours spent working on her new song, Noelle decided the snow had melted enough to go into town.

She tossed her purse over her shoulder, then grabbed her car keys, sending a silent thanks to Hank, the local mechanic, for dropping her car off sometime during the early morning hours.

Her mom had been wrong about her car. As long as the streets were plowed and she didn't run into any black ice, she'd be good. Besides a short frame and awesome gas mileage, her little go-go car got her places in most driving conditions—most being the operative word.

"You two behave." The sleeping cat and dog duo, still snuggled in a tight ball of warmth, looked blissfully happy. The pang of jealousy pricked her heart, and she sighed. "I'll be back in a few hours."

The bone-chilling house gave her the creeps. The inside temperature was fine, but the rooms lacked warmth or personality. Why, she didn't know. The doctor was kind and caring, but he surrounded himself with cold colors, devoid of warmth or personality.

On her way to the car she rubbed and blew warmth into her cupped hands to get the blood circulating. Looking back from her car, she noticed the two-bedroom cabin looked like a gingerbread house, all nestled in a grove of trees with snow on the roof. Perfect in every way on the outside, but missing the sugary goodness on the inside.

Ethan was being a gentleman, saying all the right things, and giving her a place to stay, but then why was it she felt as welcome as a fly at a barbecue? Then again, she didn't need to be overly concerned. The situation was temporary. If she could just earn enough for the gas to LA, she'd be heading out of town shortly, and on her way to bigger and better things.

She understood why her mom wouldn't let her sleep on the floor of the rental cabin. The rentals by the creek were about the size of a delivery truck, and small for one person, much less two plus a cat who liked to cuddle. Her mom could only stand cats if they weren't nearby. Knowing Cheddar, he'd most likely sleep on her mom's pillow. Plus, the single wood stove never kept the tiny cabin warm.

However, Noelle didn't need to bother with a heater. The image of the hunky male standing in the kitchen with his messed-up hair and unshaven face was enough to keep her internal heater going for a while. Her mom said Ethan's was her best option—and she believed her—plus, she felt obligated to stay. Everyone needed a little Christmas to nourish their soul, and she loved this time of year. She could contribute Christmas fun at least. Besides, he'd be at work most of the day, and she'd be looking for a job. They would hardly see each other.

She pulled into the River Creek Café parking lot and made a mental note to stop by Hank's to say thanks for dropping off her car, just after she figured out a way to wheedle health information out of her mom.

While she was brushing the snow off her boots on the welcome mat, a shrill squeal of delight greeted her, and Noelle looked up to be greeted by neon pink hair and a giant grin. "Maggie told me you were in town. I didn't believe it," Sheila bubbled, darting across the restaurant like her apron strings had caught on fire.

When Sheila's long arms wrapped around her shoulders, Noelle held on for a moment, soaking up the soothing warmth.

"Girl, I've missed you. Are you home to stay?" Sheila Gill asked, adding an extra giant squeeze.

A surge of contentment circled and tightened. She missed her friends, but she had to keep reminding herself she still had things she wanted to do. "I've missed you too, but I'm not ready to settle quite yet. I'm home for a visit." Noelle glanced around the café, returning smiles to familiar faces.

Snowflakes hung from the ceiling. Candy canes were stuffed in a jar at the reception counter. Sure enough, the Christmas tree of hope stood in its usual spot with donated, wrapped toys for kids in the area piled underneath. Wistful regret swirled in her chest. If she hadn't trusted Jon, her bank account wouldn't be bleeding out because of overdraft fees, and she could contribute, too.

Maybe she could talk her mom into letting her make some playdough. A few jars filled with fun colors and a set of old cookie cutters should make some kids happy.

Noelle slid her hands down her friend's arms. "How's your daughter?"

"Fine. Fine." Sheila tapped her knuckles on the nearest table. "So far so good. The last round of chemo seemed to work. Your mamma's been so good to me, giving me time off to run back and forth to the hospital in Denver. Now we just need to find a way to pay those medical bills. They sure have stacked up to be a heaping load. Your mom's planning a fund-raiser, bless her heart."

"That's my mom for you." The positive notes in her voice didn't match the negative doubts circling inside. Noelle always felt like a disappointment. Her mother never had agreed with her choices. On good days, she'd been strong enough to lie to herself that she didn't care. On the days when she'd failed another audition, the words bit deep. "Where is my mom, anyway?"

"She's in the back. Jenna came over to chat about next week's bakery order."

"Came over? That's right. Jenna bought the old pizza restaurant across the street."

"And you should see the place. She has a whole new line of sweet breads and baked treats. You wouldn't recognize it, except for that humongous oven." Sheila nudged her arm. "She named that old thing Fred. Sorta fits, doncha think? Plus, she put up all sorts of artwork. You wouldn't recognize the place. A lick of paint sure makes a difference."

"I'll stop by, for sure. Besides, I have to get one of her pecan rolls while I'm here. I've never had one better."

The smell of Applewood-smoked bacon, hand-cut potatoes, and farm fresh eggs permeated the air and cuddled around her with the sense of home.

Not much had changed in the years she'd been gone, other than the color of the booths and chairs. The chatter from the locals interspersed throughout the café buzzed like bees around a patch of wildflowers. For a weekday, the café was rather empty. When it snowed, most skiers and snowmobilers avoided the smaller mountain roads, opting to use the wider interstates. Even her mother's famous plate-sized hamburgers didn't tempt them into town.

"I'd better let you get back to work." Noelle took a step back. "Mrs. Bainbridge's arm must be getting a bit tired waving at you to get your attention."

Sheila glanced over her shoulder. "I bet I didn't warm up her pie enough. I'd better check. I'll see you for Christmas?"

"I'll be here."

Sheila weaved through the tables like a car swerving around pylons. Noelle pulled off her hand-knit scarf and looped it over her coat before crossing the restaurant to push open the heavy steel door to the kitchen.

"Hey, Mom. Jenna."

"You win." Jenna looked at Maggie. "She and the cute doctor didn't do the bump and rub. I would have bet a whole sheet of magic bars she would have turned his head. I guess he's still not ready."

Irritation over being the topic of conversation sent a prickle up her spine. "Ready for what?"

"Ready to start dating again. I figured three years was enough."

"Three years? What are you talking about?"

Jenna looked at Maggie. "Oops. I think I'm turning into a town gossip. How disgusting is that?"

"Totally disgusting." Noelle grabbed the edge of the prep station counter. "But don't stop now. Do tell."

Maggie tossed Jenna an annoyed look. "You can't back out now you've stepped in it."

Jenna pushed a strand of hair behind her ear. "It seems the good doctor still has a broken heart."

"He needs surgery?" Noelle looked first to Jenna, then Maggie, for an explanation.

"No. He's scrumptiously fit. However, when you lose your wife and child in a car accident, it seems nothing will mend your heart."

So that's why his place looks like it hasn't been lived in. Ethan isn't living.

"Wow, I had no idea. You say it was a car accident?"

Jenna nodded. "Sad, isn't it?"

"I bet that's why he was so insistent I get off the highway."

"Most likely."

"I can't imagine losing someone you love. *Two* someones must be a gazillion times worse."

"Trust me. It's not easy." Maggie brushed her hands down her apron, then started waggling her finger at Noelle. "Noelle, don't. Don't you dare." Her mother's gaze homed in like she had a target on her forehead. "I know that look, missy. Don't you dare try to fix Ethan. No one can fix what broke him."

Noelle pushed back her shoulders and tried to sound surprised...or at least mystified. "I don't know what you're talking about."

"Yes, you do. You see a broken toy, wounded animal, or sad person, and you do your best to fix the problem, no matter how big."

"Well, that's your fault. You raised me to be compassionate."

"I raised you to help where there's a need. Not everything or everyone can be fixed." Maggie popped the end on her retractable pen in and out in rapid succession. "No sense in getting your emotions all tangled up. You'd just have to untangle them when you leave."

Just because she wasn't going to stay didn't mean she couldn't do something to help. Noelle pulled in a determined breath, her mind crunching through a few options. "Where is everyone meeting for Christmas this year? At the grocery store?"

"Heavens, no." Maggie shook her head. "Harold and Claudia decided last year the space above the store was way too small. We'll be having Christmas here, at the café."

"How many are you inviting?"

"We're encouraging anyone who doesn't have a place to go for the holidays. So far the count is about twenty-three."

"Wow. That's a lot of prime rib. Can I help?"

"Absolutely. And before you poke your nose where it doesn't belong, I've already asked Ethan. He declined. His uncle will be here, though."

Jenna leaned in and winked. "Maybe you can get Mr. Hottie to change his mind."

"Mr. Hottie? Me?" She looked at her mom, then Jenna. "You two know him better than I do."

Jenna laughed, "Yes, but you're the one shacking up with the guy."

Noelle inhaled deeply. "Only because I can't stay at Mom's."

"Sure. Sure." Jenna flicked her hand, waving off the comment. "If it were me, I'd stay with Ethan any day of the week. I mean, just look at him. He's got that handsome, outdoorsy look going, and there's no better butt in this entire town."

"Aren't you married?"

"Yes, but I'm not dead. Besides, I'd like nothing better than for you to try out my new Sin Sugar on him."

"Sin sugar?" Noelle laughed. "I'm almost afraid to ask."

"I've discovered a whole new market for my leftover frosting. I slap it in a jar and label it Sin Sugar. I can't keep the stuff on the shelf."

"Frosting." Noelle's shoulders and arms

pulled inward. "Holy fart-sticks. What are the people in this town going to think up next?"

"It's fantastic, and flying off the shelves. I have six different flavors. I'm thinking of running an ad. Something like, 'When you and your honey play, it's oh, so much sweeter. A flavor for every mood,'" Jenna winked with a bit of wicked added in.

A tingle of heat brushed up Noelle's neck. "I can't believe we're talking about this, especially in front of my mother."

"Oh, hon. I didn't raise you right if you think having sex isn't natural."

"It's not that," she shifted and rubbed her head. "Forget it. I'm changing the subject." She hesitated.

"Well?" Maggie gave her a nudge. "If you're going to talk about something else, get started. We don't have all day."

"Is all the Christmas stuff still stored in the garage at the house?"

"It is. Why?"

She dismissed her mother's scrutiny. "I

love Christmas, and I want to celebrate, even if I can't stay at the house."

Maggie gave her the famous what-are-you-up-to eye. "You rarely come home for the holidays. Scratch that. You rarely come home, period."

"I refuse to be like my siblings and rush back every time I have a problem or need money. I'm getting pretty good at figuring things out for myself."

"You needed money? When?"

Every day since I've been gone. "You're missing the point. You raised me to stand on my own two feet. Look at you, you've made it on your own all these years."

"Oh, hon. If you think I raised three kids and ran a business by myself, you are sorely mistaken. If it wasn't for the people in this town, I'm not sure what I would have done."

"But..."

"But what? Sure, I raised you kids to be tough, but nobody makes it through life without a little help now and then."

"Isn't that why you sent me to stay with Ethan? To help him?"

"No. We needed to find a place for you to stay. Those cabins are small and a bit on the chilly side."

Her mother suddenly looked older. The ball-busting, motorcycle-riding hell-raiser she knew had softened. When did her mother become so mellow? "Maybe you shouldn't be staying in the cabins either."

"Don't you worry about me. It's not your job."

"I do worry. And, what about those lumps the Doc mentioned?"

"Hush. You're embarrassing me." Maggie pulled the pens out of her apron pocket and began sorting for blue and black ink, putting them each in a different pocket. "What would you like for your birthday?"

A way to make you tell me what's going on, and possibly make Ethan smile again. "A job would help. I figure I need about two hundred dollars to make it to LA for tryouts."

"A job. You want a job for your birthday?"

Maggie's brows hitched up a couple of centimeters.

Noelle stuck her tongue out to make her mother laugh.

"If you want to work, you can pick up any shift you want. Take mine. My back aches. My feet hurt. I'd be happy to take the days off."

Since when? Her mom always worked, starting at sunrise to well past sundown. Frustration combined with concern. Her mom looked tired, and much older.

But she didn't look frail. There wasn't a fragile bone in Maggie Conroy's body. Her mother was the strongest woman she knew. "Thanks, Mom. Before I leave the restaurant, I'll check the schedule."

"And if you need some money, I've got a little set aside for you to have."

"I don't want your money. I'm perfectly capable of working. It's just I don't know if tip money will be enough to get me to LA."

Maggie's eyes went a bit misty as she gave Noelle one of her patented bear hugs. "I love you, baby girl. You make this momma proud."

Proud? Of me? "You told me often enough that I remind you of my dad," she murmured, trying to keep the resentment locked down tight. She didn't want to be compared to some drunk loser who didn't even stick around long enough to see his child born.

"He was my Peter Pan. The world was his playground, and he wanted to play." Maggie stepped back. "I need to prep for lunch, and we need to finish this order."

And I need to find more work if I'm going to get to LA and have enough to put down for first month's rent.

A headache started at her temples, worked all the way through her head, and then rolled down her back. She lifted a long strand of hair, weaving it in and out of her fingers.

Noelle's heart jolted when Jenna ran a hand down her arm. "If you don't mind working a cash register, I can always use some help at the bakery—the pay is ten bucks an hour. It's not like waitressing, because there aren't any tips, but it would be fun working together. We're almost like adopted sisters anyway, since Maggie decided to take me under her wing."

And I'm grateful to have someone like you looking after my mom. The kindred whisper eased her heart. "I'll take it. Thank you."

Her mother did, indeed, have a soft spot for Jenna. Not that she blamed her. Jenna's story was amazing. Penniless and lost, Jenna had wandered into town several years ago. Rumor had it her mother found Jenna sleeping on a park bench and offered her a job and place to stay. Her mom would never confirm the story, but Noelle suspected it was true. Her mother was a good judge of people, and knew when to help. That's why Noelle wanted her mother to know she was okay. She'd been raised right, and could take care of herself.

A complicated swell of emotions rolled into her throat and cut off her air. She gulped down a cleansing swish of relief. "When can I start?" she asked Jenna. Then she bit her lip, contemplating her next request. "Would you mind if I borrow a mixer? I'd like to make some of my favorite recipes for the holidays."

"Why don't we work on making treats together? We could even put some out for the customers as Christmas treats."

"That would be fantastic. I could take some to Ethan." Oh, no. She shouldn't have mentioned his name. Both Jenna and her mother lasered in on her like a cat hearing the tuna can open.

"Forget I said that."

"Nope. Not happening," Jenna said with a little friendly nudge-nudge-poke-poke. "If you can find a way to get Ethan to smile, I'll give you one of my Sin Sugar jars. I'm telling you, it works."

Noelle fought off thinking about those delicious dimples she spotted this morning, his messy morning hair adding to the ooh-la-la look.

She reached into her back pocket for her vibrating phone to look at the text. "Please call me, Jon." She deleted the jerk's text, then rolled her eyes and shoved the phone back into her back pocket. "That won't be necessary. I'm done with men."

"I take it that was Jon." Maggie brushed her bangs back as her expression gentled. "You say that now, but when the right one comes along, you'll know it. I never did like Jon. Seemed awfully selfish to me."

"You mean the guy who's so into himself he forgot I was around half of the time? He is selfish. Always wanting to be the center of attention. I just couldn't see it."

"That sounds like an accurate description."

"Mom. Why didn't you say something?"

"It wouldn't have helped. I know you. You're stubborn, and would have stayed with him just to prove me wrong."

That's not true. Or was it? "Well, it doesn't matter anymore. Jon's out of my life."

Maggie puffed out a breath. "We'll see. He's the type of guy who knows when he's been offered a good meal."

"Maybe so, but I'm not his meal ticket." *Not anymore.*

"That's my girl." Maggie squeezed her arm. "Let's get to work, shall we?"

Jenna picked up her notebook full of scribbles. "Do you want to work here today or the bakery?"

"I say bakery," Maggie interjected. "We've got coverage today. Tomorrow is a different story."

"Do you want to follow me over to the bakery, then? I can fill you in on what I need help with."

Noelle pulled her purse higher on her arm. "Sounds like a plan."

Halfway out the door, Noelle realized her mother still hadn't told her what was going on with her health. She'd find out one way or another. If she had to, she'd lay down the heredity guilt thing. If her mom was sick, she'd postpone LA.

Singing was her life, but if it came down to a choice between her dreams or helping her mother, of course she would help her mother.

CHAPTER FIVE

"What are you doing?" Ethan appeared in the doorway of the kitchen.

Noelle held a frosting tube over a counter filled with trees, wreaths, and bell-shaped cookies. "Do you know Jenna? She's the owner of Dreamy Delights." She waved a dismissive hand. "It's not important. Anyway, she loaned me her bag of decorating tips. I'm decorating the sugar cookies we baked today. Do you want to try one? The cookies are a family recipe."

"No. I'm talking about that." Ethan pointed in the direction of the living room.

"Oh, that…" She set the pastry tube on the counter and wiped her hands on the borrowed Dreamy Delights apron. "I stopped by the hardware store to say hi to Bill Mason. He was grumbling about no one buying the tree because it has a bare spot. I suggested someone could set it against a wall and no one would know. I'll admit the tree didn't look as big on the lot." Her smile slipped and then rebounded. "Bill gave me the tree when I told him I was looking to get one for you. There's nothing better than a blue spruce tree for Christmas. Doesn't it smell good?"

"And who said you could set one up in the first place?"

"You did."

"I did?"

"Yes, you did when you told me I should make myself feel at home."

She had a point. That determined smile of hers was like a bottle of pain relievers. She wanted to fix him, make him feel better, but he wasn't fixable.

He went to the arch leading into the living room.

She had indeed set up the tree by the front window, but he could still see the bare spot in the back. A quilted skirt surrounded the base, and several boxes of ornaments sat nearby, waiting to be hung. On the mantle she'd hung four stockings, presumably including socks on each end for Cheddar and Trapper. On the coffee table was a centerpiece of red, gold, and silver balls. The room resembled one of those traditional Christmas cards. Too bad blissfully happy people didn't live inside. Well, that wasn't true. There was at least one joyful person inside.

She lifted a decorating tube. "I just love Christmas."

"Of course you do."

"What's that supposed to mean?"

"With a name like Noelle, I would assume it's your type of holiday." He walked farther into the living room and flicked on a lamp to illuminate the room with a soft light.

Standing in the center of the room, he

glared at the stack of boxes. "You're not seriously thinking about putting all that stuff on the tree?"

"That stuff is my family's precious collection of ornaments." Her eyes sparkled like she was reliving memories of her family standing around the tree hanging ornaments. "Want to help?"

"No."

"C'mon, it'll be fun."

"Who says?"

"I do." She walked across the room and pulled off the lid of the first box. A dark, rich vanilla scent registered as she passed. He inhaled the scent, allowing the vivid essence to mellow his prickly mood.

"Don't be a Scrooge."

"I am a Scrooge." His stubborn slipped a notch, and he struggled to plaster up his defenses. "I don't like Christmas or New Year's." *Or any holiday in between.*

"Is it because you lost your wife and child?"

Oh, please tell me you didn't just go there. If it

was Maggie... He closed his eyes and started counting the number of sutures he put in his last patient.

"I'm sorry. I didn't mean—"

He opened his eyes. The sorrow in her eyes about did him in. "I figured someone would tell you sooner or later." When the resentment eased back from a boil to a simmer, he asked, "What did you hear?"

She shrugged and tugged the edge of her apron. "Only that your wife and child were in a car accident sometime around Christmas. It's understandable for you to hate this time of year."

He didn't just hate the holiday. He hated every day. Every day memories surfaced of his little girl riding her bike, or his wife studying at the kitchen table, or the family on a tropical beach vacation. As hard as he tried, he couldn't block the memories. He couldn't even have pictures of Brigitte or Callie around. It was just too painful.

He debated whether he should just leave and let her hang ornaments, but he collapsed into the leather chair, taking the weight off his sore feet.

"You look exhausted. Would you like me to make you something to eat?"

"You don't have to wait on me, but if it will make you happy, sure."

She looked ridiculously pleased. Guilt didn't help ease the ache in his shoulder muscles. She hurried toward the kitchen, and he swore there was a skip in her step. As soon as the refrigerator door opened, she filled the house with the sweetest melody. The full, ripe quality of her voice soothed his never-ending desolation.

Although tired, he felt stronger than he had in months. The dark memories paralyzing him with remorse and guilt had receded. He expected the memories to resurge in the early morning hours, but Noelle's feminine scent and presence had kept the doom and gloom from closing in. She smelled like a county fair caramel apple. Even Trapper's behavior was different since Noelle arrived. More content. Less decrepit.

What was it about her that forced him into the present, kept him from sliding back into the robotic world he called life?

"Your dinner's ready."

He glanced at his watch to check the hour, surprised time had actually passed. "Thanks. I'll be there in a minute."

With a stranger and a cat living under the same roof, he'd expected to feel unbalanced, but he wasn't. She lived a noisy life, but he wasn't disturbed. Her presence was comfortable, even if a little bit messy.

He pushed up from the leather chair and walked into the kitchen. Trapper sat watching her with eyes full of hope.

"No more." She pointed to his pillow in the corner. "You've had enough turkey. Go lie down."

Trapper bowed his head, then slowly meandered over to the pillow, looking back a time or two, then circled twice before collapsing onto the fleece with a conspicuously pitiful groan. Some time during the day a small, colorful ceramic dish had appeared next to Trapper's metal bowl. He recognized the colorful daisy design as Callie's grade school creation, but he decided not to mention the connection.

He slid onto one of the stools at the island, content to watch her navigate the kitchen. "Where's your cat?"

She set a plate of food in front of him. "Cheddar? He's upstairs sleeping." She reached into a cabinet for a glass.

"There's green stuff on this sandwich."

"Eat it. It's not poison. I love the turkey, Havarti, and pesto. The combination is perfect. I made the pesto fresh with your food chopper. Hope you don't mind."

"You made pesto?"

"Harold didn't have any at the store, and the basil looked so lovely. I'm not sure where he got the herb this time of year, but I don't care. Ted allowed me to raid the café's pine nut stash, and voilà. Pesto. It's not that hard."

"I wasn't questioning your ability to cook. It's just I've never been around someone who doesn't make meals from a whole bunch of cans and jars, or pulls out something previously frozen."

"How can that be? You're a doctor. Doctors are supposed to eat healthily."

She said the word doctor like there was some kind of lofty expectation that always accompanied the profession. "I do eat healthy. My protein drinks have all the vitamins and nutrients I need."

He took a bite of the sandwich and reluctantly admitted the titillating combination was quite pleasant. The pesto reminded him of the color of her eyes. He took another bite, and another. Her irritation over his food choices made his muscles ease into the consistency of warm honey.

She cared.

How refreshing. And unsettling.

He counted the geometric patterns on his plate to avoid the circulating feelings. "Doctors are on call 24/7. We don't always have the time to eat and exercise the way we should."

"When taking care of people, you need to set an example."

"Is that so?" He kept his voice level, even though something on the inside of his chest cracked open, and he wanted to chuckle at her scolding.

"Listen to me. I'm starting to sound like my mother. She loves to nag."

He liked that her bold announcement came loaded with good intentions. "Maggie is an amazing woman, just like her daughter."

Her arms suspended in the air. Her mouth hung open. She didn't move, and his mind did a rewind.

How had he let that compliment slip? If he was trying to encourage her to leave, accolades didn't help. He gulped down the remaining bite of the sandwich, then pushed back from the counter. "I'd better take a shower."

"Wait. Aren't you going to help me decorate the tree?"

Trapper gave him a don't-be-a-loser stare. "One box, but that's all."

The squeal of joy and rushing footsteps caught him unprepared. She threw her arms around him. He stumbled back a couple of steps to find his balance, stiffening. He didn't have anywhere to put his hands except around her small waist. He could feel her warmth, and her curves. At least his knees locked, or they might have both ended up on the floor.

"Oh. Sorry. I just got excited."

He slid out of arm's reach. "Don't get too excited. It's just one box."

"I'll take it."

He groaned. He never should have agreed. Snared like a rabbit, he had no way of getting out. "I'm not very good at hanging ornaments. I could break one. Maybe I should just go take a shower."

"Nope. You said one box, and I'm gonna hold you to it."

The weight of expectations poked at the already tense knot in his shoulder. "Why do you like Christmas so much?"

"It's the most magical time of year, that's why."

"You believe in miracles?"

"Yes. Don't you?"

I used to, once upon time, in a land far, far away. He remembered the nights with Callie curled against his side as he read aloud her favorite storybook. He popped his knuckles, one at a time, letting the jolt in his body bring him back to the present. "Let's get this over with."

She pranced back and forth like a kid waiting in line to tell Santa Claus everything she wanted for Christmas. "You pick out a box, and I'll warm the cider."

"Cider?"

"You can't hang ornaments without hot cider and Christmas carols."

Oh, jeez. "Let me guess. That's one of your family's traditions, too."

"Every year. On the Saturday before Christmas, my family would gather around the tree and load up the branches with ornaments. My siblings and I would fight over who got to put what ornament on the tree. The next day, Mom would stack the packages under the tree. She went to great lengths to make sure we were surprised."

"Did you ever guess what your mom gave you?"

"Sometimes, but Mom was good at disguising gifts. She'd put them in odd-shaped boxes, or put a smaller package in a larger box."

"That sounds like my mom." He leaned a hip against the counter. "My mom couldn't wait to start decorating. She wanted the tree up the day after Thanksgiving, so Dad would haul up the tree bag from the basement while the rest of us went shopping. After dinner, we were all required to stick around and decorate."

"You had an artificial tree?" Her face collapsed into distaste. "That's not very Christmassy."

"My dad was worried the dogs would knock over the tree, and my mom didn't want needles tracked everywhere. I thought the whole idea of decorating rather pointless."

"It's not pointless. It's fun. And it brings people together."

Not in our family. "You think hanging ornaments on the tree will bring us together?" Anxiety clutched at him. "I didn't mean us, specifically. I mean us, meaning the community sort of us." He shoved his fingers through his hair.

She picked up his empty plates and brushed the crumbs into the sink before loading them into the dishwasher. Then she scrubbed the sink, her sweeps of the sponge becoming smaller and more desperate.

"Noelle?" He placed a hand on her back. She jerked and let out a soft squeal. "Please, look at me."

She replaced the sponge on the sink ledge and turned, knotting her arms in a tight weave across her chest.

"I'm sorry. Holidays are hard for me."

"I get that, it's just…"

"Go on. Say what you were going to say."

"Last Christmas I spent the holidays alone. All my friends and boyfriend went home for Christmas, and I stayed to earn money, taking extra waitressing shifts to save for studio time. Being alone for the holidays was one of the worst decisions I've ever made. I was there in my apartment, with only a cat for company, and it just sucked. When I called home, Mom had a houseful, and I've never felt so alone in my life. I made a promise to myself that I would be surrounded by people this year. Although at the time, I thought I'd be in my apartment having all my friends over. You shouldn't be alone for Christmas... no one should."

"I told you I'm a Scrooge."

"You are, but this year you can choose to be different."

"What if I don't want to be different?"

"Then you can live a lonely, miserable life. But I've never met a doctor who's miserable."

The statement startled a curiosity. "Are you miserable, Noelle?"

"I'm doing my best to find my happy, and

so should you. What happened to your family sucks. You're a wonderful guy, and don't try to tell me you're not. People all over town have told me stories about how you helped rescue a dog, or took groceries to Mrs. Bainbridge after her surgery. You stopped to help me when you could have driven past without a second thought. You deserve better."

His face pulled into a skeptical frown. "Maybe I'm doing those things to make people think I'm nice. I might be the biggest jerk on the planet, and you have a no-jerk rule, remember?"

"You're not a jerk. I know you're not. People like you. And Trapper is the sweetest dog I've ever met. Jerks don't have sweet dogs. That's a fact."

"Where did you read that? On some blog post?"

"No. I read it in a magazine."

"It must be true then. I bet it had the title, 'How to Spot a Good Guy in Thirty Seconds or Less.'"

"Now you're grumpy."

Her smile was so warm and fun and gracious. She resembled a cartoon with those big green eyes full of hope. And he was being a grump, although he probably should have used a stronger word.

"Believe me, I'm not one of those cute little dwarfs everyone loves. I might be a Doc or a Sleepy, but I wouldn't say Grumpy."

"Grumpy is rather cute, even if he is a bit pouty."

"Now I'm pouty."

She rolled her eyes. "Never mind. Why don't you pick out the box of ornaments you want to put on the stupid tree?"

"Now you're even calling the tree stupid."

"Has anyone ever told you you're difficult?"

"Certainly. Most of my patients. Especially when I follow up to make sure they're doing their exercises, or taking their meds, or giving them news they don't want to hear."

"I'm starting to understand why there are

very few women in your life. I can't imagine you date much."

I've never figured out a way to be lovable. "Dating is overrated. Now when it comes to sex, I've had plenty of offers."

Her eyes opened a bit wider. "Oh. Really?"

As old as she was, she still had an idealistic naivety, a belief that life could be perfect and wonderful. He crossed his arms. "Really."

"And what have you done about all those many offers?" Her brows lifted in a doubtful arc.

"Are you questioning my abilities?" He crossed his arms and leaned in. "I can still please a woman. I may not be Superman, but I'm no Lex Luthor."

"I'm sure you can. You're smart and talented when it comes to reading people. You adapt, move, change subjects. And you're going to block and deflect and fight this Christmas thing all the way to the new year, aren't you?"

She saw right though his defenses.

The disappointment staining her cheeks

wasn't hard to miss. In fact, her emotions were like her sweater—bold and bright. He could see every shifting mood.

"Probably. It's become habit."

"Well, Doctor, you're in the business of changing bad habits. Change yours." Her shoulders dropped, and her head tilted a bit sideways. "And forget the ornament thing. It's not important. What is important is you discovering the life you want to live. You should focus on that."

"I ruined your Christmas."

"No. You didn't ruin my Christmas. You ruined yours."

There was that sign again. The one that said Not Good Enough = Unlovable.

She made her way out of the kitchen and into the living room. Trapper gave him one of those disgusted looks and followed Noelle.

He huffed out a frustrated breath. "Well, crap."

CHAPTER SIX

Noelle attached the snowman ornament to the prickly branch. The cute crossed eyes and wonky smile tickled her mood, but the happy moment didn't gain traction.

The conversation with Ethan had dampened her spirits. She crossed her arms, pulling inward, tucking her chin in the folds of her chenille turtleneck for comfort.

Isolated from family and friends, she settled on the couch and questioned where her life was headed.

Pulling her guitar into her lap, she strummed a few notes, until the random strumming rolled into a familiar sequence of cords. The melody eased into her skin note by note, tapping into the buried pain, hurt she rarely allowed to show. The pain of never knowing her father, never quite fitting in, pushing to find happiness but never quite getting there. She closed her eyes and let the raw emotions surface. The personal, unfiltered song expanded. She let it build. Feeling the power until she felt full again. Then she let the song slide back into a strumming of notes until only the vibration of the strings remained.

She bowed her head and took a long, deep breath of renewed energy. Meditating again on where her life might be going.

"That was incredible."

She twisted toward the stairs but remained seated. "I thought you were in the shower."

"I was."

She set her guitar aside, then leaned over to select another ornament from the half-empty box. Yanking on the edge of the paper, she unraveled the tissue, revealing a reindeer with red and green colored lights wrapped around his antlers. The hand-blown glass reflected off the glow of the tree lights. Her mother had attached the fragile ornament to her seventeenth birthday package. She loved the whimsical lines and artistry of the design. She always hung the deer front and center.

"May I help you with that?"

She studied his doctor's mask, so carefully devoid of feeling. "It's okay. You've told me enough times you don't like Christmas."

"About that." He walked around the corner of the couch, then sat and studied the tree. "The year Brigitte and Callie died, I was working a lot."

He frowned and rubbed the edge of his thumb. When he started talking again, his voice sounded muffled and slow, like he had to drag it out of himself. "We were testing a new AIDS drug, and I was in charge of administering the trial medications and adjusting the dosage. New developments were happening every day. I was working around the clock to carefully monitor the effects. Callie begged us to put up a tree, but her mother and I were busy seeing to patients. We were going to save the world.

"A couple of days before Christmas, Callie came to our bedroom. She'd been crying. She wanted to know if we loved her anymore. In her mind, we only had enough love for the children at the hospital. The next day, Brigitte and I decided to take off work to go shopping as a family. I don't know why I answered the phone. I shouldn't have. It was the head of the study. I was needed at the hospital." Ethan pulled a hand down his face, then rubbed his eyes, then his jaw, then let his hand fall to his lap. "I never saw my little girl again. If I could just take that one moment back, change things." He slowly raised his head. "I'd buy her presents, put up a tree, make her favorite pancakes, and I sure as hell wouldn't answer that damn phone."

Her chest ached with sorrow. For the man. For the father who would never be able to hold his child again. "And because Callie didn't get her tree, you can't have one either?"

"You don't get it."

"You haven't told me what happened, only that you were doing critical, important work. So you are right—I don't get it, but I would like to."

His eyes darkened with intensity. "Nothing, and I mean nothing was more important than my family."

"I get that, but you were saving lives."

"I helped people who were HIV positive live longer. There's a difference."

"Is there?" Noelle lifted an arm, wishing she could hold his pain—take it away. "Life has no guarantees. You couldn't have predicted what was going to happen."

She reached a bit farther, wanting to touch him, let him know he wasn't alone. "I'm just asking a question. I get that you loved your wife and daughter, and I would never want to take away from those cherished memories. They are yours to treasure."

He pulled further inward and her heart

wept. She wanted him to hear her. Reach out. Be comforted. "But you shouldn't punish yourself for the rest of your life."

"Oh, yeah?"

Oh, Ethan. "So, what? You're just going to keep on working, punishing yourself for what happened. Tell yourself you don't deserve to be happy?"

His jaw muscles pulsated and his eyes deepened with rage. "You don't know me."

"You're right, I don't, but anyone with a pair of eyes can see you're in pain. I just want to do something—anything—to make you smile again."

"And you think decorating a tree would help."

She could see the wall he was building, brick by brick, made of self-recrimination and guilt. If she could distract him long enough, maybe he would reach out. Connect.

"I do." She studied the precious glass in her hand before she extended her arm. "You can start with this one."

Like a robot, he accepted the ornament

from her hand, stood, and walked stiffly toward the tree. Yet when he reached to the top branch, his actions became softer, more fluid. His breathing relaxed.

She handed him another precious memory wadded in an old paper towel.

She stepped back to appreciate the splendor.

His hair was combed back in tracks of wet strands, still not dry from the shower, but he hadn't shaved. And she was glad.

She reached for another ornament, just as her cell phone buzzed in her back pocket. Noelle brushed a thumb across the screen to display the message.

HEY, *Sugar Cube. I want to wish you an early happy birthday. Miss you. Love Jon.*

"OH, NO YOU DON'T," she muttered. She deleted the message, then tossed the cell phone onto the coffee table. Ethan glanced at her and then the phone.

"Boyfriend?"

"Jerk of the century."

"That bad?"

"Worse. He started texting me this morning. I'm sure it's to ask for more money."

Ethan retrieved another ornament from the box, slowly unwrapping it in his hand. "Here. This one's for you."

In bold red lettering, the ornament read, *Go suck your candy cane.*

The sound of something between a huff and a chuckle made her look up. Was that a smile? It was. His eyes sparkled, and his mouth seemed to have stretched and curved into shape. The tree behind him framed his face in a halo, and his amusement was infectious. Joy filled her empty crevices, brightening the gaps.

"You deserve better, Noelle."

"I know. And so do you." She hung the red ball on a lower branch. "There was nothing left for me in Nashville, so I left. I thought if I could start over somewhere new, things would get better."

"Tom told me you left Elkridge to become a singer."

She coughed out her surprise. "Seems I'm not the only one who's been listening to rumors."

Ethan blushed and shoved his hands into his pockets. "You gave me something to talk to my uncle about."

Interesting. "And just what did your uncle have to say?" She could only imagine what the blush was about.

"Not much. He just said that after high school you went to Nashville for tryouts."

"Tryouts. That's pretty accurate."

"You didn't get to sing?"

"Oh, I sang. I worked every angle I could. I paid my dues by working on the streets, in bars, and at local fairs, but nothing big ever came along. Jon, my manager, said he was working on a new record deal, but the whole spiel was just another one of his lies."

"Jon. The guy who sent you the text?"

"Yep."

"Your manager was your boyfriend?"

"He introduced me to people, got me some gigs, set up my schedule. Little did I know all he was doing was getting in my head to the point I would believe anything he told me. One day I turned around and my bank account was empty, and he'd moved on to do the same thing to someone else. I filed a police report, but the detectives said they couldn't do anything since we were essentially living together. I can't believe I was so naïve. Since my lease was up at the end of the month anyway, I sold everything I could, gave away the rest, packed my car, and left."

"Sometimes it's hard to know who to trust." His eyes flickered and flattened and the lively humor evaporated.

She couldn't help but think he was talking about his wife, which was odd, since he loved her. "We've known each other for less than two days, but if you ever want to talk, I'm a good listener."

"I'm a pretty good listener myself." He

picked up another wad of tissue from the box. "What happened with Jon?"

A turbulent vibration started in her heart and stung and bullied its way up to her throat. "I don't know."

But she knew exactly what happened. If she opened up, confided her stupidity, would he open up as well? She took a deep breath for the courage to lasso the hurt. "Jon, I suppose. He was funny and spontaneous. He was older, had money, and took me places I'd never been before. He pampered me. I felt pretty. Protected. Safe. We connected on some deep level. He was a creative like me, and I thought he got me."

"Sounds like a sociopath to me."

She exhaled a faux laugh. "Now you mention it."

"So what's next?"

Enthralled by the question, she wiped the emotional slate clean. "I'll do what my mom raised me to do." She pointed at the top of the tree. Ethan accepted the dangling ornament from her hand and hung it exactly where the little chipmunk belonged. "I'll pick myself up, dust myself off, and start again."

"Sounds like good advice." He studied her face the way he'd studied the last ornament he hung. Thoroughly. "So why don't you stay in Elkridge? Get your feet under you?"

What would I do here? Dreams of singing onstage, of hearing her song on the radio, pushed everything aside. "Nope. As soon as I get enough cash, I'm heading to LA. There's a good chance I'll get a slot in this band. It's my turn. I've paid my dues. I've worked hard."

There was that faint curling of the mouth again. "You've got an incredible voice."

"But..."

"But nothing."

Wow. There was always a but. Could it be he believed? Believed she could make it singing?

Man, she could kiss him.

A tranquil feeling settled over her. She stared at his lips, wondering how they might feel against hers. Would they be gentle or demanding? Instincts told her they'd be a little bit of both. She took a half step closer, found herself leaning forward.

The lights from the Christmas tree created a false intimacy, a fairyland of feelings that might dim in the light of day.

He stilled and seemed to pull in on himself. "Maybe we should call it a day. It's time for bed." His voice was soft, husky, deepening the sense of magic.

Was he giving her an out? What if she didn't want an out? "Are you asking me to go to bed with you?"

He brushed a thumb across her cheek. "No. That wouldn't be a very good idea. In fact, it would be a horrible idea. I'm no good for you, Noelle. Hell, I'm not good for anyone."

"That can't be true."

"Trust me on this."

He handed her the ornament in his hand, then took a step back. "Good night, Noelle."

CHAPTER SEVEN

"Hey, Tom." Ethan gestured for Trapper to sit. "Where is everyone?" He glanced around the office waiting room, which was normally full of people.

His uncle tipped his head down, glancing at Ethan over the top of his reading glasses, then placed the medical chart on the top of a teetering pile of files. "I decided to close the office and give the staff the rest of the year off."

"What?" Panic welled in Ethan's chest. "Why would you do that? What about all the patients?"

"All appointments have been rescheduled for the new year." Tom's gaze pulsed like radio waves, scanning, evaluating like an MRI machine, revealing Ethan's anxiety about not being able to work. Right now he needed the distraction of focusing on every little detail in a patient's chart so he could stay busy and numb.

"Why don't you take time off?" Ethan offered. "I can cover the office."

"Everyone needs a rest, Ethan. We only had a couple patients scheduled for general office visits, and each one said they could wait until January. Plus, between the two of us, we were only scheduled three days at the urgent care clinic. That new resident who moved here last month is looking for some hours, so I told him he could have ours. It will help him get settled in."

The seasoned doctor was like a bear in hibernation. Once he decided where to settle, nothing moved him from his spot.

"What happens if there's an emergency?"

"Then I'll handle it. Just like I always do.

Aren't you the one who complains you never have enough time to catch up on your reading? Now's your chance." Tom handed Trapper a doggy treat and patted him on the head before the corners of his eyes creased with concern. "Why are you fighting this? I thought you'd be happy to get some rest. You've been going nonstop since you relocated here."

"You know as well as I do there's always work to be done at the office."

Tom pushed his readers to the top of his head and glared at him. "Just as you know you can't work fourteen to sixteen hours a day for weeks on end and still be truly effective. I made the decision. The staff needs time to enjoy their families."

Family. Maybe that was the problem. His patients were his family. He'd gotten to know Patricia and Margaret Bainbridge and, come the new year, Patricia's sugar levels would be out of control. She couldn't resist eating her niece's homemade cookies. Then there was Bill Mason. He'd be in for back pain. He just couldn't stop helping others dig out their car or truck. He was always overdoing it. Plus, he should check up on Stella King to see how her new heart medication was working for her.

"You're right, the staff needs time off, but I don't." Ethan tried again. "What about the new billing system we're putting in? You said we need to upgrade all the medical scripts. Why wait? I could get started on it today."

"Nice try, but the software won't be installed until January."

Ethan bounced his fist on his thigh. "Then how about—"

"No. This conversation is over." Tom then rolled out his best doctor-patient intimidation tactic. He pulled his readers off his head, plunked them on his nose, and proceeded to ignore him.

"What?" Ethan crossed his arms. "Are you going to ignore me now? I'm not one of your patients."

"Maybe you should be."

"What's that supposed to mean?"

Tom crooked a finger over the bridge of

his glasses and pulled them down to the tip of his nose. "You know full well. Come December, you start working more hours, stop eating and sleeping. You're a brilliant doctor, and in high demand, and people let you work yourself into the ground." Tom matched Ethan's cross-armed ante and raised him a frown. "Well, not this year. This year, you'll take time off. Reflect. Figure out what's what. Doctor's orders."

"You mean about Brigitte, Callie, and the baby? I still don't understand why Brigitte didn't tell me she was pregnant."

"Have you ever thought that maybe she didn't tell you because you didn't want to hear it?"

Ethan sucked in a mountain of air. "You don't know what you're talking about. You weren't there."

Trapper sat on Ethan's foot and nudged his hand. He reached to soothe the dog's ear.

"I don't know what I'm talking about? You sure? I seem to recall about the time you started grade school you began to close yourself off. With every passing year, you had less to say. You started building barriers. Pushing people away. Rebelling. First with your father. Then your brothers. Finally your mom. Why do you think you were sent out here to stay with me for the summer between your junior and senior year of high school?"

Ethan remembered that restless summer. Tom had worked him from sunup to sundown, clearing logs off the parcel of land where the cabin now stood. It was hard work, but it managed to work the rage of trying and failing over and over and over again out of his system.

Tom helped him see he could accomplish things, and that someone he respected would appreciate his efforts, even if his parents never did.

Ethan scratched under Trapper's chin. "I learned a lot that summer, thanks to you."

"But you didn't learn the lesson I wanted you to learn. You found solace in your studies. You even convinced your dad you could get better grades in college if you lived alone.

Don't get me wrong, Ethan, you're an amazing doctor. Brilliant. You heal people. And they love you for it. But that's not real love."

Years of stubborn resentment fought against the rational. "What lesson did you want me to learn?"

"I wanted you to learn to love yourself. Love who you are, not what your parents want you to be."

Maybe he didn't know how to love. He'd been angry as a little boy. He watched his friends' parents hold hands and sneak a kiss when they thought no one was watching. But not his parents. His parents were about as sterile as a medical tray. They never raised their voices. There was no passion. No love. Even his younger brothers felt the absence.

The void of feeling felt scorching.

As a teen, when he couldn't stand the isolation, he tried justifying and compartmentalizing, and when that didn't work, he became numb. Apparently that wasn't working for him either.

"You're right. Brigitte tried to help me figure out how to let go, to love and be loved. If I had placed family above my work and let someone else take the emergency call that day, my wife and both my children might still be alive."

Tom pulled a couple lollipops out of his shirt pocket, and offered them to Ethan. "You don't know that. You need to stop beating yourself up about something you had no control over."

"I'm not discussing my marriage again." Ethan selected the lemon-lime flavor. "Not with you. Not today." *Not happening.* "I think I'll go make house calls. Check on some patients."

"I knew you'd feel that way, so I've checked on most of our patients already. There's nothing left for you to do except enjoy the holiday season. Now get out of here and start enjoying life."

"I *am* enjoying my life." He pounced on the word *am* hard and fast, as if trying to prove to himself he knew what he was talking about. "I'm doing what I love to do."

"Yes, but being a doctor and caring for your patients, versus having a family who nurtures and supports you are different. Trust me, I know. I thought being a doctor was enough. Let me tell you it's not. There are days when I arrive home and it feels like I'm walking into a jail cell. Life gets lonely. Trust me on this."

"Then why don't you date, or find someone special?"

"I could ask you the same question."

"I've tried, and it didn't work out."

"Really? Were you really invested in your marriage? My understanding is you and Brigitte spent every waking hour at the hospital until she got pregnant and you decided to try out marriage."

His stomach muscles and hands clenched. "What do you know about love and marriage?"

Tom flicked a hand at him dismissing the rage. "Fine. Get defensive. Deflect my comments." Tom sat and leaned back in his chair as if they were discussing football. "One of these days, Ethan, you are going to find a woman who gets under your skin. You'll try to shut her out because you don't believe in love. Your parents certainly didn't show you what love could be like, so you don't know it exists. But love does exist. And, when you experience it, it can transform your soul. You'll fight it, of course. You can't trust the feeling."

"Let me get this straight." Ethan pointed his lollipop at his uncle. "Are you saying I don't know what love is?"

"You know what it looks like, but my guess is you don't know what it feels like. You've never allowed yourself to truly be vulnerable enough to let someone love you."

"I think you should stick with medical practice. You're full of shit when it comes to psychology and figuring people out."

Tom removed his glasses and stuck one end of the frame in his mouth, his eyes narrowing. "Fair enough." He pointed with his frames. "But let me ask you this. You've been here...what, two years? How many times have you invited me over for dinner? or to a concert? or for a run?"

"We did the Boulder marathon last year together."

"Yes, we did. We've run together once, but both of us run two, maybe three times a week."

"We work opposite shifts." The excuse rolled off his tongue easily. Too easily. So easily it started guilt whirling in his chest. He held out his hands. "That sounded really lame, didn't it?"

"Yes, it did."

"I see your point. You're right. I don't really have a connection with my family. And I don't have many friends. However, I do love what I do. I'm good at being a doctor. There's nothing more satisfying than saving a person's life." He heard himself repeating the same worn-out phrase he'd been repeating all year. Ethan brushed a hand over his hair. "You have to know how grateful I am you gave me this job."

Tom snorted. "I didn't give you squat. This town is lucky to have you, and I'm lucky to have you in my life. Although the look on your face tells me you're surprised to hear it." Tom stood and took a step closer. "One of these days, Ethan, I hope you'll let me in—let us be more than just partners."

Tom opened his arms.

The leery, untrusting sensation Ethan felt as a boy crawled up his arms like a million marching ants. As much as he tried, he couldn't brush the feeling away.

He knew what his uncle wanted. More than anything, he wanted to give the one person in his life who got him—who understood him— what he wanted. But he hesitated, unsure whether he could trust the feeling, and before he could conquer the anxious fear of trying and failing to connect, the moment passed.

"See? That's what I'm talking about." His uncle picked up and opened a file.

"Tom, I'm sorry."

"Don't worry about it. But, please, think about what I said."

"I will. Promise. Oh, and by the way, I called Mrs. Cranston back. She's fine. I think she just wanted someone to listen to her complain."

"Someone needs to give that woman an enema. She's crankier than a pregnant woman about to deliver."

When Ethan stepped forward, Trapper, ever faithful stood by his side. "Tom, I—"

"I'm good." Tom glanced up from the file he was pretending to read. "I love you, Ethan." He tapped his chest. "In here. I feel the love. I hope I've been able to show you what I feel."

"You have." Ethan pushed through the feeling of remorse for not being able to show the man what he truly felt. "I'll call you. We'll go running."

"I'll be home, with the fireplace going, watching some football. You are welcome to stop by any time you like."

His uncle tried to mask the

disappointment, but the pull of muscles downward and the despondency welling up in his eyes was crushing.

"The same goes. Tell you what. Why don't you stop by the cabin? Noelle set up a Christmas tree, and she's made fudge. Two kinds. You can help me eat it."

Surprise ignited Tom's expression. "Really? This I will have to see."

When Tom's expression softened, relief fueled Ethan's determination to follow doctor's orders and take a vacation. "Come on, Trapper, let's go find something to do."

"Don't forget to stop by the grocery store sometime today," Tom called after him. "There's a bad storm coming in—and before you ask, the answer is no. The urgent care clinic is fully staffed, and neither you or I are on the schedule."

"I don't ever remember you being so—"

"Protective?"

"I was thinking more along the lines of a part of the male anatomy."

Tom chuckled. "It seems to run in the

family." Tom flashed a grin, then returned to studying the files in his hands, a clear signal it was time for Ethan to go.

What in the heck was he going to do for ten whole days? He turned toward the exit.

He needed to replace the garbage disposal...then there was the light in the upstairs closet needing a new socket. He looked at Trapper. He would stop by and surprise Tom. Maybe he'd get Tom and Bill at the hardware store to go ice fishing. Maybe he could ask Noelle if she knew how to snowshoe.

Noelle. There she was again.

She slipped so quietly into his thoughts.

He lifted Trapper into the back of his SUV, then settled behind the wheel, pointing the car toward the grocery store.

A vibrating buzz caught his attention, and he pulled his phone out of his pocket and swiped with one fluid motion.

"Tom? Did you change your mind?"

"No, it's your mother."

He closed his eyes. The sound of her voice

filled him with a longing to quietly sit with her in the sunroom, reading. When he was little she'd prop a hardbound atlas in her lap and show him all the many places he could travel. She loved to read history, and when she could get away with it, she read historical romances. His father only read nonfiction, considering anything beyond business and biographies worthless trash. Maybe that's why his father couldn't think his way out of a box—no creative imagination.

"Hi, Mom."

"I thought I'd call to see how you are. I know this is a tough time of year for you."

"Mom..." His breath faltered. "I'm good. There's no need to worry." He tried infusing a bit of peppy in his answer to calm her concerns. "How are Grandma and Dad?"

"Nan slipped a few days ago. Thankfully she didn't break anything this time."

"Are you sure? Did you take her to get X-rays? With osteoporosis, her bones are brittle and can crack."

"Relax, Doctor." His mother chided

casually. "She's being taken care of. She's been resting comfortably, and has been asking about you."

The large, gray clouds rolling in over the mountain ridge matched his mood. "We talked about me coming home this spring."

"Yes, but I always think of you, especially at Christmastime."

He ignored the implication. "You know how it is. A doctor's work is never done." He was talking about catching up on his technical reading, not working with his patients, but he'd invent work just to avoid listening to Dad tell him how he was wasting his time working in a small town. He didn't need the hassle.

The news about his grandma, however, unsettled his determination to avoid the trip home. He'd call her later to make sure she was okay.

"I just worry about you, that's all." His mother's voice held a delicate concern that he tried to block. He didn't need to add more guilt to the already overflowing pile.

"I know, Mom. I do know." His hand tightened on the steering wheel. "So, what are you getting Dad for Christmas?"

"Did I tell you he's taking golf lessons at the club? He wants to get his game under eighty, so I bought him a driver he's been eying."

"I'm surprised he hasn't bought a golf cart."

A sarcastic laugh puffed through the speaker. "Don't encourage him. He's already been eying a custom-made one that looks more like a racecar than a golf cart. Can you just see him racing around the neighborhood in one of those?"

He could. His dad always wanted shiny new things. Thanks to Ethan's grandfather's trust, he could afford pretty much everything that caught his eye. "Maybe he should stick with buying golf clubs for now. Nothing ever holds his attention long."

"True." His mother's voice was soft, contemplative. When Ethan opened his mouth to ask what was wrong, she added, "Maybe you and your brothers could arrange to go to Florida this summer. It would be fun. When's the last time you got together?"

He dropped his head. "Mom…"

"Ethan. I know William always pushed you boys to compete in grades and sports. He's proud of the fact he's got a doctor, a lawyer, and a banker in the family. And he's proud of the work you did in Tanzania."

"But, he's not proud now, is he, Mom? He hates the idea of me wasting my education working in this Podunk town."

"He just wants you to live a good life."

No, he wants me to live a rich and famous life. "I'm helping people, Mom, one person at a time. Tom taught me that. I don't need to save the world."

The conviction in this statement startled him. They weren't just words any longer. Working with Brigitte in Tanzania had been euphoric. Side by side they worked, day in day out. It was her passion to find drugs to slow the spread of HIV and malaria. The drive to find a cure kept them going. Once she was gone, the desire to keep writing articles and publishing medical findings and pushing to save the world died.

"As long as you're happy."

I just need to get through the next ten days, and then I'll be able to breathe again. "Don't worry about me Mom. I'm fine."

"I've put a package in the mail for you. Just a little something for Christmas. And don't forget to call your brothers."

"I will." He controlled his breathing to keep the irritation from puffing into the phone. "And Mom? Your gifts should be arriving tomorrow. Take care."

He did care about his Mom. However, the relationship with the rest of the family was strained. His brothers were a mini version of his dad, and, while he liked them all well enough, he couldn't find it within himself to respect them, and without respect, the love just wouldn't follow.

"I love you, Son. I hope you know that."

"I do. And tell Grandma when I come this spring, we'll go dancing." The trill of laughter made him smile. "Later."

"Later." The phone disconnected.

Family. His father's demands and his brothers' competitive pressure to get a high-powered job and be immensely successful was a long haul to the top of that mountain, a path he wasn't sure he wanted to travel anymore. The price was too steep. The drive to succeed had cost him everything.

Trapper leaned in and licked his ear.

"It's okay, buddy. I know."

He glanced at the entrance to Valu-Shop, the only grocery store in town. Maybe time off was warranted. He needed to figure out what he wanted out of life. For the past three years he'd been working hard to stay numb, drifting from day to day, skimming the surface and no more.

"Ready to go shopping, Traps? You like Harold." His pooch blew hot air onto the back of his neck. "Harold's your buddy. He gives you treats. That's why you're so fat. Everyone always gives you treats. That's because you're lovable." *Unlike me.*

He opened the car door to let Trapper

maneuver into the front seat. To his surprise Trapper jumped down. "Good boy! Look at you go."

He studied the mountain ridge ahead of him, watching the clouds hover and swirl just above. The air felt damp, cold, but for the first time in a long while, he felt warm.

"Okay. Let's get to the store before this storm kicks in. Then we can find out what Noelle's been up to."

Hearing Noelle's name, Trapper barked. His tail wagged, his body wiggled with excitement, and matched Ethan's feelings, even if Ethan couldn't show it.

He couldn't wait to get home to see Noelle.

Heaven only knew what she'd been up to.

She was always full of surprises.

CHAPTER EIGHT

Noelle shoved harder to force a small suitcase in her trunk.

Ethan rolled down his car window. "I thought you were working today."

And here comes Mr. Personality. She shoved her hands into her back pockets and suddenly became interested in a pinecone that had rolled next to her foot.

"I worked the morning shift at the café until Jenna called and said she needed help with the morning rush. It seems everyone wants baked goods for their Christmas parties."

Ethan pointed. "What's with all the luggage? Are you leaving today?"

"I still don't have enough to make it to LA, so I need to stick around for a few more days. I'm going to stay with a friend. Ashley said I could sleep on her couch."

"A couch? I know the Bryants' house is large, but it's not that big."

"Yes, well, it's the best option I have. I've overstayed my welcome here."

He closed his car door and shoved his key fob in his pocket. "If it's because of the tree thing..."

"It's not about the tree." *It's about you not being able to let go of the past, and making everyone around you miserable.* She rubbed Trapper's chest.

It's about me always picking the jerks, and I don't want to be around jerks anymore.

"I promised you I would try to find a place to stay. Ashley Bryant—I mean Daniels, I keep forgetting she got married— invited me to stay with her." Noelle stuffed the apprehension she felt all morning back into the corner of her mind where it belonged.

Why had she waited for Ethan to return? Why?

But she knew why. She didn't really want to go. If she stayed, she could get him to smile —she knew she could. "Anyway," She tugged on the thread of confidence that had helped her get this far. "Ashley stopped at the bakery yesterday and offered to let me sleep on her couch. I should have told you, it's just that…" *I wanted to help you find your bliss.*

"You can't go."

"Excuse me?" Her heartbeat picked up the pace as she straightened. "Why not?"

He considered the road, then sky, then glanced at the house. "The roads are already starting to get icy. Your tires are not all-weather, and I don't want you to get stuck again."

Are you just being protective, or do you actually care what happens to me?

Irritation sliced right through her previous excitement. *He'll never be able to enjoy life. Just get in the car and go.* "For your information, snow tires are not needed in Nashville, nor are they needed in LA."

His face squeezed in like he just chomped on something sour. "That's my point, and why you shouldn't be out in this kind of weather. You're out of practice. Besides, why sleep on a couch when you have a bed and a private room?"

A little spark of hope flared. *Maybe I don't always pick jerks after all.* "Are you asking me to stay, Doc?"

"Just for the holidays. It's only ten days before you leave, right? Besides, you're the one who reminded me it's no fun being alone for the holidays."

He looked so darn cute and flustered that her aggravation over him not being honest eased.

He reminded her of the day Brad Clairemont paced on her porch and asked her to the junior prom. Brad was so nervous. Too bad she was only a check mark in his little black book. Ethan, on the other hand, didn't have a black book. He was in love. The only problem was, the love of his life was gone, and he hadn't rejoined the living.

In fact, he was barely surviving.

"I'll stay on one condition."

He took a few steps toward her then stopped. "I've always found the word *condition* rather unsettling."

"Conditions are not illnesses. They don't kill you." She crossed her arms. "I want you to take me to the café on Christmas Day. I'm not sure my car will make it there, so I need a ride." She fibbed a little, so just in case, she made sure to add a bit of bold to convince him she meant business.

"You mean for the town's Christmas party."

A snowflake hitting her nose startled her, and she tipped her head back to study the sky. When she looked back, he was standing directly in front of her. His eyes had softened, and the dark circles under them didn't seem as pronounced. "I don't want to walk into the café alone," she continued. "Your uncle will be there. Along with Hank and a few others."

"By few. You mean a few dozen." He hung his head, debating, his thumb rubbing across the knuckles of his opposite hand. "Why do you want me to come? I'm no good at parties. What would I talk about? Dislocated shoulders and compound fractures aren't on the top of most conversation-starter lists."

"Just because you don't know how to start a conversation doesn't mean you should sit home on Christmas. Tell you what. I'll look up five conversation topics, and we can practice before we go. You'll be okay. Besides, being surrounded by people who care about you shouldn't be that hard. Tom and Maggie speak highly of you. Bill gave me the Christmas tree for you. Harold asked about you when I was at the store. Jenna—"

"Okay. Okay." He spread his arms, palms out in surrender. "I get it."

A bounce of joy ricocheted off the walls of her chest. "Did you just say okay?"

She held out her hand to catch several snowflakes.

His shoulders were covered with frosty crystals, and his cheeks were turning pink. The temperature was dropping, but he looked so damn content, she couldn't help but fill a tinge of joy. However, she wasn't about to tell him about the jar of Sin Sugar Jenna sneaked into her bag.

"Why don't you take Cheddar back inside while I grab the groceries?"

"Do you need any help?"

He shook his head. "I'm good. I'll help Trapper after I get this stuff inside."

"I got him." Trapper placed his front paws on the bottom step and looked at Noelle. She walked up the steps, turned, leaned over, and clapped. "Come, Traps." She clapped again. "You can do it. It's just a few steps."

The dog leaned forward with a soft whine and struggled up the bottom step, then the next one. "That's it. That's my boy." Noelle clapped her hands for encouragement.

The geriatric dog struggled up the last

three steps and nuzzled her hand. "What a good dog you are. Yes, you are. There's some turkey left in the refrigerator. Let's go get it for you."

Ethan followed her into the kitchen with grocery bags in his arms. "Trapper hasn't made it up any steps in weeks...no, more like months. I'm already amazed that you got him to go down the outside steps. How did you get him to climb up?"

"We've been practicing, plus I've been massaging his hind legs and hips. I found with a little bit of encouragement and pieces of turkey, he'll make the effort. He won't do acrobatics any time soon, but he's been able to make it up a few more stairs each time he tries."

The look on Ethan's face gave her the impression he wouldn't mind a massage, but she wouldn't go there. Ten more days and she'd be out of Elkridge, and she might not be back.

"Just to confirm, you are taking me to the Christmas party, right?"

Ethan set the groceries on the counter. "I'll go as long as there are no emergencies and the roads are clear."

She opened the kennel and lifted her cat to face her. "Did you hear, Cheddar? Ethan's promised to take me to the Christmas party."

"As long as there are no emergencies."

She set the furball on the floor. "You didn't learn any snow dances while you were in Africa, did you? I wouldn't want to think you could conjure up an emergency to get out of going."

"Nope." He let the p in the word pop like a cork.

Oh, my. She sighed. His whole face had changed. Every feature had evolved into a softer, more handsome, more casual state of ease. Today he looked more approachable. Gentle. Sexy.

Maybe her jar of Sin Sugar would come in handy after all.

No. no. no. She couldn't go there. Although wasn't every girl's dream to date a doctor? She'd watched enough of those television medical series to be convinced half the population had a secret doctor fetish. She didn't need to fantasize. She had a real-life hunk in front of her, and he was better than any television character. Plus he had the alpha, moody thing down pat.

Trapper nudged her hand, thank goodness. He gave her an excuse to open the refrigerator and rearrange the bottles and cartons and storage containers on the shelves. She grabbed the lunchmeat package, and turned.

Umph.

Her arms connected with a solid chest, and Ethan's muscles bunched beneath her hands. He smelled scrumptious, like a stretch of river on a warm, sunny day. She inhaled and let the scent tingle its way down to her core. Mm-mm-mmm. Her head tilted forward.

"Noelle?"

Don't interrupt my fantasy. It's beautiful.

"Um. Noelle?"

"Uh-hun?"

"Do you mind if I put the steaks in the refrigerator?"

"What?" Her eyes snapped open. There was that lopsided grin. Was he laughing at her? No, he couldn't be laughing, he didn't know how. She slid sideways just as her phone buzzed in her back pocket. *Saved by the buzz.*

"Jade. Hi."

"Where are you? And don't tell me you haven't left Nashville yet."

"No. I'm all packed and headed your way. I decided to come home for Christmas and see my family for a few days," *because I didn't have enough cash to make it to LA.*

"Family is such a drag. Get here soon, okay?"

"I'll be there as soon as I can."

"Before I forget, they found a lead singer."

Stitches of envy threaded around her heart. "That's right. Last week was tryouts for the lead vocal." Not that she could forget. Her mind churned with ideas and worries about the band audition since she decided there was nothing left for her in Nashville.

She originally planned to go to the open call for lead, but chickened out at the last second. Based on prior feedback, she decided her voice wasn't unique enough, and the producers wanted someone who could hold an audience—whatever that meant—and she didn't have it. Besides, she was more interested in writing songs. That's what she kept telling herself, anyway. She leaned a palm on the counter and closed her eyes. "Who did they get?"

"Candy Foliday."

"Candy? You've got to be kidding." Noelle started counting even numbers in multiples of two.

"I heard she's from Austin," Jade continued.

"I know who she is." Noelle's heart folded inward. "We auditioned together in Nashville." She didn't even get through the second verse before she was shooed offstage.

"I looked her up on the internet," Jade

grunted. "Couldn't find much, other than her posts on Twitter and Facebook—which looked pretty lame. I don't think she knows how to market herself. What's she like?"

Noelle pushed past the jealousy. She hadn't even tried to win the position, so she had no right to be snotty. "She's pretty. Nice. She'll look good for the cameras. I can see why they picked her." Her chirpy summation was weighted with years of trying and failing. Month after month of being turned down by every producer in town. Eating scraps. Singing on street corners just to make enough to pay rent.

Little gnats of doubt nibbled at her self-confidence. But she would never give up. She couldn't. Singing was like breathing.

"They haven't started filling the other positions, have they?" she asked.

"Nope," Jade said with a snap of her gum. "Tryouts still start the second. I talked to the organizer, and he said our best chance is for me to try out for bass, and you to audition for one of the backup singer slots."

"What did he say about the songs?"

"He said what all the other jackasses say. Make a demo. However, he did say he'd listen to the songs. Not that I believe him."

"We've both heard that before." A demo was a nice way of saying, "I'm not interested." She rubbed her eyes.

"Hey, Christmas, you still there?"

The nickname made her smile, even though the sting of never being in the right place at the right time hurt, and put a nick in her life's mission to stay positive and upbeat no matter what.

She dragged in a deep breath. "Yeah, I'm here. Listen, Jade—"

"Don't say it. Don't you dare. Get your ass in the car and get here. All right? We're in this together, remember?"

"I'm not giving up. I just don't know if this is the right opportunity for me. You're right, though. I just have to keep putting myself out there."

"Snap—same goes, girlfriend," Jade encouraged with a you-go-girl attitude. "I'll send you the music, and we can set up a web chat or something to practice."

She'd help Jade because, unlike so many others, Jade understood. Her former bandmate had been there to celebrate the small wins and helped pick her up off the pavement when she'd been beaten down.

"Send the music sheets, and I'll start learning the songs tomorrow." Today she just wanted to take a step back and make sure singing in the band was the right thing. If the producer didn't like her songs, then what? Would she settle for just singing backup?

"Get here soon," Jade pushed. "I need someone to practice with."

Typical, self-centered Jade. It was all about her. "I'll do my best." Noelle disconnected the call and tossed the phone on the counter.

"Is everything okay?" The concern in Ethan's tone made her guard her hurt.

She waved a hand in front of her face, hoping he wouldn't see the forming tears. "A friend called to give me a tryout update. I guess the producers already found a lead singer for the band."

"Why didn't you try out?"

I'm not good enough. "I wanted to come home for Christmas."

"And?"

She sighed, and her shoulders drooped while she stared at the floor. "I didn't have the gas money to get to LA. Don't tell my mom. She'd just shove money in my purse. I had the cash saved up until Jon took it out of my dresser drawer. I should never have kept that much cash in the apartment."

"Okay, so Jon took your money. But I get the feeling that's not why you didn't try out."

She shrugged. "And, I'm not good enough to sing lead."

"Who said?"

"Other people."

"You mean idiots. I heard you sing. You could win any of those talent shows I've seen on TV, especially when you're singing one of your songs. That's when it comes out."

She pulled a hair band from her pocket,

bunched and twisted the hair out of her face. "What comes out?"

"Your passion. There's a raw quality to your voice that makes everything else not matter. You're very talented."

"I love my songs." The swirling snowflakes outside the kitchen window matched the rhythm of her thoughts. Swirling, churning in circles with the change in the wind. "There's so much talent out there. Unless I can catch someone's attention, I'm just another singer/songwriter."

"Is that what you really believe?" Ethan took a step too close for comfort. "There are hundreds of thousands of doctors in the world, but there is always room for one more. It might be that one doctor who finds the cure for diabetes, or another major disease. So don't say you're just another anything. You just might be the one."

She rubbed her nose, leaving a streak of snot on the back of her hand. "I know. I just have to keep pushing, and grow a thicker skin."

He touched her shoulder, his fingers tugging lightly. "Nobody gets used to being rejected."

"It's so hard, going out there, putting everything I've got into a song, only to have it...have it..." She took a deep breath and shrugged, looking everywhere but at Ethan.

His expression shifted and cleared. "It sounds like the cases I had in Africa. I worked day and night trying to diagnose a cause, and then when I nailed it down, I went to work trying to do everything possible to extend a life for another day, a month, maybe even a year or more."

He shoved his hands in his pockets and rocked back on his heels. "Sometimes the patient died. When that happened, I felt cheated, like there was always something more I could have done."

She wrapped her arms around his waist, wanting to feel close—listen to the cadence of another human heart. Eventually his arms wrapped around her loosely. She calmed her breathing to hear his rhythm. "I've tried to stay positive about things, but days like this, I just feel like crawling into bed and calling it a day."

"That's how I've felt every day since Brigitte and Callie died."

His wife. Right.

She brushed her palms across her eyes and stepped out of his arms. "Would you like to talk about it? I mean, their death and what happened."

"Not really."

Right. And you never will want to talk about it. She pointed over her shoulder. "I should go check my computer to see if Jade's files came through."

"Let me know if there's anything I can do to help. Come to think of it, I know a man who might be willing to listen to your songs."

If she had a dollar for every time anyone mentioned a friend of a friend who might know someone who could help her, she wouldn't be broke. Jon had vowed the same thing. She wanted to believe him, believe someone could find a way to promote her dream, and Jon made promise after promise. He hadn't kept one of them.

"Don't worry about it. Right now my only chance at getting my songs heard is at the audition in LA."

"And if you don't make it, what then?"

"I guess I get a waitress job and keep trying." For the first time since they met, he didn't look sad, but she couldn't stand to see the sympathy. He shouldn't feel sorry for her. She didn't want him to. "I had better get my stuff out of the car."

"I'll help."

She waved him off. "I got it in there, I can get it out. Thanks for the offer." She picked up her pace and was out the front door and down the steps in seconds.

In the middle of the driveway, she stopped, letting the snow and exhaled breath swirl around her. She crossed her arms and shivered.

"What am I doing?" She pushed the snow on the ground into a little pile with the toe of her shoe.

Could she give up writing songs?

No! her mind screamed. She couldn't give it up. Singing was her passion—her soul's nutrients. Singing helped her through lonely times, happy times, and trying times. She couldn't stop singing any more than she could stop breathing.

The cabin and the warm glow eased her fretting.

Ethan understood the drive, the wants, the needs to be fulfilled.

He got it, and that was why she felt compelled to do whatever she could in their remaining time together to help him, for no other reason than he deserved to be happy.

Although he might not appreciate the plan that just popped into her head.

CHAPTER NINE

While Ethan added another piece of firewood to the stack on his arm and whistled for Trapper, dark streams of clouds moved west across the ridge. In the past hour, the snowfall had doubled, half-inch flakes pelting nonstop from the night sky. Over a foot had fallen, and the updated forecast predicted another several inches before the storm ended.

He'd checked the portable generator and made sure there was plenty of gas just in case. Trapper came around the corner just as he reached the back steps. Ethan pushed open the back door to stack the wood in the wrought iron rack. Last winter he learned his lesson when he hadn't been able to make it to the shed for additional wood and one of the water pipes froze.

"Can I help?" Noelle appeared in the doorway leading to the kitchen.

He stomped the snow from his boots. "I'm good. Something sure smells good."

"I made apple cider. Would you like a mug?"

The cinnamon apple smell wafting from the kitchen wasn't what he was talking about —it was her. She made everything smell like a bag of Halloween candy. "Sounds perfect. Give me a minute to remove my boots and wipe Trapper's paws."

He closed his eyes to shut away an appealing fantasy of her standing in his kitchen wearing nothing but an apron. He groaned, doing his best to block his immediate reaction.

In the past few days she had made her mark. A bowl of pinecones decorated the counter, caramel creamer invaded the refrigerator's top shelf, and vanilla shampoo stared at him from the bathroom windowsill, to name just a few. She filled every room in the house with fresh smells and bright colors. She was the rainbow beneath his storm cloud, and he didn't quite know how to deal with her.

Even Trapper had taken to following her from room to room. Sure, he liked anyone who gave him treats, but the affection went beyond the usual. The grumpy old man even had taken a liking to her cat. Like Cheddar, Noelle had nudged and cuddled and settled into his life whether he wanted her to or not.

He walked into the kitchen to find a mug of steaming apple cider on the counter, but no Noelle. Picking up the mug, he followed the sound of her voice. Nestled into a chair, she sat with paper and pen in her lap, her guitar within easy reach.

"Working on a new song?" He sat on the couch across from her.

She shrugged. "I'm supposed to send a demo of my songs in before the audition, so the band can check them out." She tapped her pen on the notebook. "You might be able to help."

"Me? I don't know anything about writing music."

"You don't need to. That's my job. All you need to do is talk."

The way she looked at him with that innocent smile that wasn't so innocent made his gut churn. She was up to something. He'd like to know what. "Talk about what?"

"I need to write a ballad. Jade thinks the song about my dad is good, but recommends I have a backup in case the judges don't like it."

"What does your song writing have to do with me?"

"Well..." Noelle bit her lip and started fidgeting with the edges of the fleece lap blanket that once had been Callie's. "The best ballads are about love or a lost love."

He shoved away from the sofa so fast Trapper launched to his feet, the hair on his back ridged, and he looked right and left and barked a warning.

"Wait." Noelle held out her hand. "I'm sorry. I didn't mean to be insensitive, but I thought talking about your wife and daughter might help."

His gaze snapped to her. "How would talking help? They're gone. Nothing will bring them back."

"I know that." She placed the notebook on the coffee table and pulled her knees to her chest, studying him over the top. "I can tell you loved them, and I would never do anything to diminish their memory. In fact, that's why I want to write the song. It's my gift to you and your wife. Your story can be preserved forever in a song."

The snow outside the window swirled just like his thoughts. Part of him wanted to walk up the stairs and lock himself away. Ignore Noelle. Pretend his life wasn't in shambles. But he couldn't ignore the hurt in her eyes. He'd caused her sparkle to dim. He'd been careless.

He paced back to the couch, slowly sinking into the leather.

"I owe you an apology," he raked his fingers through his hair.

"What for?"

For being closed off? Rude? Unable to feel? Take your pick. "For being difficult."

"You aren't difficult. I'd say you're more like moody. Besides, this is your home. And, you're allowed to be yourself when you're in your own home. I'm the one who's intruding."

Did she just imply it's okay to be an ass simply because this is my house? Really? "Are you always so accommodating?"

She laughed. "Jon said I was needy."

"You're kidding."

Judging from her expression, she wasn't kidding. The bastard. Noelle didn't have a needy bone in her body. "It's good you're no longer with that jerk."

"I have my flaws."

"We all do. But yours are sugar-coated."

She flashed him a sublime smile. "Oh, dear. You've got me all wrong. I get obnoxious if I've had more than one drink, I rarely make my bed, and people tell me when I get excited I talk too much. When I'm driving, I yell at other stupid drivers, and…" she peeked his way, "well, that should be enough to prove I'm not always kind."

"No one is perfect. However, there are some who are closer to perfection than others."

Less than five minutes ago he had every intention of leaving her to write. But what would happen if he stayed? Noelle's positive energy was infectious. While he was around her, his empty life gained a tinge of color. But what about her? He wanted her to remain happily untouched by his moodiness, as she called it.

"If I agree to help you with your song— and I'm not saying I'll do it—what would I need to do?"

"We could start by you telling me what you loved about your wife. What made her special?"

Right. All I need to do is rip my chest open and spill my guts. "And then?"

"Then, if you want, you can tell me how you felt when you lost her."

He pulled and squeezed at his fingers. "I don't think you would want to write a song about feeling angry and guilty and completely lost. If I had only known…"

"If you had only known what?"

"If I had only known it was the last time I would ever see them again, I would have done things differently."

She grabbed her pad of paper and pen. "Go on."

"I would've gone with them, or asked Brigitte not to go. I definitely wouldn't have gone into work. I wouldn't have been so distracted…would have paid more attention." He pounded his fist on his knee. "I would have cherished the time we had together more."

She pushed her feet to the floor, grabbed her guitar, and strummed a few chords before closing her eyes. "If I had only known it was our last moment, I would have taken more time." Her fingers paused and then began strumming again, this time more slowly. "I would have lifted your hand in mine and hugged you close. I would have whispered your name and told you my secrets. I would have made you laugh, and kept you safe. If I had only known it was the end, I would have taken more time."

"That's amazing." He rubbed his sweaty palms down his jeans. "You got all that from what I said?"

"You like it?" A ray of pure joy lit up her face.

For the first time in months, he felt lighter. His gaze latched onto her hopeful smile, and he wondered what made him feel like he wanted to drag her into his arms and protect her the way he hadn't been allowed to protect Brigitte. His wife felt suffocated whenever he tried, insisting she was capable of taking care of herself. And she was. She was the type of woman who didn't need anyone or anything, including him. When she pushed him away, it reinforced his old insecurities, the conviction that he wasn't wanted—wasn't lovable.

Never had been.

But he wanted Noelle to know he cared.

"I do like your song." He increased the volume of his positive comments to make sure she heard, and believed, his praise. "You have a magical way of capturing the moment."

"Thank you."

Her smile broadened, and the smile made him think about intimacy. Why her smile triggered those emotions he wasn't quite sure, but he liked the feeling. A curious interest expanded, but not enough to explore.

"Is there anything else you can tell me?"

There were a lot of memories, but none he wanted to skim through again. "I'll have to think about it." Right now all he was thinking about was her.

"There's time. We've got a few days."

But only a few days. She was leaving to pursue her dream. He had to keep reminding himself she was only there temporarily.

Then what? What was he thinking? Somehow she'd managed to open the door to his heart.

He slammed it shut.

Never again would he let anyone into his life. It hurt too much, plus the feeling was only temporary.

"I had better find something to eat for dinner," he said, to get himself out of the room.

"My mom let me raid her supplies, and I made a pot of chili yesterday. The crockpot's in the refrigerator on the bottom shelf."

He braced his foot against the door of his heart, working hard to find the lock. "It's not your job to cook for me."

She set the blanket aside and got up from the chair. "I know. Chili sounded good, and since it was going to snow, I thought it might make the perfect meal. I also made cornbread, which I stored in the oven." She crossed the room toward the kitchen, then turned. "Cheddar likes to take bites out of anything left on the counter."

The sparkle in her eye appeared, the one he couldn't resist. The passive attraction had begun to transform into an intense awareness when she took a step closer, her lips slightly parted. But she turned and went into the kitchen.

"Would you like to join me?" she asked while pulling the crock from the refrigerator.

The word *join* got stuck in a repetitive loop. His mind interpreted the word correctly, but his body decided to use a somewhat different definition.

He forced his legs to carry him backwards toward the cabinets to get out bowls for the chili. "I'll warm up the chili if you want to set the table."

"Do you have a spatula for the cornbread?" She accepted the bowls he handed her.

"It's in the far drawer. Over there." He pointed to the four-drawer cabinet next to the oven, then opened the refrigerator and looked at the crowded space to shift his thoughts to the more mundane. He slid the milk jug aside and reached for a beer. "Drink?"

"Beer would be great."

He grabbed a second bottle, twisted the

top, and handed her the lager. She tipped up the bottle, taking a long swig.

"Oh, this is good. What is it?"

He retrieved side plates from the cabinet and handed them to her. "It's a microbrew from Boulder."

"If you ever go to Nashville, stop by Yazoo, and have a Hop Perfect. Then again, the India Pale Ale may be a little citrusy for you. The HOPRY might be more your style." She set the plates on the table, then aligned the silverware, just like any seasoned waitress would do out of habit. "Listen to me being all informed. Back in high school, there were only a handful of breweries in the area."

"Things change."

She looked at him intently, nodding. "You're right. Time always seems to keep traipsing on, even if you don't want it to."

"Is that another line for your song?"

She shrugged. "Maybe. Are you ready to talk some more about your wife after dinner?"

"No."

"Are you sure?"

He liked her stubborn persistence, although not when it came to dealing with his past. "Why do you think the first song you wrote isn't good enough?" He tested a spoonful of hot beans and meat and spices, then pressed the microwave start button again.

"It's too personal."

"You mean the song isn't commercial, and may not appeal to a broader audience."

"It's commercial, but I haven't been able to put the song in a box yet."

He leaned in, knowing what she was trying to communicate was significant. "I don't understand. Tell me more."

"Singing in a box is like putting walls around the emotions. If I'm singing a song about a breakup, I can tap into the emotions easily since I've been through the experience personally. I've put boundaries around those emotions. I can tap into them, feel them without letting them get out of control. With my dad, I'm still processing a few things. I don't know how I feel exactly, and I have a hard time tapping in to write them down. The emotions are too raw. It's like I keep hiding behind a wall, not ready to let myself be so vulnerable."

Her explanation resonated deep within his open wound. He'd been putting things in boxes all his life, only his boxes he'd padlocked, never to revisit. He didn't feel the need. It was too late for him, but not for Noelle.

"Can't you just tap into a similar feeling?"

"Not really. I've tried, and it doesn't work.. The song ends up flat, or at best two-dimensional. Either way, it's never good enough to get a producer's attention."

He set the bowls on the table as she handed him the plate of cornbread. "If you watch reality singing shows, the judges are always telling the artist to push harder. Is fear holding you back?"

"I don't think so, but then again fear is a funny thing." She folded the lumps of beans and meat and sauce over in her bowl. "You aren't aware of it until something happens and it's revealed." Her cheeks splotched with a touch of pink. "If I'm making any sense."

"I get the gist." He spread butter on the cornbread to melt. "I had this challenging medical case. We needed to operate, but there were a lot of risks. The chief medical officer knew I was nervous. He gave me the best advice I've ever been given."

"Oh?" She studied him.

"He said fear can't sabotage you if you believe in what you're doing."

"In other words...believe in yourself." There was that sparkle he loved to see. If she had a switch he could turn on, he'd keep her sparkle lit all the time.

"I wish someone had told me something similar for when I've been onstage."

"Stage fright?"

"I'm okay when I'm in front of the crowd, but once I'm backstage, I get in my head and start believing the audience hated my music, or I was flat, or I wasn't good enough.

"By whose standards?"

"Mine."

"Ah," He picked up his beer to wash down the tasty bread. "Well, if you don't make it as a singer, you can always open a restaurant."

"That's just it. I can't imagine doing anything else. Singing and writing songs is the only thing that feels right."

"Then I suggest you tap into your determination the next time you're onstage and stop caring what other people think—especially producers and other singers, who are probably just jealous."

"Every creative has doubts." She poked at a breadcrumb that had fallen on the table. "But you're right. Have no fear." She shoved a large spoonful of chili into her mouth, then chewed and swallowed. "I really like where the song is going. Will you help me work on it again after dinner?"

Ethan felt the tension surge into his shoulders and pinch his neck. "Does it mean that much to you?"

"It does. I've always found it helpful to open a box of memories with someone else.

That way the other person is there to talk things through. I always feel better afterward."

He stared at her for a long silent moment. "Is helping me why you asked me to assist you in the first place? You think talking about my wife will make me happy?"

"I think talking about your wife will help you stop avoiding dealing with the past."

His stomach clenched and rejected the bit of food he was about to put in his mouth. He dropped his spoon into his bowl. "I'm not avoiding the past." But he was, and he knew it.

"Maybe not, but you *are* avoiding your future."

"I'm working, healing people." His stomach did another flip and flop. "Why is it you think I'm avoiding anything?"

"Everyone in town says you're burying yourself in work."

"So?"

"So, people are worried."

He folded his arms and leaned back

against the wooden chair rungs. "Worried about what?"

"Never mind." She shoved from the table, but he caught her arm.

"Noelle—"

"They are worried you might give up, stay angry, never find a way to be happy. They like you. Harold, my mom, Jenna—lots of people hate seeing you so sad."

"And you thought if you decorated a Christmas tree, made me cookies, and permeated my house with your luscious scent and gorgeous body, that life would be grand again?" He let his frustration settle. "Damn. Drinking when I haven't slept in days wasn't a good idea." Weeks. He hadn't slept in weeks, but no one had been there to count.

The silence grew fat and thick. She eased back into the chair, studying him quietly. Thoroughly.

"I'd better go read my medical journals. Then I have a 50/50 chance of falling asleep."

"If you're worried I'm offended by your

last comment, don't be. I already told you I don't date jerks."

He was starting to think he might be the biggest jerk in the state. Then he caught the slight lift at the corner of her mouth, and a sparkle settled in her eyes.

"It's probably a good idea you've decided not to date idiots, either."

"I didn't say I don't date idiots...just jerks. Idiots are fine as long as they are hot, have good rhythm, and have a big penis."

He coughed and sputtered. "Did you just say penis?"

"Are you having trouble with the technical term, Doctor?"

"No. I'm okay with the word. I just didn't expect you to use such a...clinical term."

"Well. If you hang around backstage after concerts, you'll hear all sorts of sparkly terms."

"Good to know. It's no wonder you hate men."

"I don't hate men, just the ones who don't know how to be gentlemen. I believe in love, and that life trades up. Someday, I'm going to find a man who treats me with respect and love. A man who's strong, yet gentle. Sure of himself, yet seeks advice. Can both communicate and listen."

"You mean one of those fairy-tale princes."

Her brow and nose scrunched in unison. "No. No way." She shook her head. "Why would I want pristine and perfect when I can have reckless and wild? There's someone out there for me. I just have to find him. Just like there is someone out there for you."

"Been there, done that...can't go back."

"So you believe you can only love once in your life?"

He searched for a response, but nothing felt quite right. "Maybe."

"That's a shame. You have a lot to give, if only you were willing."

"I give a lot to my patients every day."

"It's not the same, and I'm pretty sure you already know that. I'm talking about finding a person to spend your life with, to share the ups and downs, to explore. You can't have that type of relationship with your patients."

His foot vibrated under the table. What she was telling him was pretty much what the hospital psychologist told him. Then why did it irritate him so much?

"And you think you'll find your Mr. Forever in LA?"

"I'm hoping to find a career in LA, and if I bump into Mr. Forever, then it's a bonus. I can't stop living my life just because Mr. Forever hasn't decided to knock on my door. Besides, if I don't put myself out there, I'll never find the right guy."

Maybe the right guy's in front of you and you just can't see it. Whoa! Where did that come from? He tapped a finger against his temple. "You think because I'm not out there dating a different woman every night that I'm not happy."

"A whiskey bottle doesn't make for very good company."

"Touché, Miss Conroy." He nodded, but he wasn't sure he agreed. "I need to put another log on the fire." He should have left, but here he sat, gazing into her eyes, filled with hope. His fingers itched to tuck the strand of fallen hair behind her ear, but he didn't.

"I'll take Trapper out." She patted the old dog on his side. "It sounds like you have medical journals to read."

She disappeared through the doorway, and another piece of regret was plunked down on top of the already teetering stack.

Outside the kitchen window, he could see several feet of snow, but the buildup was the least of his worries. The spunky woman staying in his house was his biggest concern.

She'd pushed him, tested him, and found him unworthy.

His parents found him unworthy a long time ago, and he found a way to stop caring.

However, Noelle was different. For some reason he wanted to prove her wrong.

CHAPTER TEN

"Freshly fallen snow…snow…snow," Noelle played with the lyrics and melody, then placed her palm over the guitar strings, letting out a frustrated growl.

Why couldn't she get into a writing groove?

Nothing sounded right.

Writing songs had always come easily, but not lately. Lately everything seemed so darn hard.

She leaned back in the leather chair and stared out the window at ice crystals hanging like daggers from the eaves. Cheddar jumped on the arm of the chair and rubbed his head against her leg. She set the guitar against the end table to make room for her fuzzy buddy. She lifted the cat into her lap and rotated him toward the window.

"Look at all the snow. There must be at least two feet. It doesn't look like I'll make it over to Mom's today."

Disappointed loneliness settled around her heart while Cheddar kneaded his way into a ball on her lap. The sound of water racing through the pipes in the thin cabin walls stopped, announcing Ethan would be down for breakfast shortly. She wished she hadn't said anything about his manly parts. Just thinking about the conversation made her cringe. What had she been thinking? She needed to install a zipper on her mouth.

What was it about him that made her go on and on like a babbling idiot? Every time he was around, she wanted to climb aboard, feel those solid muscles between her thighs, and take a Caribbean cruise.

She stroked Cheddar. "I'm such a fool.

Why is it that I'm always attracted to unavailable guys? What's with me?"

Whether or not he was available didn't matter. Her body reacted like a drunken local to an open Karaoke mic.

She just needed to be more careful.

The house was big enough, so she should be able to avoid him, at least on an emotional level.

She stared out the window at the untouched, romantic landscape. The large spruce trees bent with snow stood sentry along the mountain ridge. The wind caught the snow and sent it swirling into the air. A lone deer grazing on the edge of the tree line popped her head up, listening for movement. Noelle's heart sang a silent lullaby.

A few minutes later Trapper wandered into the room and settled at her feet. "Hey, old man." She rubbed his ear, then stroked his head. "This cold weather is hard on old bones, isn't it? Poor baby."

"Is everything okay?" Ethan asked from the stairs.

"Trapper's fine. He's just a bit stiff."

"I was talking about you."

"Sure. I'm fine." She sat back, but couldn't manage to strap on her happy face today, even for Ethan. "I've been trying to write most of the morning, and nothing is working."

"Maybe you're trying too hard. Blame it on your muse."

"If I waited for my muse to wake up and get out of bed, I'd be sitting around twiddling my thumbs for a long time. I need original material. I can't use my muse not cooperating as an excuse. I must write. Otherwise, I have no chance of making an impression during the audition."

He walked toward her. "Come on. Let's go find some inspiration. Since we're stuck here today, we can at least enjoy the snow."

Blue jeans hung low on his hips. A blue T-shirt peeked out from under a blue flannel button-down. And the heavenly smell wafting her way spelled trouble. He was a whole stack of blueberry pancakes with creamy butter and cinnamon syrup. If he got too close, she was confident she'd overindulge, and she didn't need the calorie count.

"I think I'll pass. I need to get this song written."

"I'll make you a deal. I picked up bird and squirrel feed while I was in town this week. If you help me load the feeders, when we're done, we can continue down memory lane. How's that sound?"

"Are you talking about your song?"

"Yeah." He shifted uneasily. "I'll see what I can do to help."

His rippling jaw muscles told her he expected the discussion to be as much fun as a tooth extraction. She might not be able to write the song, but talking about it might do him a little good.

"Okay. Just give me a few minutes to change, and find my scarf and gloves."

She tucked Cheddar on the chair beside her and threw back the pinecone print blanket. When Ethan's eyes brightened with humor, she followed his stare down to the gold double-w on the bright red cotton stretching across her chest.

"What? You don't like Wonder Woman?"

"I prefer Cat Woman. The skintight black leathers leave a lasting impression on a guy. Then again, Wonder Woman has a golden rope."

She'd like nothing better than to kiss the smirk right off his face. She rolled her eyes and escaped quickly to avoid doing the one thing she shouldn't.

Halfway up the stairs, she heard an odd sound, and stepped back a stair to listen. Was that laughter? She waited. Sure enough, she heard it again: an actual chuckle. The sound was a bit rusty, like it hadn't been cranked over in a while, but that didn't matter. He wasn't going to get away with laughing. Not at her expense. Paybacks were in order.

Ten minutes later, she scooped a ball of snow, packed it tight and let it fly. Bull's-eye.

He turned. His focus targeted. "Oh, babe, that was the wrong move."

Babe? Did he just call her babe? She'd show him.

The way his eyes tracked his every move made her want to play. He leaned forward.

Run. She squealed, her heart pounding in time with her feet. A splat on her back knocked her forward, but she used the forward momentum to reach for more ammunition—a tactical error—and lost her balance, tripping face-first in the soft powder.

A hand grabbed her arm, helping her roll over.

"Are you okay?"

She brushed snow off her face. Her skin puckered from the cold, but his gaze could have melted snow. All she could see were his lips, those lips she wanted to feel against her skin. Oh, man, she was in heaps of trouble. She pushed on his chest. "Seriously? It's just snow. Are all doctors so overprotective?"

He leaned close, breath warming her skin. "Only when there's a need to be." He pushed up off the ground and left her stuck in the snow. He whistled for Trapper and headed toward the house, his long strides making it difficult to catch up.

"I was teasing. Would you wait?" she called after him.

He stopped but didn't turn around. She lifted her feet higher and trudged around him.

"I'm sorry. I'm just not used to being with someone who really cares."

His jaw rippled again. He looked at her, then at the ridge. "Brigitte was the same way. She often accused me of being overly protective. I worked hard to let her find her way, but now I wish I hadn't."

Anger bubbled and burned the back of her throat. "I'm not Brigitte. And besides, you can't protect everyone."

"Obviously." He waved her off. "It's just that Brigitte was spontaneous. She went barreling through life. She was reckless. Fearless."

"In other words, she was perfect. She was independent, which in turn allowed you to do your work." *She wasn't needy in ways I've been accused of.*

"No. That's not what I'm saying."

"Then what are you saying?"

He tromped down the driveway toward the tree line where she'd seen the deer earlier. She fell into step beside him.

He glanced at her, then away, letting the silence and air swirl. "The day Brigitte and Callie died, a haulage bus lost its brakes and slammed into several cars. Brigitte saw the accident happen. She apparently left Callie in the car and went to help the victims. She was like that. Always wanting to help others. Giving everything she had to others. She was always pushing limits. Once in a while, she'd try again to give her love to me, but I never let her in. I always held back."

Noelle slipped her mitten-covered hand into Ethan's and squeezed. He returned the squeeze, but didn't let go. They walked in silence for a few more steps.

"I could never let myself be vulnerable. Why, why couldn't I give them what they needed?"

Noelle ached for the man, the father, the

husband, but he needed to take a look inside that locked box. He needed to heal to find his way back. "What happened to Brigitte and Callie?"

He squeezed her hand, hard, and her fingers went numb, but she held on. "A mini-bus slammed into our car and flipped over, hitting Brigitte. Callie was killed instantly. Brigitte lasted three days, but never came out of her coma. I donated her organs. She would have wanted me to." He hiccupped back a sob. "Traffic in Tanzania is atrocious. I told her to be careful. To never get out of the car. But she never listened." He kept walking, kicking at the snow to make a path. "I'm sorry. I shouldn't burden you with this."

"Who says? Besides, it's not a burden when you share with friends."

"Is that what we are? Friends?"

"I'd like to think so."

"Friends." He tried out the word like he was trying on a pair of jeans.

"You sound disappointed."

"No, not disappointed, so much as…"

"Relieved?" She camouflaged the hurt with a smirk. "Don't worry. I get that you're not interested. I'm not your type."

But you're certainly mine.

His eyes grew dark as the winter storm clouds and he pulled on her arm, turning her toward him. "Don't you get it? Noelle, I'm protecting you."

"From what? You?" She scoffed at his sacrifice. He didn't need to be the defender of her pride. "In case you haven't figured it out, I'm doing okay taking care of myself. I've been on my own for years. Sure, my life has had its speed bumps, but I've managed okay."

"You're doing better than okay. You're going to LA to play in a band, get married, have kids."

"You're painting a pretty tidy picture," she said around her suddenly heavy heart, "but I don't think you have it quite right."

"No? Then tell me where I went wrong."

"I'm the type of girl who wants to believe in fairy tales, but I'm also realistic. Love hurts. I already know that. But I still believe it's better to share a life with a person you care about than never to have loved at all. You may not believe it now, Ethan, but love just happens, and can smack you upside the head. You won't be able to avoid it. One day you'll wake up and be blissfully happy. Life trades up, remember?"

He didn't believe her.

The look on his face proved it.

The concept of a second chance at love was too far out there for him to believe.

"And you say you don't believe in unicorns and fairies." A harsh underlying current had surged into his tone. "You live in an idealistic world where only positive things happen. I hate to pop your bubble, but truly loving another person isn't all puppies and kittens and kites. Loving someone hurts like hell."

"You feel that way because you lost Brigitte and Callie, but—"

"Unless you've been in love, truly in love, then you have no idea what I'm talking about." The anger in his voice made her take a step back, but she wasn't afraid. He didn't frighten her, he just made her want to shake him.

Her fists tightened into dogged knots of denial.

Doubt swirled in her chest, and she swallowed back her response. Maybe he had a point. Did she really know how love felt? Her dad died before she was even born. She hadn't grown up witnessing the love between a husband and wife. Maybe he was right.

She looked into his eyes. "I may not know what love is, but I won't stop singing about it, or trying to find it. I believe love is a worthy pursuit, for everyone."

"Then let's write a fairy tale."

She sucked in a breath. "I already told you, I don't write songs about puppies, kittens, or kites." She let her bold stride extend as she approached the house.

The buzz in her pocket made her reach for her phone. If it was Jon, she'd gladly give him a piece of advice, but unfortunately it wasn't. "Hi, Mom. Sorry I couldn't make it to the café today." I could have used the money. *I need to get out of here.*

"Hi, honey. Happy birthday."

She inhaled a long breath like she was going to blow out candles, but there was no cake or presents, only an irritating, belligerent man lecturing her on the finer qualities of love.

"Is everything okay? Do you have everything you need?"

Her mom always remembered the important things. "A winning lottery ticket would help." She laughed. "I'll manage, Mom. I always do."

"Stay warm. Hopefully the plows will be up your way soon. I'd love to see you, but I think it's safer if you stay put. I'll see you tomorrow for Christmas, even if I have to send up a snowmobile. We'll celebrate your birthday then. Okay, hon?"

"Sounds great, Mom."

After the age of thirteen, Christmas, birthdays, New Year's seemed to roll into one. Slipping into her pajamas and cuddling up with Cheddar and a good romantic suspense where the heroine kicked butt and shot the bad guys was sounding more and more tempting.

"Did your brother or sister call?"

Are you kidding? They don't call unless they need something. And I'm done trying to stay connected with them. "I'm sure they're busy. They'll call when they get a chance."

"I asked them to call. Tell Ethan I'm glad he decided to join us this year."

"I will." She wasn't about to argue with the only person who remembered today was her birthday. "'Bye, Mom. Love you."

"Love you too."

Noelle swiped her thumb across the screen, shoved the phone in her pocket.

"Was that your mom?"

"Yep." She lifted and dragged her feet through the deep snow toward the house, thinking about Ethan and what he told her.

"What was that about a birthday?"

She shrugged. "Mom's upset we can't

celebrate today. Tomorrow will be soon enough."

A mass appeared in front of her. She couldn't stop in time and collided with his chest.

"Why didn't you tell me today was your birthday?"

"It doesn't matter."

"Says who?"

"Says me."

"Birthdays are special."

Here we go. Frustration bubbled just below the surface. "For an educated man, you seem pretty confused. You don't believe in love, or celebrating holidays, but you believe birthdays are special. Doesn't that strike you as odd?" She held out a hand. "No, don't answer that. Now I'm being a jerk, and I hate morons. I'm going to take a hot shower and warm up. Then I need to call a few friends." She took a step, then turned back. "And before your hero gene kicks in, I want you to know I'm fine. You don't have to worry about me. In fact, you don't have to worry about anything at all. I'll be outta here in a few days, and you can go back to ignoring life."

Her hands were shaking so hard she shoved them into her pockets, took one step, then another, determined to make it to the house before one tear fell.

Who was he to tell her love didn't exist?

Her father and boyfriend had all abandoned her, not to mention all the guys in between who didn't last. The last three guys she dated did their best to make her believe she wasn't lovable—but their opinions didn't matter. She didn't need anyone to lecture her about what it was like to hurt.

She was alone. On her birthday. And that just sucked.

Lying in bed that morning, she reaffirmed her commitment to be a successful singer/songwriter, and to live a positive life.

Too bad the good intentions didn't last.

CHAPTER ELEVEN

Ethan assumed the always positive and perky Noelle would have wandered down for lunch after she showered.

There was no evidence she'd eaten breakfast.

She hadn't retrieved her guitar.

And Cheddar was nowhere to be found.

The old familiar feeling of guilt came to visit. Some days he wished the feeling of inadequacy would take a permanent vacation. He told her the truth about what a failure he'd been. A failure as a husband, father, friend, but she hadn't wanted honesty—or his version, anyway. The only thing he'd ever been good at was being a doctor, and he was a helluva good one.

Then again, maybe the truth was like fear. Both got in the way.

Just after six o'clock, he exhaled a long, gusty sigh and climbed the stairs of shame to knock on her door.

He waited. Listening.

He raised his hand to knock again, but hesitated.

His breathing stalled.

"Come in." The fragile voice was tucked behind the door.

Relief pushed the gloom of guilt aside. He opened the door slowly. Noelle sat on her bed with a book in her lap and Cheddar curled by her side. The optimistic, buoyant, passionate Noelle had disappeared. Only sadness remained. She'd been crying. The tissue shrapnel scattered on the bedside table spun his moral compass and landed on guilt.

Even though she was hurting, Noelle's eyes were still kind. She probably had no idea how to be cold-hearted and heartless like him.

"I came to see if you want some dinner."

"I'm not hungry. Thanks anyway."

He stared at the planks in the wooden floor, disgusted with himself for ruining her birthday. He should go, leave her alone, yet he found himself walking into the room and sitting on the edge of the bed.

"I'm sorry, I—"

"Please." Her gentle tone increased the angst. "You have nothing to apologize for. I shouldn't have pushed. You loved your wife. Anyone who sees you would be blind not to notice."

"We were both so much alike. Driven. Focused. She had a passion for medicine." He rubbed at the palm of his hand. "My dad always wanted me to be a doctor. To be honest, being a doctor wasn't a profession I would have chosen for myself. It wasn't until I met Brigitte that I fell in love with being a doctor. When she died, the passion disappeared."

"Then you not only lost your wife and your child, but you also lost direction." She blinked as she processed the additional information. "I can understand why you withdrew and took time out to find your way again."

"After they were gone I felt like I stopped breathing."

"You were right. I have no idea what losing a loved one feels like. To be loved completely, unconditionally must have been amazing."

Brigitte and Callie had loved him, yet he didn't see it. "I didn't realize how much I loved them until they were gone."

She tipped her head to the side to see his face. "She loved you. How could she not?"

"Brigitte loved everyone, and gave everything she had to everyone else." *That's why I never truly believed she loved me. It was just what she did for everyone.* "As a doctor, we take an oath to heal the sick, to take care of human life. Those simple words come with a burden. The drive to heal leaves very little room for anything else in our lives. Brigitte gave everything she had to her profession, and to Callie and me."

"But, she—" Noelle traced a finger around the design on the bedspread. "You must have been proud of her."

He reached for the box of journals he'd lugged up the stairs. "You asked me to tell you about my marriage. I think you will find what you need in here." He lifted the lid off the box. "A couple of months after the accident I was angry and eaten alive with hate. I couldn't focus. I had all these thoughts running around in my head, and I needed to make them stop, so I committed to writing down all the things I could remember."

Noelle reached for the lid and placed it back on the box. "I can tell you don't want to read the journals." The gentle notes in her voice only amplified her compassion. "I'm sorry I've pushed. You will read them when the time is right."

"But what about your song?"

"You mean *your* song?" She leaned forward to touch his chest. "You're holding the song safe, in here. It will reveal itself when it's ready."

Placing a hand on top of hers, he let her warmth seep into his hand. He wanted to feel the connection. Embrace the affection that hadn't been there before.

For the first time, he wanted to crack open the bottle holding his hurt and let out the pain.

He opened the box again and lifted one of the journals to turn to the first page.

BRIGITTE, *love.*

I MISS YOU. *I miss feeling your warmth next to me when I wake up. I miss having someone who understands and pushes me past being a realist. I miss holding you in my arms. I'm not sure you ever realized how much.*

. . .

YOU TOUCHED SO *many lives with your healing hands.*

THE BEST DAYS *we had were working side by side, problem-solving, working to find treatments and cures. There was nothing more special than watching you and Callie curled together sleeping. Each moment is a snapshot in time, to be saved and preserved. I mourn the day you were ripped from my life.*

YOU WOULD LAUGH *at me and call me foolish for thinking such a thing, for you were always one to live your life to its fullest. I live alone with memories of you and Callie, my loves. Tell Callie I love her, and I'm glad you are together, and please know I'm so, so sorry.*

ETHAN

. . .

212 | LYZ KELLEY

A COCKTAIL of emotions mixed and stirred. He shifted uneasily. "Maybe I shouldn't have read you that one." He closed the book.

Noelle touched his shaky fingers. "You don't have to backspace or edit your life for me, or anyone. You get to choose what you share, how you feel, what you do."

Not always. He didn't get to choose when he was young, and so he'd chosen to shut out the world. Live inside himself, where life was safe.

"I always felt like I was walking on eggshells with Brigitte. She always wanted more from me, but I never could figure out what she wanted."

"Have you ever thought that maybe all she wanted was you? Not the brilliant doctor. Just you. The man."

"What if I don't know who the man is? What if I'm only the doctor?"

"Being a doctor is only part of who you are. You care about people. You want to protect them. My guess is you've learned to block out their pain by protecting them. You've become so good at avoiding emotional involvement that when it comes to your personal life, you don't know how to reengage."

She was right. Instinctively he knew her point was solid, but it went way beyond just being a doctor. "I never thought of it that way."

"She gave you Callie, and you can't tell me you didn't love that little girl with everything you had."

"Callie." His daughter's name grew wings and floated into the room.

An ache as pure and resonant as crystal ran from his head to his toes.

How could she possibly have known how he felt? It was like she could read his emotions and thoughts. The heat of her hand warmed him, and he couldn't accept the sympathetic warmth. He paced to the window, pressing that same hand against the cold pane.

"For months I blamed myself for Callie's

death." *And for my unborn child's.* "If I had only been there."

"Oh, Ethan. If you had been there, you might have been killed as well."

"That might have been easier," he uttered softly, hoping she didn't hear his truth.

Noelle's face appeared as a reflection in the glass. She stood behind him, her arms outstretched. His fingers tightened on the window frame. The guilt of being with Noelle gnawed at him, but he didn't want to feel guilty anymore. He'd felt guilt. Remorse. Bitterness. And he was damn tired of feeling angry, so he'd worked hard to feel nothing.

"You shouldn't feel sorry for me. I need to blame myself. Who else is there to blame?"

Her hands dropped to her sides. "Ethan, it doesn't do any good to place blame. All those negative feelings can do is prevent you from being happy."

"I deserve to be unhappy. I should have been there. I shouldn't have taken the call." She gasped, but he continued. "I've gone over and over and over everything that happened.

Every word. Every action. Every excuse. Brigitte begged me not to go. Like an intricate surgery, I assessed each stitch, each gesture, trying to figure out if I could have done anything different. Searching for anything I could've changed so both of them would still be alive."

She placed a hand on his shoulder. "Their death is not your fault." Her body pressed against his. "Is this why you bury yourself in your work, to make amends for something you think is your fault?"

"Yes. Can't you see? I don't deserve a second chance. I had it all, and I blew it." He took her hand and threaded his fingers through hers. "I'm sorry if I've ruined your fairy tale. As I said, love hurts."

"I have to believe love can heal and be good."

"Why do you need to believe?"

"If love doesn't exist, what are we here for?"

Some of us aren't really living—just working hard. "I thought you were an idealist."

"Maybe, but I'd rather be an idealist than just going through the motions. There has to be more to life than the daily grind." Cheddar rubbed his head against her shin.

"It's time for dinner," Ethan said, for lack of anything else to say, trying to find a way to wade out of the deep, suffocating waters. "And I think someone else is hungry too."

She ran a hand down the cat's back and up its tail. "He didn't get his supper."

"I made Pilau if you're hungry. I left it to simmer."

"What is Pee-lah?"

"Pilau. It's a rice dish, although I've added meat. Maggie would have cooked up a special meal for your birthday, but it's all I've got."

"You cooked me dinner for my birthday?"

"And I have apple pie for dessert. Don't be impressed. It's one of those frozen jobbers."

Jackpot. There it was. The little flicker of joy that started at her mouth and swarmed upward until the light flashed in her eyes and made her whole face light up.

"I'll be down in a minute to help. If you're

cooking me dinner for my birthday, I want to change."

A thrill of excitement zinged up his arms and down the length of his body. "Great. The table is already set. Come down as soon as you're ready."

"Okay."

When he looked at her this time, he didn't see any similarity to Brigitte.

He'd been wrong.

Noelle wasn't anything like Brigitte. Sure, she had the same inner strength, but she connected with people in a very different way. Noelle gave people around her a soft place to land. She didn't push a person to be what she believed was their best selves, and that's what made people feel safe with her.

He stared after her, admiring the slim curves of her hips, and swing of her hair before she disappeared into the dark hall heading for the shared bathroom.

He rubbed at his chest. The chronic ache didn't feel all-consuming today. Maybe her healing warmth had melted the crack in his heart.

Yet he was still broken.

He had to learn to stop caring about Noelle.

She was fun and bright and happy, and the last thing he wanted to do was extinguish her light.

CHAPTER TWELVE

"Whatever you cooked smells amazing." Trapper greeted Noelle with wags and wiggles as soon as she entered the kitchen. The neatly set table, complete with matching pottery, stainless steel, and crystal, touched her heart. Ethan had centered the bowl of pinecones she collected from the yard in the middle of the table and placed a cream-colored candle in the middle.

"What's this?"

Ethan shrugged. "Since you're stuck here, it's the least I could do for your birthday."

Knowing he willingly worked so hard to

make her birthday special spread warm appreciation limb to limb.

Ethan lifted a wooden spatula from the simmering skillet. "Want a taste?"

He lifted the rice mixture higher, allowing the steam to swirl into the air before aiming for her mouth.

Their eyes met. His breath caressed her skin with soft strokes. She closed her eyes and opened her mouth to receive his gift. "Oh, my. What a unique flavor."

The spice reminds me of you.

"The first time I tasted the dish, I was in love."

"Me too." The idea slipped so casually into her mind, but she wasn't talking about the meal.

Love? Holy crap. Was she really in love with him?

Yes, her heart responded.

The feeling couldn't be love...could it? The desire to lean in for a kiss was real. It had to be her rebound brain leading her astray. Disillusioned lovers hopped from the frying pan into the fire all the time. Jumping in bed with the first guy after a breakup, decent or not, was nuts. She didn't want to get involved with anyone, and sex made her brain believe crazy, wonky things.

She had things to do.

A career to get off the ground.

Yet there was something about him that filled her to the brim. Nooo. She couldn't think like that. She wasn't his type. He wasn't available. She took a step back to let the magic fade.

With the thread broken, Ethan picked up the wooden spatula to stir the thick mixture. "Pilau is an African rice dish spiced with a little bit of cumin, black pepper, cinnamon, cardamom, and just a touch of cloves. I like to add meat, carrots, and raisins to the basmati rice, although it's not traditional."

Act normal. Breathe. "Whatever you put in that stuff is amazing." She pushed her shoulders back, pretending he hadn't caused her heart to flutter. "Thank you for cooking dinner, and setting the table, and for making my day special." She sat on one of the counter stools to watch him cook, even though she should be thinking of ways to avoid him. If she allowed herself to get invested in a relationship with him, he would change her life.

Yet she had plans.

She couldn't get distracted or deviate from fulfilling her dream.

Look where trusting got me.

While she enjoyed the instant connection of family and friends, she wanted more.

Yet here, in the kitchen, he looked like the savory dish he was preparing, spicy, hot, and yummy.

"Did you work on your songs this afternoon?" Ethan pulled two wineglasses from the cabinet and poured her a glass of red.

"I tried, but nothing seems to be working. I used to be able to bang out a song in an hour. The past few months, I haven't been able to tap into my well of creativity."

"Does it have anything to do with your former manager?"

"I don't think so. I'd have plenty of material for breakup and stupid-girl songs. I feel so dumb. Months ago, Jon started staying at work late. The excuse seemed plausible. I was busy. He was busy. I didn't notice his absence. When several of my friends saw him at a bar with different women, he easily explained the sightings away. He told me it was a business meeting, and I believed him. Or at least I wanted to believe him. Trust is so fragile."

"Was he dating someone else?"

She took a long draw of the wine. The dark red fruits tantalized her taste buds and quickly slid down her throat, leaving a lingering tang. The alcohol seeped into her pores and soothed the ache of deception.

"Several someones, actually. I learned his office couch was used quite often."

"Ouch."

"Exactly." She took another sip of wine to clear out threatening tears. "The pathetic part was I believed him when he said he wouldn't do it again—that I was his one and only—that he'd made a mistake."

"There are guys like that." His tone was even, nonjudgmental, kind.

"Please tell me you don't condone such behavior."

"I don't understand that type of behavior, but I can't judge someone else, because I wasn't the type of man I should have been for my family."

"I'm sure you were doing important work."

"Yes, I was saving lives, but shutting out the rest of the world in favor of my career isn't a good excuse. If I could get a do-over, my family would be the priority."

The self-loathing in his tone about ripped her heart out. She wanted to reach out and touch him, take away the pain, but instinctively shied away from the dangers. She'd give and give and give, and he wouldn't be able to give back.

His hurt and pain tossed her about like a stormy ocean. She needed to grab onto something—anything—positive. A change of direction was warranted. "What was Tanzania like?"

"Hot." Ethan's laugh was crisp, short, but there was an underlying sense of pleasure she hadn't heard before. "The culture is rich. There are a bunch of ethnic groups, and everyone speaks a different language. People rely on the land. Living there can't be compared to anything here." The lightheartedness faded. "The poverty makes you want to give everything you have. Especially when kids line the side of the road crying because they don't have enough to eat."

"I bet it was hard."

"Hard?" He shook his head. "More like inspiring. A good majority of people in the US have clean water and access to food and medicines, while more than half the population in Tanzania lives below the poverty level. And yet they work the land, and their culture is strong."

"What was it like living there?"

"Crowded."

"But, I thought…"

"You thought lions, zebras, and giraffes, and miles of space, oh my." His eyes lit, accompanied by a cute little smile. "No, we lived in Mwanza in the Lake Zone. It's a big, crowded city where a lot of the research is done for malaria and AIDS." The gratification returned. "Nature's beauty at its best. To me, Tanzania is one of the most beautiful places in the world."

"Would you go back?"

"To work? No. To visit. Definitely. This time, I'd hike and fish and do a little exploring." He laughed. "I'd go on one of those tourist safaris."

"You say you loved the culture, the people, but there is nothing in this house, no paintings, little carvings, pictures, to remind you of your time there."

He pulled the skillet off the burner and shoveled the rice mixture onto the plates. "Ready to eat?"

She slid off the high back chair. "There I go again. Putting my foot in my mouth."

"You didn't." He collected the plates. "Since it's your birthday, let's eat in the nook this time," he added, and carried the food to a small, round oak table by the large picture window just off the kitchen.

"You're being polite, but I did. I get curious and poke inappropriately into peoples' lives."

"Your question was legitimate and insightful. Most of the stuff I brought back was given to me by patients and friends. There's a hand carved mask that's quite impressive. Then there's my daughter's soda can lizard. It was made from recycled material and given to Callie by a nurse at the hospital." He sighed a laugh. "I should have my mom ship me my ostrich boots. Everything is stored in South Carolina."

"South Carolina. Why there?"

"It's where my parents live. My dad still hopes I'll take an attending position in one of the research hospitals there." *Which will never happen.*

"Why didn't you go home?"

I didn't want to be suffocated. "I became a doctor because my dad pushed us kids into what he considered worthy professions. After meeting Brigitte, I realized that even though I graduated top of my class, and had my choice of places to take up residency, I didn't have the passion, not like some of the doctors, who wanted nothing more than to dedicate their life's work to solving a single problem. I realized working in a large hospital with the sole purpose of making a name for myself was my father's dream, not mine."

"I've got the opposite problem. My mother never wanted me to go into the music business. She'd rather I was a waitress or a hairstylist, but I always wanted to sing."

"It could be she's just afraid for you. Singing is a tough way to make a living." His expression narrowed, became contemplative. "Maybe that's why my dad wanted us to be doctors, lawyers, and bankers. The jobs pay well."

"There is something to be said for putting food on the table." She slipped another bite of splendor into her mouth. "This is so good. Will you teach me how to make it?"

"I'll try. I've never been good with recipes. I tend to toss what I like into a pan and hope for the best."

"You sound like my mom. If she doesn't like the ingredients in a recipe, she changes them."

"Tradition is the only thing that matters in my family. My mom would never dream of altering a recipe. Every ingredient is measured with precision. My Nan always said perfection couldn't be improved upon."

"You don't talk about your family much."

"No, I guess I don't."

Disappointment eased into her chest, and she reached for her wineglass. Asking pointed questions and shutting down conversations had become her specialty. "So...what's your favorite sports team?"

His whole being perked up, and she silently laughed at her witty change of subject.

She didn't care what his sports team was,

only that he kept talking, opening up. Living. The conversation meandered from sports to politics to world events, and back to Elkridge and how much he liked it here.

He scooped the last of his meal and put it in his mouth, then drained his wineglass. "Ready for pie?"

"Sure. I'll clear the table." She reached for his plate just as he stood, their faces passing within inches of each other. His smell tickled her senses, and her soul whispered *yum*. She leaned in and absorbed the scent.

He closed the distance and his lips pressed against hers. Her flash of surprise quickly settled into an ooh-la-la tingle. His mouth was warm, demanding, yet reserved. The sweet sensation made her toes curl. She almost whimpered when he pulled back.

"I shouldn't have done that." He straightened, his face going pale.

"Maybe not, but it was a beautiful gift."

His blush got an even brighter red. "Gift?"

"It's my birthday, remember?"

The plate she was holding disappeared from her hand.

"If you think that was your birthday gift," he studied her mouth, "I'd better make sure your actual present is more memorable."

Her skin warmed when he placed a hand on the small of her back. He pulled her closer. His mouth lowered to hers. He paused and hovered just above her lips. "Are you ready?"

She should have stepped back, made an excuse, but all her brain could process was: *ready*.

His mouth consumed hers. His tongue outlined her lips, teasing, pleasing, tempting her to open to him. When she couldn't resist anymore, her lips parted. Instantly his tongue sought hers. A tango of emotion. Back and forth. Dips and swirls. She pressed in. He made a sensual noise, then pulled back.

Her head dropped to his chest. "Holy crap."

"Did you like your present?"

"If I say yes, will you still kiss me again?"

His shoulders shook and chest bounced

with a laugh. "Do you want to be kissed again?"

Yes!

Her limbs buzzed.

Her cheeks tingled.

The wine. It had to be the alcohol making her so reckless.

"Um, I better say no. I don't make good decisions after I've had a glass of wine."

"Gotcha."

The heat switched off, and he grabbed the serving dish like nothing had happened.

Had she been dreaming? The way he leaned in, searching, playing...he felt something. She was positive he did.

"Hey, I was going to load the dishwasher," she objected.

He lifted the scrub brush from the back of the sink. "That's okay. I need to keep my hands occupied and off you."

"So it wasn't just me who felt it."

Ethan looked down at the tent in his pants. "Isn't it obvious?"

"Now you've pointed out the facts," she

snickered. She took two steps closer and lifted her hand, but he backed out of her reach.

"I don't think we should complicate things." He held the scrub brush in front of him like a sword. "I mean...I'm staying here, and you're leaving for LA."

She placed her wineglass on the counter. "In that case, I think it's best if I finish my book. I was just getting to the good part."

"What about pie? I have vanilla bean ice cream, too."

"Pie's always good for breakfast." She hoped her disappointment wasn't posted on her emotional billboard. She enjoyed his company and would have liked to hear more about his travels, but more talking would lead to more kissing, and he didn't want more. Even though she did.

"Good night, then, and happy birthday."

"Thanks for the meal and my gift." She leaned down to pet Trapper. "See you in the morning, old man, and no getting into your stocking. I have a surprise for you."

Trapper lifted his head and lapped at her chin. She didn't look back while she made her way to the stairs.

She had to be careful. Staying with Ethan under the same roof after a kiss that curled her toes wouldn't be easy. But she was strong, just like the people of Tanzania. She'd make the roommate situation work until she got enough money to head for LA.

Although she wished she could find a way to reciprocate his gift. The tender, needy, memorable kiss would stay with her, and be the one against which all future kisses would be measured.

CHAPTER THIRTEEN

Maybe attending the Elkridge Annual Christmas party was a good thing. It was an opportunity to prove to Tom he wasn't a total anthropophobic. He could handle interpersonal relationships and social interaction. He could. He wasn't shy.

Then again, there was Noelle, with her endless smile. She distracted him. Her strength was camouflaged and had sneaked up on him. Underneath the silly, bright red Wonder Woman top was a true woman of steel.

He opened the café's front door and made

the effort to plant his feet on the welcome mat when the rowdy sound of "Jingle Bells" made him want to turn around and go home.

He wouldn't leave her. Thanks to Tom and Noelle, he was learning what was important. For some reason he had the impression she was nervous about tonight, and he was here to make sure nothing went wrong.

A seven-foot nutcracker stood sentry in the corner of the café, a Christmas tree balanced out the room at the opposite end, and small white twinkle lights hung from every booth and table.

A long table pressed against the far wall was jam-packed with potluck meats, salads, and breads, while townspeople gathered in clumps of twos and threes, laughing and talking. The comfortable exchanges appeared normal, as if it was just another ordinary day.

But today wasn't just an average day.

Today reminded him of the bleakest moment of his life, and he didn't want to celebrate it.

"Ethan, Noelle, you made it." Maggie's

voice carried over the conversational noise. A couple of people waved, others continued their conversations, and a few, like his uncle, nodded a greeting.

Ethan felt like a pack mule, he was carrying so many packages. Noelle handed her mother the seven-layer Jell-O salad and a plate of gingerbread cookies. Bill Mason lifted the gifts from his arms.

"You two look festive." Maggie winked. "I don't think I've ever seen you in a sweater, Ethan. Very handsome."

He fought the urge to scratch at the wool irritating his neck. The only red object in his closet was this sweater, which his mother gave him years ago for Christmas. He only kept it to wear during his annual video call, to please his mom, and then it came right off, to be stored for another year. But this time he got smart and put on a T-shirt first, so only his neck and wrists suffered. At least he didn't have to dress fancy. Jeans and boots were the best he could do, since not all the roads had been plowed, making the drive a slippery challenge, and he needed to be dressed for possible driving emergencies.

"Hi, Mom." Noelle pulled the wool scarf from around her neck. "What can I help with?"

"Hang your coats, then find a place to sit. We're just about ready to open the buffet." Maggie rushed toward the crowded food table with Noelle's layered Jell-O salad.

Noelle inspected him like a critical care nurse might examine a patient. "Are you okay? I'll stay with you if you'd like."

"Noelle, I'm old enough to manage on my own. I don't need a chaperone." But he liked knowing she wouldn't be too far away.

"If you need me, just stick your hands in your pockets with your thumbs out and I'll come rescue you. And before you ask, it's a trick my girlfriends and I used at a bar or party."

"Interesting." He leaned in closer, mostly to get a whiff of her vanilla shampoo. "And what if you didn't have pockets?"

"Then we put our hands on our hips with

our thumbs forward. It's an odd position, but it works." She pointed to a group of women gathered around a table. "I'll be over there if you need anything."

Tempted to try out her rescue method to see how she reacted, he shoved his hands in his pockets...and at the last minute tucked in his thumbs. If she was into rescuing, maybe she could give him CPR lessons. He regretted ending their mouth-to-mouth session. In fact, he'd dreamed about the gift kiss all night, only his fantasy didn't end with the kiss.

She continued walking toward the table crowded with the women he referred to as the local women's club. Several had giggling babies bouncing on their laps.

The joy of lifting Callie to his shoulders to hang the Christmas tree top came rushing back, and he had to work to breathe in and out. He could still feel her giggle vibrate through his arms and bounce on his shoulders. Hear the joy in her laughter. See the delight on her happy face.

He sucked in the cherished memory. *You can do this.*

He spotted Tom talking to Harold, the owner of Valu-Shop. Every few seconds, Tom shifted his gaze in his direction to check on him.

He was fine.

This whole Christmas jingle-all-the-way thing was his uncle's fault anyway. If his uncle hadn't placed him on forced leave, he'd be at the office working—a very convenient excuse to miss all the holiday festivities, and the uncomfortable feeling of being where he had intimate knowledge of just about everyone in the room.

"Ethan." His uncle greeted as he approached. "I see you haven't learned how to smile yet." His uncle's whispered statement was louder than Ethan would have liked.

"Know any good plastic surgeons?"

"Funny, but plastic surgery won't fix your crankiness. You need to learn to find the joy in life."

"Seems like we're repeating a conversation we've already had."

"We wouldn't keep having it if you listened for once."

"Look, Tom. You were right. I needed to take a bit of time off. If I'd kept pushing, I might have made a mistake."

"Everyone makes mistakes, Ethan. You're a brilliant doctor, but you are human." Tom crossed his arms and rocked back on his heels. "I know this is a tough time of year for you. For two years I've stood by and watched you run yourself into the ground, taking on extra shifts, volunteering for the emergency crew, working nonstop. Pretty soon you'll run out of runway. You're headed for a crash, and I care about you enough to help you avoid going headfirst into the ground. I know you love Brigitte and Callie."

"Stop. Stop right there. You know what I went through."

"I do. And that's why I'm telling you to take some time." Tom leaned closer. "You're like a son to me. I care about you, Ethan."

"I know." He took the opportunity to wrap his arms around his uncle's shoulders and gave them a couple of good manly slaps to make up for his previous hesitation. Tom stiffened, then relaxed into the unusual embrace. "I care about you, too."

Ethan stepped back, not sure what to do next.

Tom's intense stare didn't help either. "It will all work out, Ethan."

"It's just losing Callie, and then discovering Brigitte was pregnant." Ethan pulled at his collar. "I would have wanted her to tell me. I would have." Sorrow burned the linings of his chest.

A glistening sorrow filled Tom's eyes. "I know you want answers, but you'll never know the why, Ethan. Stop beating yourself up."

"Easier said than done." Ethan pulled again at the sweater's collar, grasping for anything to give him a sense of normal. He pointed at the table where Noelle had settled. "What is up with all these Christmas carols? And what's on everyone's heads?"

Tom looked at the booth with a half-dozen women crowded around the table, then chuckled. "This year's theme is Rudolph, and Ashley Bryant brought antler hats. The baseball caps light up."

"You're kidding."

"Have a beer. It gets easier with a beer. Besides, there are benefits to being off—you can drink as much eggnog as you like."

"Did you warn Maggie about salmonella poisoning?"

Tom placed a hand on his shoulder. "Ethan, there are certain things you simply cannot tell a woman. Telling Maggie Conroy her family recipe is a health hazard is one of them."

"I see your point."

"Why don't you mosey on over and see what your roommate is up to?" Tom urged with a little head nod in the direction of the corner booth.

"Who, Noelle? She's not my roommate."

Tom's brow arched in an uh-huh kind of way.

"She's just visiting, and hasn't given me a second thought."

Tom continued the placating nods. "Right."

"She'll be leaving in less than a week."

"Uh-huh."

Not buying it, huh? "What?" he asked, working the innocent angle.

"In the past three minutes, every one of those women has looked over here, and Noelle's blushed a time or two." Tom placed a hand on his shoulder. "I think there's a thing or two you need to learn about women."

"I suppose you're going to teach me." Ethan poked at his uncle teasingly.

"Nope."

"No?" He laughed and nudged his uncle with an elbow. "Come on. I'm sure you're just dying to impart all your manly wisdom."

"Nope. There are things a man has to learn on his own."

Ethan leaned in closer. "Come on, now. Won't you at least give me a little hint?"

Tom turned, yet all the humor had faded from his eyes. "Your dad wasn't always right, you know." His expression deepened into a serious attitude. "In fact, William was wrong about a lot of things. Lots of people marry more than once."

"Not in our family. Look at you. You've never married." An odd emotion flashed across Tom's face, then floated away.

"I was in love once. It just didn't work out." Tom's voice had softened. He scratched at his ear, and then coughed to clear his throat. "You need to follow your gut, Ethan. Talk to Noelle. Don't listen to your dad." Tom slapped him on the back with a friendly whack, then wove through the tables toward the buffet.

What was that all about? And what does my dad have to do with Noelle?

Seconds later, Noelle threw her head back and laughed, then the whole table started laughing. She'd left her hair down, and the blonde curls fell just below her shoulders, the blush of her cheeks, the way her gaze met his, she was rapturous. At that moment, the music faded, the lights dimmed. The light above the booth highlighted her presence. She was amazingly beautiful.

Why hadn't he noticed before?

She'd transformed from cute to stunning.

With each laugh or glance his way, his body did the oddest thing. His muscles relaxed. He almost felt human.

If he wasn't more careful, he'd end up a limp pile of flesh and bone on the floor.

But why did she keep looking his way?

He'd love to know.

CHAPTER FOURTEEN

Noelle rushed to the corner booth to visit with Ashley and Mara. "Kym is that you? Color my toenails purple." Noelle leaned in to hug her high school friend. "And look at you. Where did you get that tan?"

"Zach and I have been working in LA the past few weeks. He just started working on movie cars for a new show, but wanted to fly in and surprise Hank for Christmas." Kym scooted over to make room. "Luckily we got here before the big storm hit. Zach's been working nonstop to help Hank with car repairs. Does anyone in this town have a car that runs?"

Mine's working. It just can't deal with the two feet of snow.

"I was wondering who the good-looking guy is that Hank was talking to. Nice catch." Noelle gave Kym the thumbs-up. "I'll be in LA in a few weeks, and I'd love to get together. It will be nice to know someone there. Maybe I can talk you into doing my nails. I haven't had a good mani-pedi since I left town."

"I'd love to get together. I miss everyone."

So do I. She'd been texting or chatting with everyone at the table for the past few days. It was like everyone just picked up where they left off. She had forgotten what it was like being around people who'd known her from the time she took her first steps. There were no secrets. Only acceptance.

Kym reached for her drink and Noelle grabbed her hand. "Wow. Look at the rock."

The whole table froze like mannequins. Mara's head snapped toward her best friend. "Did you get engaged?"

"I was going to tell you. Zach proposed on the way here. He stopped in front of the nail salon. He said it was where we first met. I reminded him we actually met at Lookout Point, but who cares? He's such a romantic." She wiggled her fingers, showing off the sparkling diamond. "It got me all choked up and ruined my mascara."

"And you've waited until now to tell us?" Mara chided. "I would have run into this place screaming."

"No you wouldn't have. You don't run anywhere. And it's not like I can text you."

"Yes, you can. I have text to voice." Mara tried putting on airs she didn't possess, which made her haughty expression even funnier. "Joey bought me a new phone."

"Fine. Just call me out why don't you?"

The back-and-forth banter between Mara and Kym was just for giggles. Kym had stayed with Mara after her parents and sister were killed in a car accident. It took months of rehabilitation to get Mara back on her feet, and Kym was with her every step of the way, one of the many reasons Kym and Mara were best friends, and nothing could separate them.

Kym made a clicking sound with her fingernails and looked uncomfortable. "Don't make me apologize." She added a bit of attitude. "You know I'm not good at saying I'm sorry."

"We've been friends since grade school. There's no one who knows you better than I do. And don't you pretend sorry isn't in your vocabulary." Mara threw her arms open. "Now wrap those scrawny arms around me, give me a hug, and promise me you will at least tell me when you get married. I bet it will be on the beach on some exotic island."

"You're so needy," Kym whined, with a little snicker thrown in.

"Zach's a wonderful guy." Mara pulled back. "We took a vote, and we like him, so you can keep him."

"Thank dog-farts for that. Otherwise I'd have to kick him to the curb like a piece of wet trash."

Ashley choked on her drink, giggling. "Seriously, though, I'm so excited for you."

Noelle studied each face at the table. Each friend was about her age, and either engaged, married, pregnant, or had kids. What was wrong with her? Was she always picking the wrong guy out of a misguided need to find the relationship she couldn't have with her father? She looked at Ethan. There had to be a reason she always fell for ineligible guys.

Mara sat in the far corner of the booth rubbing her baby bump while Ashley breastfed her newest. Jenna kept everyone entertained, talking about her most original Sin Sugar flavors. As Noelle quickly learned, besides chocolate, cherry vanilla was fast becoming a best-seller.

Jenna nudged Noelle's arm. "What are you doing to your yummy doctor? He looks dangerous."

Noelle glanced past Ashley. Sure enough, Ethan looked like someone had just stolen his Christmas stocking and he was looking for the thief. Poor guy. Maybe she shouldn't have forced him to come.

"It's a hard time of year for him," Noelle offered as an excuse.

Ashley adjusted her cotton nursing blanket. "Hasn't it been three years since his family was killed?"

"Yes, but, there's no time limit on healing the heart."

"Did you try the chocolate Sin Sugar I gave you?" Jenna winked.

"Leave poor Noelle alone," Mara said in her defense. "She's not responsible for fixing Ethan. Besides, Maggie mentioned you plan to leave shortly for a singing job in LA."

A ball of frustration wadded in her gut. "It's not a job yet. It's just an audition." She pulled a corner piece off the nearest napkin and rolled the paper around and around in her fingers. If only she could bundle the restlessness plaguing her for the past several days into a small ball, she'd flick the disquiet into the trash.

Ashley's eyes narrowed. "The last time we

talked you were so excited about the opportunity. What's changed your mind?"

"I am excited."

"But?"

Noelle tore off another piece of napkin. "Living in LA is expensive. I don't even have enough money to make the trip yet, plus I'm supposed to have a couple of songs ready and haven't had time to practice."

"Why don't you sing at Mad Jack's on Friday?" Mara suggested.

Enthusiasm pumped her heart a bit fast, then stalled. "I was going to talk to Jack, but I'm sure the schedule is already set."

"I know for a fact it isn't. He asked me to sing this week, but can you imagine me trying to fit a guitar on my lap with this bulge?" Mara folded her hands on top of her swelling stomach. "Jack will be thrilled if you say yes. There's usually a big crowd by 7:30 when I start my set. I bet Jack will give you the same deal. I get three percent of the bar tab, plus we can pass around a collection hat."

"I'll sing, but I couldn't ask people to just give me money." *It seems so wrong.*

"Why not?"

"Yeah, Why not?" Jenna gave her a look.

"I love to sing, and would sing for free just to get up onstage and play some of my new songs."

"I'm thinking Noelle doesn't remember how good she really is." Mara placed a hand on Ashley's forearm. "She's always been way too nice"

"I agree. Too nice." Ashley's accusing brows lifted. "We're going to have to rough her up a bit."

"Oh, I don't need to be roughed up. I've whacked a few bartenders upside the head with a beer glass when they thought sex was included in the bar fee."

"That's more like it." Ashley chimed.

"So, how about it?" Mara circled the conversation back around. "Will you sing for us Friday night?"

Noelle's fingers tingled with excitement. Her mind started preparing a song list. "It would be a lot of work to get the songs ready."

"You can do it." Ashley's eyes sparkled with encouragement.

"My take-home is usually somewhere between one-fifty to three hundred bucks," Mara added.

A swirl of possibilities pumped up the excitement. "That's a lot. I could make it to California and have a little left over."

"So? What do you say?" Jenna prompted.

"I'll do it."

The hoots and hollers and whistles sent tingles of joy bouncing through her chest. God, she missed her friends. The late-night chats over a gallon of ice cream. The pajama parties. Getting ready for high school dances. She missed having their unquestioning support.

Sure, her friends in Nashville were always available for a movie, or dinner, or meeting for coffee. There was always friendly banter, but never the unconditional, unending, uncritical support.

"Sounds like you ladies are having way too much fun," Ashley's husband, Chase, appeared at the table. He placed a burping pad on his shoulder and held out his arms. Ashley lifted Bobby, her two-week old, from her breast.

"I was thinking the same thing." Ethan came to stand by Chase.

The longing in his eyes when he looked at Bobby almost broke Noelle's heart.

"Noelle's singing at Mad Jack's Friday night." Ashley handed Chase a blanket. "We need to get the word out."

"I'll help." Joey, Mara's husband, joined the group, holding Caitlyn, Ashley's firstborn. "I'll have it added to the town's event calendar."

"You don't need to do that, Sheriff." Heat crawled up Noelle's neck.

"It's not a problem." Joey dismissed her misgivings.

"And I'll post something on the community's Next Door page," Grant, Jenna's husband, joined the group along with a smiling little boy she and Grant called Kyle.

Overwhelmed, Noelle began to push out

the booth, but a warm, calming hand landed on her shoulder. She eased back into the booth.

"And I'll help in any way I can." Ethan squeezed her shoulder and sent a clear message of support.

She looked around at the smiling faces surrounding her. "I can't thank you enough. Although you might live to regret it. Once I get started singing for a crowd, it's hard to stop."

"You make this mamma proud." Maggie nudged her way into the circle. "Now get your butts over to the buffet table before the food gets cold."

"Yes, ma'am," several of the group said in unison.

Maggie blocked Noelle's way. She put a finger under Noelle's chin and lifted. "I'm proud of you."

"For?"

"Doing your thing."

Really? Tonight was the second time this visit that her mother had said she was proud.

A merry-go-round of joy circled, spinning faster and faster. "Thanks, Mom. That means a lot."

"Don't be getting sentimental on me. Join your friends and load your plate. I don't want to pack leftovers."

Maggie stepped back and allowed Noelle to climb out of the booth. She wrapped her arms around her mother. "Merry Christmas, Mom."

"Merry Christmas, and happy birthday, baby girl." Her mom lovingly cupped her chin with her warm hand, then released her. "Now go before you turn me into a blubbering idiot."

Noelle took a couple of steps, then stopped when Ethan cut across her path. "Are you okay?" he asked.

"Just a bit overwhelmed." She studied his face. He didn't look so tired today.

"I can set a broken arm, but I sure can't figure out what you need."

Where did that come from? She searched his eyes for a clue, but didn't find any answers. "If I could make one wish for you, it would be that you figure out a way to be happy. You're a good man, Ethan Brennan. You have way more to give than medical advice."

"That's a mighty big wish." Ethan faked a gag and cough. "I thought you might ask me to do something hard."

"Happiness is a worthy pursuit."

"Yes, it is." Ethan pushed out an elbow for her to take. "Shall we?"

Noelle didn't hesitate, slipping her hand into the crook of his arm and wrapping her fingers around his scrumptious bicep. They joined the line. In a few steps, she would have to let him go to fill her plate. The thought struck her as odd. In a few days she'd have to walk away, but for tonight she wasn't ready.

She studied his stone-hard face, once so unreadable. Now she could see the subtle changes. Ethan was a series of opposites. Serious yet gentle. Moody yet sympathetic. Hard yet soft. In the past few days, she'd begun to understand the dynamics of Ethan Brennan.

He wasn't a jerk. He was a generous man, yet complex.

The kind of man she could spend a lifetime getting to know, and enjoying every moment of it—yet for some reason she couldn't quite trust her heart.

CHAPTER FIFTEEN

Noelle scanned the long table on the far side of the room for an empty space. Not finding one, she approached the next nearest table. Her mother had hijacked Ethan, saying something about helping her get more prime rib.

"Is this seat taken?" Noelle waited behind the seat next to Harold Talbott, a retired Air Force veteran and owner of the only grocery store in town.

Harold shoved away from the table, stood, and pulled out the chair next to him. "This seat has your name on it."

Noelle returned the older man's smile, then set her wineglass and plate overflowing with turkey and stuffing and German potato salad on the white tablecloth her mother used for special occasions. "Thanks." She sat as Harold helped slide her chair under the table.

"Do you mind if I sit here?" Ethan asked from the other side of the round table that could seat six.

"Help yourself, Doc," Harold said before she could respond.

Ethan settled in, setting his silverware aside, and placing the napkin in his lap. "How's Claudia doing?"

Typical Ethan, she thought. His first concern was always to check on his patients.

"The dementia is getting worse." Harold's somber voice was colored by a strong edge of concern. "She's having trouble remembering what day it is, and keeps forgetting where she put things. She's getting confused and frustrated more often. Plus, she's continuing to withdraw."

"Is that why she didn't come tonight?"

"That, and her specialist put her on Donepezil. She's lost her appetite and is tired all the time. I didn't want to leave her alone, but she insisted I come tonight, so our daughter came up from Denver to keep her company."

Ethan nodded, his eyes distant, contemplative. "That's to be expected. Why don't we have lunch next week? I'd like to show you an article in one of my medical journals. Then maybe you can discuss the options with your doctor." Ethan scooped a combination of prime rib and mashed potatoes into his mouth.

"Thank you for caring."

Ethan swallowed his food. "You're welcome. And I mean it about talking to your doctor, okay?"

But Ethan went far beyond his role of doctor. She'd overheard the phone calls over the past few days—him fighting with the insurance company on behalf of his patient, and listening to Mrs. Cranston tell her stories. He sincerely cared, and his empathy made him different. She laid her hand on top of Harold's. "Is there anything I can do while I'm here?"

"Maybe you can stop by the hair salon and sing her a song. She'll get her hair cut on Thursday."

"Sounds like a wonderful idea."

"I'll call Sue at the salon and set things up. Claudia loves your singing. Always has. It will be a treat."

Drops of gratitude pooled in her heart, pumping her full of confidence. "She also loves Christmas carols. Maybe I can throw in a few."

Harold's eyes went a little misty as he talked about all the Christmas music he loved. The conversation meandered into holiday traditions, then stories about Christmases past, with Harold carrying most of the conversational weight. She added a sentence or two now and then, but Ethan was quiet. He watched. Listened. His typical monosyllabic responses whittled down to silence. She caught herself more than once twirling her hair around her finger. A dumb-blonde habit she thought she'd broken.

Harold pointed his fork at her after he swallowed a bite. "Your mom says you're on your way to California."

"That's right. I'm meeting a friend there."

"Your friends here miss you. I hoped you might consider staying."

"Just passing through." She worked hard to hold on to the stubborn conviction that had become slippery recently. Lately she'd begun to question why she was really going to LA. Yes, she wanted to sing and write songs, but why LA? Was it the right move?

There were studios in Denver. In fact, there were big names recording in Colorado. Plus, these days, with the internet and social media, she could create, record and distribute music from almost anywhere, as long as she was willing to travel. Money was the issue, and LA had to be the most expensive place to be. Then again, Colorado wasn't a megatropolis of opportunity.

Decisions. Decisions.

Fears of making the wrong decision doubled the doubts. Fears of staying brought on the feeling of failure. What had she said to Ethan? Something about never being able to see fear until it reveals itself.

She dragged her cranberry sauce around her plate with her fork, making a swirling design.

"Noelle?" Ethan set his fork on his plate. "You said you were looking for different material. What if you write a song about Alzheimer's? It affects about six percent of the senior population. Researchers think the disease is genetic, but more research needs to be done to prove the theory. Writing a song might help the cause, and help you connect with new audiences."

"I'm not sure it's what the producers in LA are looking for."

Harold wiped his mouth. "Why not? If Kenny Chesney can sing about the disease, why not you?"

"There was another guy, too. Tim

something." Ethan pointed his fork at Harold, his gaze on the ceiling, his mind working.

"Tim Rushlow?"

Ethan pointed at her. "Yeah him. He wrote a song about Ronald Reagan."

She took a deep breath. "He did, and he got some radio air time."

Harold leaned her way. "I heard they played the song at 5K running events."

"Charities do tend to adopt theme songs."

She looked up at Ethan. "Is this your way of getting out of helping me with your song?"

"I said I'd help."

"Yes, but—"

"You can do this, Noelle." He spoke with more confidence than she felt at the moment.

What was *wrong* with her? Normally she was all-out confident. Never asking why. She always went for it, hoping something would stick. But lately. Lately, she was questioning everything. Thank heaven gratitude filled the gap self-doubt ate away. "You think so?"

"I know so."

"And so do I," Harold added. "You've always been determined and driven."

Maggie took the chair next to Ethan. "Why are you all looking so glum?"

Ethan relocated the water glass so Maggie could set her plate down. "We were just talking about—"

"How great this food is," Noelle interrupted quickly, not wanting to talk about singing or music around her mother. Until tonight, her mom hadn't embraced her career choice, and Noelle didn't want to delve into the sour subject tonight. It was Christmas, after all.

Ethan studied her for a moment before turning to Maggie. "Mrs. Conroy, this meal is delicious."

"Ethan, I told you before. Don't you dare call me Mrs. anything. You do, and I start looking around for some old lady, and I refuse to be old. So you call me Maggie, or Mags, or nothing at all."

"Why are you getting so fussy, Maggie Mae?" Harold pointed his fork at her mom.

"Your daughter, Ethan, and I were having a pleasant conversation."

"Of course you were. Noelle is the kindest, sweetest person on this earth. She doesn't have a mean bone in her entire body. I'd wonder if she was my kid, except for the fact that I popped her out the night before Christmas. Fastest and easiest delivery of my three kids."

"It's usually the other way around." Ethan pointed out. "Usually the more you have, the easier it is."

"Not in my case." Maggie thrust her knife a couple of times in Noelle's direction. "My eldest was my perfect child. I swear she came out smiling. It wasn't a month before she was sleeping through the night. Too bad my other children didn't follow her example."

"Now, Maggie," Harold chided, "you can't pick favorites."

"I'm not picking favorites. Noelle can be stubborn as a jackass. Takes after her father that way."

There it was again, her mother comparing

her to that loser. "Let's change subjects, shall we?" Noelle added with a faux bit of Christmas cheer. "What's your favorite holiday treat?"

The three groaned in concert.

"How about them Broncos?" Ethan supplied with a grin and a wink.

"That's better." Maggie grabbed the metal water pitcher and filled the glasses on the table.

At some point during the night the conversation turned its focus on Ethan. He answered question after question about his travels. With every passing minute he became more animated, the tension in his shoulders easing, and he even managed to smile now and then.

"I think Tom mentioned you were working in Nepal at some point." Harold prompted.

Ethan swiped a napkin across his lips. "I worked there for a little over a year."

The way he pulled at his collar when

nervous tickled Noelle. "Why did you choose Nepal?"

"The country was rebuilding after its Civil War, and there was a great need for medical services. I was young and idealistic, and wanted to help. Besides, working in an emergency ward overseas, I got to see and do a lot of things other physicians starting out don't normally get to do for years."

"I get the impression you changed your mind."

"One of the world's leading infectious disease experts talked me into leaving Nepal and joining him in Tanzania. He said my skills were being wasted."

"That's a nice compliment." Maggie tapped him on the arm.

Ethan chuckled. "It would've been if I hadn't known he was short-staffed and needed another warm body."

"But, still…" Noelle supported her mother's statement. "It must have been nice to be asked."

"It was," Ethan nodded. "As it turns out, he

was right. In Nepal I saw everything from gastrointestinal disorders to parasites to tuberculosis. Couple that with the lack of medication and nutritional disorders, and there was often little I could do to make patients comfortable. The hospital I was assigned to lacked structure, and I was doing very little in the way of prevention.

"In Tanzania, I was assigned to help with a malaria study. Several of the leading diagnostics experts were trying to develop a way to accurately diagnose malaria. We gained access to a rapid diagnostic test, but were forced to do more outreach than studies. We believed the country's practice of overprescribing antibiotics was contributing to the spread of drug-resistant malaria strains. Our tests were inconclusive, but every year we were finding containment of the disease harder and harder."

"Weren't you afraid you'd get infected?" Noelle's attempts to keep her concerns dialed back failed.

"No, not really. There's a list of things you

can do to prevent infection, like using treated mosquito nets, covering your body with loose clothing, using repellent, covering windows and doors with screens, plus there are anti-malaria medications."

"Fighting malaria is important work. Why did you give it up?"

"I came to realize that while fighting malaria is important, I enjoyed working directly with the patients. Once I understood my calling, I decided practicing in Africa or overseas wasn't required."

"Is that why you ended up in LA?"

Tom placed his hands on Ethan's shoulders, effectively stopping the conversation. "Actually, that's why he ended up here." Tom squeezed his nephew's shoulder. "Is everyone ready for gift opening?"

"Oh, goodness. Look at the time." Maggie pushed her chair back. "I had better help Jenna put out the desserts."

Harold reached for several empty plates.

"I'd better get in line before the cheesecake is all gone."

The table emptied faster than a nut bowl at a football party.

"Doc B, will you join us?" She hoped he would, since she was having a hard time avoiding being alone with the sexy hunk across the table. She didn't need dessert. All she needed to do was spread Jenna's Sin Sugar on Ethan, and she'd be good to go.

The fantasies of working off the calories kept getting more and more elaborate and frequent.

"Just for a moment." Tom set an envelope on the table. "I want to give Ethan this."

Ethan stared at his uncle, who was sitting on the edge of the chair vacated by Maggie. "I thought we both agreed we were going to donate to charity this year."

"We did, and I did, but this is something extra."

"Do you want me to open it now?" Ethan glanced at the envelope and then his uncle.

"Your choice."

Ethan ran his fingers under the edge of the flap, then pulled the official-looking piece of paper from the envelope and scanned the contents. "I thought...are you sure about this?"

"I've been sure since the first day you came to work for me. I've just been trying to find the right time."

"This is unexpected. Thank you. Your vote of confidence means a lot."

Noelle's curiosity expanded. She leaned forward to get a peek at the paper.

Ethan tilted the paper in her direction. "Tom's giving me his medical practice."

"I'm not just giving it to you. You've worked hard for it. It's yours if you want it."

"But, why now? Did something happen?"

Tom scooted the chair in closer. "The kid they brought in after the car accident on the highway got me thinking."

"You mean the guy my age thrown from the car—the one who wasn't wearing a seat belt."

"Yeah, that one." Tom pointed at the

envelope. "You're not young, and I'm getting old. If you sign on to take over, then we'll need to get you in a position to fully take over when I snuff it. That takes time."

"You're too young to snuff it," Ethan made the statement in a way that left no room for argument.

Without thinking, Noelle reached for his hand. "You'll do great."

Ethan grasped her fingers and didn't let go.

Tom pushed back his chair. "I'll let you two get on with your evening."

Ethan studied the piece of paper. Noelle squeezed his fingers to get his attention. "I guess this means you're going to stay in Elkridge."

"I like the people here. Between working at the office, the urgent care clinic, and volunteering for emergencies, my life is full."

Meaning there will never be room in your life for anyone else—like a girlfriend or a wife. "You can't work all the time. Maybe you should find a hobby. I know. You should take cooking classes. That way you wouldn't have to resort to drinking those nasty shakes all the time."

"If you love what you do, there is no need for a hobby."

"True." She pulled her hand back, as disappointment ebbed and flowed. "Should we go watch people open presents?" She put on her concert face, the one she'd perfected over time in front of the mirror.

Ethan shoved his hand in his pocket and pulled out a little box. "This is for you."

Her lungs expanded with surprise, then deflated. "But I didn't get you anything."

"Are you kidding? You put up a tree and have been baking all week." He pointed at the box. "It's just a little something. Open it."

She tugged at the red bow, and slowly opened the white box. Inside was a silver metal pick, with the words, "When words fail, the music remains." A stinging sensation attacked her nose and eyes. She pressed her hand against her chest to stave off the onslaught of emotions.

"You get it. You get me." The awe in her voice swelled. "When did you have a chance to shop?"

"One of the nurses at the hospital stamps jewelry, and I thought… Do you like it?"

"I *love* it. It's wonderful." *Just like you.*

She'd never meet anyone else as heroic as Ethan. There weren't enough Ethan Brennan's in the world.

"Thank you." She said with an emphasis on the word "you," and hoped he understood how much she appreciated that he believed in her.

He pointed a thumb over his shoulder. "Shall we?"

The majority of people had gathered around the tree, yet she wished it was just the two of them. There were so many things she wanted to express to this honorable man, but now was not the time or place. She picked up her napkin and stealthily dabbed the corner of her eyes and blinked.

"Sure." She glanced at the tree again. "I

hope everyone likes socks, because that's what everyone's getting this year."

"A practical gift is always good."

Another supportive comment from the caring doctor. She had better guard her heart, since the smart, kind, gorgeous, addictive man would certainly wreak havoc with her heart.

She pushed back from the table. "You go ahead. I'll be there in a minute."

"Is everything okay?"

No. My head and heart are having a tug-of-war, and I'm afraid my heart's winning. "Everything is fine. I'll see if Ted needs any help in the kitchen."

She turned away from the skepticism in his expression, and hurried down the staff hallway, past the kitchen, and out the back door. She needed to chill, and the below-freezing temperatures would help. The wind had blown a six-foot snowdrift against the fence. Maybe she could bury her head in the snowbank and pretend she didn't love Ethan.

How had she let it happen?

She drew in a breath, letting the frosty air settle around her.

"What in the hell are you doing outside without a jacket? I raised you better."

She held up a hand, hoping her mom would go back inside. "I just needed a minute, Mom."

"Don't you dare get the flu just because you can't figure out what to do with that sexy doctor of yours."

"How did you…never mind." She could swear her mother was a mind reader.

Maggie laid an arm across Noelle's shoulders. "I can tell you like him, but you're leaving. It's not smart to start something you can't finish."

"I know, but it's a little too late for that." Her heart squeezed at the thought. "Why does my timing always suck?"

"You could always stay."

And give up my dreams? No thank you. "I know you would like that, but I can't."

"I'll give you the same advice my mother

gave me. You don't have to travel the globe to find what's already in your heart."

Noelle groaned. "Grandma was always giving advice, but I could never figure out what she meant."

"You will. Give it time." Maggie's arms tightened around her. "Ready to come inside?"

"I think I need another minute."

"I'll give you two before I send Ethan out here. That cutie-pie will chase you back inside quick enough."

"You wouldn't."

Maggie pressed her lips to her forehead. "Watch me." She swore her mother giggled. "I love you, baby girl, and I'm glad you came home. I've missed you."

"I've missed you too."

"Come inside when you're ready. I'll save you a mug of apple cider."

Maggie disappeared through the back door. Noelle crossed her arms and shivered, then looked up toward the heavens. *What am I supposed to do now?*

CHAPTER SIXTEEN

Ethan placed the letter his uncle had given him in the desk in the corner of the living room. Gratitude, wonder, optimism, and a dozen other feelings rolled into a ball of excitement. For the first time in years he had a clear direction.

Not of his father's choosing.

Not of Brigitte's choosing.

But his. He wanted nothing more than to work at building this practice, and becoming more of a part of this wonderfully quirky community. There was no decision to make.

His cell rang, and he hesitated,

recognizing the number. If he had worked through Christmas, he wouldn't have been available to take the dreaded phone call. He let the phone ring again, then expelled a heavy sigh. "Hello."

"Ethan. Merry Christmas, son."

"Merry Christmas to you too, Dad." Ethan closed his eyes and took a slow breath, knowing his father had been drinking by the way he slurred his words.

"Your brothers are here. I expected you would be home for Christmas."

No doubt his siblings were home with their wives and kids—each group a perfect family portrait. "I know. Trying to get to Hilton Head this time of year is tough. There are always closures and delays. Even getting out of Denver this year would have been tough."

"Your brothers make it every year. Next year try harder, would you?" The statement was more in the tone of a command, an order Ethan no longer felt the need to obey. "And," his father continued on like a bulldozer, "we still need to discuss your career."

Not happening. "Maybe we can catch up in the new year, Dad." His chest tightened, knowing full well he didn't want to discuss anything with his father, but he placated his father to ensure his mother didn't get hit with the brunt of his father's temper.

"Dr. Hamlin tells me you haven't returned his calls. University Medical is an honor roll research hospital. The best in the Carolinas. Working with a team of top-tier doctors would be an excellent opportunity, better than where you are now."

"I'm not sure I agree. I like working at the office and urgent care clinic, and doing a bit of search and rescue."

"Putting Band-Aids on elbows isn't what you went to school for. If you're not going to put your education to use, you might as well have taken creative writing."

"Dad—"

"Listen to me, son. With student loans and

bills to pay, you'll regret not taking your career more seriously."

And who says I haven't already paid off my loans? "I'm not sure I will, Dad. I love what I do. And I like helping people."

"Such a waste of talent. Did I tell you your brother was just promoted to Vice President of Operations at the bank?"

Typical. His dad couldn't wait to tell him about his younger brothers' accomplishments and tighten the screws to apply more pressure. He'd received two emails forwarding the press release announcing his brother's prestigious promotion, the first from his brother, the second from his father. "Congratulate David for me, would you?"

"Hold on, your mother wants to talk to you."

"Ethan?"

"Hi, Mom."

"Hold on. Let me close the door so I can hear you better." The clicking of high heels crossing a tiled floor and a door snicking shut reached him through the phone's speaker. "There, that's better."

"Sorry, I couldn't make it home, Mom, but you know it's for the best."

"Don't let William make you feel guilty for not coming home, honey. You just keep doing what you're doing. I want you to be happy."

"I'm working on it, Mom."

"And how's Thomas?"

His dad would never consider asking how his older brother was doing, but his mother had always been the peacemaker in the family. "Tom's fine. In fact, he's looking to retire next year."

"Oh?" His mother's voice swung up an octave.

"He's leaving me his practice if I want it."

"If? Is there a question? You love Colorado."

"Blue skies 360 days a year, skiing, mountains. It's not a bad place to live."

"Tom's always been a kind man. His offer is generous, and I'm sure you'll make the right decision. Happiness is priceless. Just remember that."

Ethan gripped the phone, holding it tight against his ear. "Has dad been treating you well?"

The silence told him more than words.

"He's not drinking as much these days," his mother's voice had pulled inward, "but you know your father. He's always had a temper, and he always wants what he wants."

"I wish you hadn't stayed with him for the sake of us kids."

"Oh, Ethan. It was my job to protect you and your bothers. I did the best I could."

"But still. If anything happens to you, Mom—"

"I'm fine, honey. It's not your job to worry about me."

"I know it's not about the money. I've put enough in your personal bank account to give you a cushion in case you ever decide to leave. You could start over. Find contentment."

"I know you disagree with my decision to stay. But staying was my decision to make. As cantankerous as William is, I still love him. He provided a good life for me and all you kids, and I can't imagine my life without him. I think you know what I'm saying."

Love. Damn that feeling. It could rip a person's heart in two. But in his mother's case, he thought protection was a more appropriate word. Really? Who could love a man like his father, who'd been raised to exhibit no feelings. To suck it up. To be unemotional. The man who raised him. Ethan's soul wept for the young boy who never got to play. "I do. Just know if you ever need anything, I'll be here."

The background noise suddenly got louder. "Here's your father."

"Mom. Please don't tell Dad about Tom's offer. It will only cause more trouble."

"I believe you're right, honey."

"About what?" his father's voice boomed through the speaker. "Give me the phone."

"Take care of yourself, Ethan." His mother's fragile voice made him regret not booking a flight home.

"Ethan?" His father's voice made him clench his jaw to keep from saying what he'd really like to say. But he couldn't. For his mother's sake. He'd have gone home if he had been sure his presence wouldn't create unnecessary tension. But he stayed away for the sake of his mother.

"Yes, Dad?"

"Think carefully about what I said." *Here it comes.* "I will not have one of my sons be a burden to society. You won't get a cent from me, or the trust. You haven't earned the right."

"I know, Dad."

"As long as that's understood."

The virtual poke of his father's finger could be felt hundreds of miles away.

The first time he'd overheard his Nan, his mom's mother, say something about his dad being desperate to get his hands on the trust money, and getting married to seal the deal, he'd been about ten. He learned Grandpa Brennan had established a trust with the stipulation his boys earned their first million by the time they were twenty-five. Otherwise the money would go to charity.

Granddad and Nan, his mom's parents, owned several restaurant chains in South Carolina. Several were in his mother's name for tax purposes, and were enough to meet the trust requirements when she signed the restaurants over to her new husband as a wedding gift.

Young and naïve and in love, his mom didn't know any better. The socialite wedding was the event of the summer. Everyone on the who's-who list had been invited. His father had no idea Ethan knew the truth, and since that day he'd lost all respect for his dad.

"I hear you loud and clear, Dad."

Money and position were all his dad cared about. The same with Grandpa Brennan. But Ethan saw how money made people do foolish things, and had vowed to end the vicious cycle. Money corrupted. Stole a person's soul. Left only hatred and a bitter taste behind.

"Ethan. Take care of yourself. I need to

run. The family is waiting for me. We're attending late mass, and need to leave."

I'll pray for you, Dad. "Say hi to everyone for me."

"Call your brothers next week. They will be expecting your call."

"Yes, sir."

He lowered the phone from his ear, disconnected, and tossed it onto the coffee table, his hands shaking.

He stayed on the couch and studied the ornaments on the tree, then became mesmerized by the blinking lights. A hand touched his shoulder, and his body lurched.

"I'm sorry. I didn't mean to startle you. I called your name, but you didn't hear me."

When he didn't respond, she sat down next to him.

"Are you okay?"

She shouldn't be able to read his expressions. He'd worked years to mask his true feelings. Men avoid showing sissy emotions. Men were tough, powerful, resilient—according to his dad—not crybabies.

"I'm okay."

"Could have fooled me. You look like a person who's just had all the marshmallows on their hot chocolate stolen."

He shouldn't have found the childlike sentiment endearing, but he did. In fact, he found her charming. He ran the back of his hand down her warm, soft cheek. She leaned into his touch and closed her eyes. Oh, God. He was in trouble. He should've gotten up and left, yet Christmas magic surrounded them. He slipped a hand around the back of her neck and pulled. He wanted to feel her soft mouth, taste her sweetness.

He shouldn't indulge.

"Tell me you want this."

"Ethan?"

"Tell me to stop and I will."

"I can't."

"Then I'll just have to be strong enough for both of us."

She reached for him. "Please don't."

He kissed her forehead, her cheeks, her eyes, her nose. "You're pure heaven."

"I don't want heaven, I just want you. I want to show you what you've been missing. To show you what life can be like again."

Her breath sent a fiesta of chills across his skin. "But you're not staying."

"No. But I want to give this to you. It's your Christmas gift."

He could taste the rum from the eggnog on her lips, but he knew she wasn't drunk. "Are you sure?"

"Absolutely."

With a groan, he pulled her to him, his arms circling her waist, lifting the fabric of her shirt to touch her heated skin. He leaned back just a fraction of an inch to look at her face. Her darkened gaze, full of desire, made him want things he shouldn't want. She shuddered before she pressed her lips against his as she reached and searched and pulled him closer. She wanted this as much as he did.

His tongue traced along the lower edge of her lips until she allowed him entry. He ran a hand along the edge of her panty line, diving below the elastic, trying to touch every inch of skin.

She reached for the edge of his sweater and lifted. The wool and undershirt hit the floor. He hissed as she traced a finger down the center of his chest. Seconds later, she followed the same line with her tongue.

"Noelle?"

"Shhh. I'm imagining you with frosting smeared on your chest."

"Chocolate or vanilla cherry?"

"How about both?"

He chuckled, then pressed his lips to her neck. "You already taste good enough to eat."

"Then take me upstairs."

He thrust his fingers in her hair and gently tilted her head back. "Noelle?"

Her eyes locked with his. "Doctor, stop being so practical and protective. I'm a grown woman. I know what this is."

"A bad idea?"

"It's two consenting adults, enjoying each

other's company and each other's bodies, and sharing pleasure."

He blew out a breath and shook his head. "That sounds rather clinical."

"Stop it, Ethan."

"Stop what?"

"Stop living in the past. Stay with me. Here. In the now."

"Fine, then let's do the wild-and-sexy on the floor, in front of the fireplace, under the Christmas tree. I want to indulge. It's Christmas, after all."

Her breath caught. "Sounds like fun."

He wasn't even sure if she'd ever experienced wild-and-sexy on the floor, but he'd like to be the one who showed her.

"Then let's get rid of these clothes. I need you. I need this."

Amazement skittered across her face. She blinked up at him. Without saying another word, she reached for the hem of her shirt and pulled it up.

"Well? What are you waiting for?"

You...I've been waiting for you.

CHAPTER SEVENTEEN

No one had ever told Noelle she was delightful before.

Her mom always said she was kind, and her siblings said she was a brat. Delightful seemed so formal. Stiff. She didn't know whether to be offended or indulge and play— but play she did.

She licked, and nuzzled, and giggled her way to the floor.

He needed to play.

He needed to let go. The only way to keep him from sliding back into his gloomy, painful past was to give him a playground full of a wonderland of toys.

Surprisingly, having sex and making him forget about his past made her feel better.

She wasn't rebounding.

And being with him wasn't a fling, or a one-night stand. The decision to be together was specific, purposeful. Just like him, she needed to help. To be wanted. Desired.

"Oi, I think my hair got tangled in the tree." She grabbed the hair strands and pulled.

"Hold up." He grabbed her hand. "You'll pull the tree over."

"That wouldn't be good."

"No." He kissed her temple. "But you taste good."

"Mmmm. So do you." Too good. "Maybe floor sex isn't a good idea."

He slid her bra strap off her shoulder. "It's a terrific idea." Her bra clasp suddenly popped open, and he lifted the edge of the fabric. "You're so sweet." His hot breath puckered her nipple.

She pushed at his shoulder. "I thought *we* were getting undressed. Not just me."

He looked up at her, and a wicked smile crooked the corner of his mouth. His clothes disappeared faster than her ginger cookies at the party.

Seconds later he returned for and indulged in a kiss. "Better?"

If he didn't look so darn cute, she might have laughed. But he was playing, and she didn't want to say or do anything to ruin the moment.

"You forgot something." She pointed at the long-leg boxer briefs hugging his thighs and his growing bulge.

He pressed his midsection forward to make sure she understood what she was in for. She wasn't frightened. In fact, she was intrigued.

"Take them off."

His brow lifted. "You first."

Looping her thumbs underneath the elastic, she slowly slid her panties down her legs, and hung them on a tree branch. She would have mirrored his sexy smile, but he kissed her again, and continued until she nearly forgot to think.

She fought to draw air into her lungs. His gorgeous hazelnut browns mesmerized. "Your turn."

He hung his briefs next to hers on the tree, then braced himself above her and pressed into her while she became acutely aware of his size. Her head fell back on the carpet, and she moaned. "What are you waiting for?"

He kissed her collarbone, her neck, her jawline, then licked her pulse point. "I'm waiting for you to change your mind."

"Not gonna happen."

He reached for his wallet, and slid out a crumpled condom packet. "This poor fella has been around awhile. It's past its expiration date, but I'm clean."

"I went to the doctor to be tested before I came home, just to be sure Jon didn't give me an STD. I'm clean and on the pill, but enough with the technical. Let's play."

A big, warm hand slid down her back and

around her butt cheek. "How hard do you want to play?"

"Let me show you," she leaned forward and bit his peck.

A slow smile crossed his face. "Now that *is* fun." He kissed her shoulder, then ran his tongue around her nipple and sucked in air. The nipple puckered.

She groaned, and her back arched up to meet him. He squeezed her butt cheeks, then stroked around her thigh and between her legs.

"Too bad that Sin Sugar isn't readily available." He shifted lower.

"Ethan..." She reached for his shoulders, but they were out of grabbing distance.

His facial hair scraped across the inner thigh. His tongue flicked and circled and caressed. Ethan Brennan sure knew how to frolic and take his time. His hand flattened on her stomach. She jerked.

"Relax." He kissed one thigh, then the other, then settled in between.

Relax, he says.

He got busy demonstrating the rules of the game. Her pulse raced. Her heart pounded. Her head pressed into the carpet. A scream welled in her throat and she opened, but no sound came out.

She reached toward him, but he continued to explore, his tongue drawing new designs on her folds. Who knew doctors could be so creative? Her fingers intertwined into his hair. She pulled gently, but his focus was unmovable.

If Santa existed, he just granted her Christmas wish.

A tingling sensation started at her toes and sizzled up her legs. His hot tongue lavished. He pushed her up, and up, and up—and finally over the edge.

"Ethan!" she screamed.

He braced an arm on either side. "Wrap your legs around my back." He lowered one inch at a time. His need was raw. His eyes hot and fierce. He pushed in, holding steady, then again, waiting for her to relax around him.

Then he thrust forward, pinning her to the floor.

A delicious sensation sizzled throughout her entire being. Cherished. Wanted. The emotions circled and combined and expanded into bliss. She wanted to give him everything and more in return. Rocking into him, she opened wider. When he began to move, she matched his rhythm pulse by pulse. Her breathless scream echoed through the living room as her body took over. Ethan continued to romp, and she wasn't about to stop him.

Noelle dropped a forearm over her head.

Two feet of freezing ice and howling snow pummeled the windows. A draft of cold air blew across the floorboards, but she didn't feel the least chilled. She was lying bare naked on top of a man she'd known less than a week. There were pine needles in her hair, but she didn't care.

Of all the reckless things she'd done in her life, this one was the most reckless and the most satisfying. It felt right.

The aftershocks of making love kept her warm. Her body quivered, and she dared not move to spoil the moment. Ethan stirred and rolled her to his side, propping his head on one elbow.

"Don't you dare ask."

"Okay, I won't ask."

"Good, because that was the best sex I've ever had. I think you melted my bones."

A slow smile formed—a real one, not one of those he plastered on his face when he wanted people to think he was happy. "Bones break, or get crushed, they don't melt."

"Oh yes, they do. Trust me. I don't think I'll ever be able to get off this floor."

"I'd better come to your rescue. You're already starting to get cold."

She glanced down to see goosebumps spreading across her torso.

In one fluid motion he pushed vertical to put another log on the fire. She took in his magnificence as he grabbed a throw from the basket by the couch, tossing it on the chair. Lifting her in his arms like she was light as a pinecone, he settled into the large leather seat. She curled into his arms, nestling in close while he tucked the blanket around them.

Trapper changed positions and settled next to the fireplace. Seconds later, Cheddar hopped up and settled in on top of the blanket. A gentle peace settled into her heart.

He didn't speak, and she let her breathing synchronize to his.

She laid her head on his shoulder.

"Noelle, I—"

"I read a study online that men should have an orgasm at least every other day to protect against prostate cancer." A deep breath of courage nestled into her lungs.

"Noelle—"

"Having sex is a much better way to keep the man-pump working properly, don't you think?"

He drew in a heavy breath.

"Apparently if you don't use your thing

regularly, fluid gets built up and can cause problems down there." She risked a peek at his face. "You masturbate, right? I'm assuming every male..."

The hitch of his chest made her stop.

"What? I'm serious."

"I know. That's what's funny."

How was it he made her so comfortable she wanted to stay in his arms forever and smack him, all at the same time?

She laid her head on his shoulder.

"Ethan, it was just sex."

He picked a pine needle from her hair and set it on the side table. "Noelle, we didn't have just sex."

"I know." She blew out a breath. "I don't know what I'm supposed to do now. I'm leaving, and you're staying."

He pressed his lips to the top of her head.

"Follow your dreams, Noelle. You need to find the life you deserve."

Her heart shuddered. What if she didn't know what she wanted?

"But—"

"You need to see if there's something for you in LA. I promise, I won't let this happen again. You don't need the added confusion."

And he wouldn't. His whole life was about staying in control, being deliberate and methodical. He didn't welcome people in his life, and she counted herself fortunate to be one of the few he allowed inside. "What if I don't get the spot?"

He wrapped a protective arm around her shoulders. "Then you'll be free to decide what's next."

A quiet part of her spoke up, questioning why Elkridge always seemed small and suffocating—why she'd never felt content living in the small mountain town.

Had Elkridge changed? Or had she?

At the moment, in his arms, her whole life became comfortable, perfect—even a little predictable. She surprised herself by thinking it felt wonderful.

CHAPTER EIGHTEEN

Noelle was up before dawn the next morning, shoveling out her car to head into Elkridge to help Jenna, then put in another shift at the café.

She was careful not to wake Ethan. In fact, she made every effort to ensure he slept in by letting Trapper out, feeding Cheddar, and brushing her teeth in the kitchen.

She couldn't allow herself to get hung up on the cute doctor. She needed to focus on her goals and build up some cash. She might not be sure LA was the perfect plan, but staying in Elkridge wasn't in the forecast either.

Sure, Ethan did scrumptious things to her body, things no other man had done, but she was mature enough to know the difference between sex, love, and commitment. She took responsibility for the part she played in what happened the night before, and didn't have any misguided notions of permanence.

There were no jobs for her in Elkridge, and she wasn't about to rely on her friends' goodwill. Jenna didn't really need help. That woman was a business machine. She was just kind enough to make up stuff for Noelle to help with so she could reach her travel fund goal.

Plus, she wasn't naïve.

When she walked down those stairs last night, she knew perfectly well what would happen. And every single second of what had happened between them was now tattooed on her brain. Evidence of what could happen between a man and woman when both partners' first goal was to please the other.

The feeling of being valued could be addicting.

Doctor Brennan was like a drug, and if she took too much, she'd never be able to rehab from his effect.

She drove into the alley behind the bakery and parked next to Jenna's Jeep. As she got out of her car, the snow whipped across her face. She adjusted her scarf higher, knowing full well the shiver running through her had nothing to do with the temperature. Ethan had unsettled her world, and she needed to figure out how to create more distance.

"I didn't think you would make it in today." Jenna slid a pan of bread into her oven. "Let me see if I can figure out something you can help with."

Jenna lifted another pan from the seven-foot rack. Her French braid trailed halfway down her back, and she looked cute—too perky for the pre-dawn hour. Noelle hung her jacket and scarf on a hook by the back door, then washed her hands. "I can always go

310 | LYZ KELLEY

over to the café and see if they need help there."

"No. No. I could use your help filling a batch of the Sin Sugar jars. The ladies in town decided they were great for stocking stuffers. I'm out of or low on all the flavors."

Noelle's jar was still sitting on top of her suitcase. She should have tried the chocolate-flavored spread on Ethan. Now it was too late.

"I bet the husbands love the idea," Noelle said, still groggy from lack of sleep. She placed a hand on the butcher block to hold steady.

Jenna's eyes danced. "They do. The whole idea started as a joke. Ashley, Mara, and I had an impromptu pizza/movie night, and let's just say Mr. and Mrs. Smith gave us a few ideas."

"The movie with Brad Pitt and Angelina Jolie?"

"Yep. Ashley questioned whether she could fit into that black leather outfit. Then Mara suggested she'd need petroleum jelly to get into those boots. That's when I said I had a better idea, and then it went from there."

"I'm bummed I wasn't here."

"Me too. But hey, we can hang out after your set Friday night."

Noelle's stomach tightened to the point of being nauseous and uncomfortable. She wasn't scared to sing. The response was more related to the fact she hadn't had time to put her song list together, and she didn't like hitting the stage unprepared. Put her in front of a hundred strangers and she could fake it. Put her in front of friends and family and she got nervous—mostly because she cared what they thought of her work.

"You're turning green. Don't tell me you're gonna back out." Jenna placed a large box of jars on the counter and a stack of labels.

"No. Not backing out. I was hoping to try out some original songs, but they aren't ready. I'll have to do cover songs, and that's not really going to show off the portfolio of work I've compiled. And without a band, you don't get the full effect of the sound. I'm just a bit disappointed, that's all."

"Did you talk your cutie into coming?"

"Who? You mean Ethan?"

"Who else would I be talking about?"

"He's not mine." *He's not anybody's.* "He said he'd be there."

"Good. I'll make sure we buy him a few drinks. Then you can jump him when you get home and spread on the Sin Sugar."

"Won't happen." She believed him when he said it would never happen again.

"I wouldn't be too sure about that. You're gorgeous, and he's single. I'm surprised you haven't bumped boots already."

She wasn't about to tell Jenna she'd already indulged. Jenna would tell Ashley, Ashley would tell Mara, and before she could even blink her mother would find out.

"Double-fudgesicles. I forgot to ask your mom how many pies she wants this week. Would you mind running across the street and asking her? I'd call, but she…"

"…never answers the phone this early in

the morning." Noelle and Jenna finished in unison.

"No problem. I'll run over now."

Noelle wrapped her scarf around her neck, grabbed her coat, and headed out the back door. A couple of minutes later, she pushed open the back door of the café and headed for the kitchen.

"Good morning, Ted." She peeked behind the grill's door, finding the huge man prepping his workstation for the day. "Have you seen my mom?"

Ted pointed with a scary big knife in the direction of the bathrooms without turning.

"Thanks."

She chuckled at Ted's typical response. Some things never changed. He'd never been much of a talker. Getting him to say anything before noon was like getting the toaster to sing.

She wove her way through the tables toward the other side of the café.

"Mom?" She called when she got close enough to the restrooms.

"In here," a loud voice boomed out from behind the door.

Noelle peeked around the heavy metal door. A toilet flushed, and Maggie walked out of the nearest stall with a plunger in hand. "This stupid thing keeps clogging. I need to call a plumber." Maggie dropped the gadget in a bucket to wash her hands. "It's early. I thought you hated mornings."

"I don't hate mornings, I just haven't convinced my brain and body to function before the sun is up and I've had several cups of coffee." She handed her mom a paper towel. "I promised to help Jenna with some baking, but she needs your pie order."

"It's on the counter." Maggie tossed the wad of wet paper in the trash and picked up the bucket. "Let me get it."

Typical Mom, she barreled through the café, always in a rush. If she'd been in a farmyard, the geese would have scattered, squawking and hissing and running in all directions. She pulled a pen out of her black apron, sliding the ballpoint down the extensive list.

"This should do." She handed Noelle the lined piece of paper.

"Sheila said she'd cover the café Friday evening so I can hear you sing."

Anxious misgivings made it difficult for her to swallow. "Mom, you didn't need to do that. You've heard me sing before."

"Of course I'm coming to hear my baby sing."

"The café is always so busy on Friday nights. Are you sure?"

"The staff can handle it without me for one night."

Noelle tugged on the end of her scarf. The multicolored yarn squeezed tighter and tighter around her neck, cutting off her air. "You don't like the food at Jack's."

"They got a new chef." Maggie leaned a palm on the counter. Her head tipped slightly at an angle. "What's this all about? You don't want me to come hear you sing?"

Dangit. "It's not that. You've always been

supportive, but I know deep down you never wanted me to sing."

"That's a bunch of bull-frogs." She scooted around the counter. "Who told you that?"

"You did."

"I never said any such thing." Maggie pointed at the swivel chair. "Sit."

Noelle slowly climbed onto the red rotating chair at the counter while saliva clogged the back of her throat.

"Seems you've been storing up a pile of hurt, so out with it."

Noelle twisted the mug on the counter to the left, then right, then released a long sigh. "You keep telling me I remind you of my father."

"You do. You've got his eyes, his ability to sing. And both of you are stubborner than an overloaded donkey."

She couldn't stifle her sigh. "My point."

"Now you wait just a minute, missy. Your father was a fine man."

"Yeah. The guy should have won the father of the year for knocking you up and leaving you in a hotel with no money and no way to get home. Plus, he got himself killed when he knew you were pregnant."

"Oh, hon. That may have been what you heard, but that's not how it was." Maggie pulled the scarf away from Noelle's face and brushed her hair back behind her shoulder.

Noelle nodded, unable to meet her mother's eye.

"I loved your father. More than I ever wanted to admit." Noelle could see emotions swelling and overwhelming her mother's ability to speak. She patted her chest above her heart. "Oh, lordy, that man was funny. He could make me laugh—oh, how I laughed. When he walked into the room, everybody looked his way." Maggie's voice softened into a sentimental rhythm. "Your father, he made me feel special. And boy, could he belt out a tune. Makes my heart pitter-patter just thinking about it." Her mom closed her eyes and swayed back and forth before again opening her eyes.

Wow. Didn't see that coming.

Maggie tapped Noelle on the thigh. "Now, you listen to me. I want there to be no mistake." Her mother's tone broadened and couldn't be ignored. "I've never, ever had anything against you singing." Noelle's mouth fell open, but her mother held up her hand to stall anything she planned to say. "As your mother, I have every right to want to protect you. When I was young, I spent years following your father and the band from city to city. We never had more than two dimes to rub together. There were times we didn't know where our next meal would come from, but we were mostly happy. Forgive your mama, but I wanted to keep you safe. I wanted you to have an easier life."

"But why did my father leave you in that hotel?"

"You got it wrong, hon. He's never left me. He died."

"But, you said…"

Maggie's eyes misted. "He was so excited after I told him I was pregnant. He talked about finishing the tour, maybe settling in

Nashville or Austin, doing studio work. He wanted to get married and start a family."

"Wait. He wasn't mad that you were pregnant?"

"Heavens, no." Her brows drew into a single line. "The idiot drove off to get a six-pack of beer so we could celebrate. A semi ran a red light and hit him on the way to the store."

Noelle leaned back in the chair, stunned. "So he wanted me? My father wanted me?" She pulled at the fringe on her scarf. "I thought I reminded you too much of him."

Maggie leaned in to get a good look at her face. "Is that why you left? You thought you reminded me of him?"

"Yes. Well, no. I left because I was young and foolish and wanted to prove to you I could make a living singing."

"Honey. Why didn't you say something?"

Her mom brushed at a tear that managed to find a path down her cheek. She'd never seen her mom cry. Ever. Concern welled in her core, and she touched her mom's hand.

"I didn't know where to start. You never talk about the past."

"Why should I? It's the future we need to look after. No one can change the past." Maggie squeezed her fingers. "If you want to know the truth, you sing better than Fowler ever did, and your father was a great singer."

"I'm not sure that's true. I've tried, but I can't get a contract. Every time I try out, people tell me I'm not what they're looking for."

"You're so much like your father. You have to learn life's lessons the hard way. It takes talent..." Maggie lifted Noelle's chin and looked directly into her eyes, "...which you have, plus a lot of luck if your goal is to land a record deal. In the meantime, you just have to love what you do enough to keep doing it until the moment comes."

"Do you ever think it will happen for me?"

A slow smile crept across her mom's face. "I guess you'll have to keep singing and writing to find out."

"Is my father the reason you never remarried?"

"Partially. After I had you, I was lost. I stayed with the band a few years. Held onto his memory. I was even stupid enough to sleep with Jimmy. He was your father's best friend."

"Uncle Jimmy knew my dad?"

"He was the bass player in the band."

"When did you meet David?"

"I met David a few years later at a concert. He was good to me, but we just didn't have the spark Fowler and I had. The best things that came out of the relationship were your brother and sister, and I had someone to hang out with. Life can get lonely, you know? However, I never could see myself being married, or putting up with another person for long."

"And here I thought you raised me to be independent because you hate men."

"Boy, you sure got a pile of funny ideas in that head of yours. Who stole my kid and replaced her with an alien?"

"Funny." Noelle scratched at a spot on her mom's apron and brushed off the dried food. "Fowler was good-looking. I mean, for an old guy."

"Hey, your father and I were the same age, and I'm not old." Her mom picked up a strand of hair and wrapped it around her finger, playing with the ends. "I don't think there's anyone more proud of you than I am, but he would have been proud of you too. You picked a hard road to travel, baby girl, but you've done well."

"You think so?"

Her mom straightened. "Where's that can-do spunk I taught you kids? You go out there, put your shoulders back, chin up, and you show them what you can do."

"I love you, Mom." Noelle leaned closer, and instantly her mom wrapped her arms around her. A dryer-warmed blanket of love settled around her shoulders, as the false belief she'd held on to for too long crumbled and drifted away.

Her non-hugger mom held on a couple of

seconds more than usual. Most likely to make sure Noelle got the hint. "I know, Mom. You don't have to say it."

"You'd better know I love you. I've said it enough. By now it should have stuck."

Noelle rotated her mom's hand over and drew a heart with her finger, then closed her mom's hand. "Will you please tell me what's going on with you? Are you sick? Do you have cancer?"

"There you go again, making mountains out of molehills. I've just got lumpy boobs. That's all. Grandma had 'em. I have 'em. I suspect you'll have 'em too. Just the way we're built, but it doesn't hurt to make sure."

"Are you positive that's all it is?"

Her mom brushed her bangs aside. "Always the worrier. I don't have the Big C or anything like that. When's the last time you had your boobs smashed?"

"A couple of months ago. I had a Pap smear too. I figured I'd better get it all done before I quit my job and didn't have any medical insurance."

"Smart girl." Maggie swallowed several times, and a smile gained momentum before her eyes got watery.

"Don't you have someplace to be?"

Her mother's gruff question she understood and appreciated. Now she understood her mom's heart had been broken and never fully healed. The knowing explained a lot of things.

"I'd better get this list over to Jenna. She's probably wondering where I wandered off to."

"You go on, then. I'll see you on Friday. I'll stay in the back where you can't see me, so you'll be fine."

Noelle folded the list and placed it safely in her pocket. "I'll save you a front row seat."

Maggie's shoulders pushed back. "You never liked me sitting in the front row."

"Time changes things."

"Yes, they do. You're a grown woman." Her mom's eyes went misty again, and she swiped off the tears with the back of her hand. "I gotta do something about that toilet."

And, just like that, her mom grabbed the bucket and disappeared down the hall.

Noelle eased out a healing sigh.

How could she have been so wrong all these years? Self-doubt had gnawed at her confidence, fraying the edges and making it smaller. Making her hesitate. Question everything. Was she good enough? Could she make it as a singer? How could she make her mom proud? She didn't need to worry about the last one anymore.

What else had she been wrong about?

CHAPTER NINETEEN

The house was too quiet. He woke up at sunrise to find Noelle gone and Cheddar lying on the pillow next to him.

Odd that he didn't hear her leave. He never slept. Not lately. But she'd managed to slip into his life so thoroughly he hadn't heard the shower running.

Then later he caught himself standing in the bathroom, just breathing in the smell of her shampoo and studying all the brushes, tubes, and boxes of stuff she didn't really need. She was beautiful, with or without them.

Although catching himself daydreaming about her things did make him question his sanity.

For years he'd worked hard to park in neutral. Now his mind churned with imagery of a spunky blonde.

With the practice closed for the holiday, he'd made a few phone calls to check on patients.

Mara Gaccione was still feeling pregnant with no signs of contractions, but she needed a refill of her prenatal vitamins. Her niece, Sophia, was getting over her cold.

Stella King said the side effects from the heart medication were minimal, and her grandson was feeling fine after he had his tetanus booster. She assured Ethan her grandson would think twice about trying to pull another squirrel's tail, which made him laugh.

Ethan also called Ernie to remind the deputy he was due for an annual physical in the new year.

When he finally ran out of people to call,

he figured a day of reading sounded like the perfect way to pass the time, yet he couldn't seem to concentrate.

He scratched Cheddar's chin, then stared at the office's copy of the medical journal with curled corners and ripped pages. The magazine, flipped opened to an interesting article on the effects of altitude change on anemia patients, sat unread. He smoothed the edges. A reminder he needed to find a way to pull Tom into the twentieth century. Electronic versions were available, yet his uncle insisted on receiving paper copies.

As he smoothed the edges of the pages, the sexy singer's sensual curves kept interrupting his rational thoughts.

Usually the consummate student, he sat staring at a page filled with incomprehensible words. He chided himself.

Trapper nudged his leg. "Hey, buddy. You miss her, don't you, boy? You better get over it. She's going to leave us both soon."

The sound of a car pulling into the drive produced a firecracker thrill. *She's home.*

Trapper made his way to the front door while he slid out of the high back leather chair to follow. He opened the door at the same time she reached the upper step.

"Hey," she offered with her usual cheerful smile.

His heart did a tapitty-tap-tap upon seeing those beautiful green eyes so full of glee.

"Here. Let me help you." He lifted the bakery box and a bag from her hand. "How was your morning?"

"Busy. I filled in at both the café and bakery. Jenna sent home bear claws. She said they're your favorite."

He could smell the cinnamon and brown sugar and the buttery cream sauce. "I don't have a favorite. All her stuff is good."

Noelle pointed at the bag. "Mom sent me home with Christmas leftovers. I think we'll need to freeze some of it. Otherwise, it will go bad before we have a chance to eat it."

We. She said the word we. His heart did a fist-bump with his chest.

Yet her mood suddenly changed and

dragged a bit. Her steps slowed and lacked energy, and she shuffled across the wood planks toward the kitchen. He watched and waited. Could she be regretting last night? He hoped not. Touching her. Feeling her move. Being inside her. It was magical.

"You're quiet today."

Her dull, lifeless eyes met his. "I've got a lot on my mind."

Oh, no. Disappointment surpassed his delight from the previous moment. "If it's about last night…"

She waved him off and concentrated on stacking the to-go boxes in the refrigerator. "It's not."

He shoved his hands in his jeans pockets, refusing to reach out. Touching her would lead to things he promised himself wouldn't happen. Sex confused things, and he didn't want their intimacy to force choices that weren't right for her.

"Do you want to talk about it?"

Her face creased into thoughtful lines. She folded the paper bag and placed it in between the refrigerator and kitchen cabinet, then scratched Trapper's chest. The lines next to her eyes deepened.

"Have you ever been in a situation where everything you thought you knew about life was wrong?"

"That's a pretty complicated question. Do you mind being a tad more specific?"

She paced back and forth along the kitchen island. Realizing she needed more space, he relocated to the stool at the counter.

She stopped to stare out the kitchen window, toward the mountain ridge. "My mom..." The desperation in her voice escalated, but her tone had sobered.

He leaned closer so he could hear her.

"...all my life I thought my mom didn't want me to sing. I mean she supported me, sure, but deep down, I thought she never wanted me to sing."

"But singing is part of who you are. I can't imagine Maggie asking you to give up the thing that's most important to you."

Shuffling back into the kitchen, she

hoisted herself up on the counter, her legs dangling over the side. "She didn't. I've been going over every conversation I can remember. Not once did she ever say, 'I don't want you to be a singer.' I just made an assumption based on how she felt about my father. He was the lead singer in a band. On the rare occasions he came up in conversations, she'd always change the subject, or get emotional."

"And you thought if you sang, it would make her feel bad."

"I hated my father. A guy I never knew. He made my mom sad, and I thought she never remarried because he'd hurt her." She swung her legs, her feet beating against the cabinet doors. "I wanted to be nothing like him. I didn't want to look like him. I didn't want to sing like him."

Oh, I totally get where you are. "Yet when you looked in the mirror, you were both the things you didn't want to be."

Her startled eyes lifted to his. "Exactly."

She rubbed at a spot on her jeans while a

sullen cloud hung over her, sending her inward. Cheddar, sensing her mood, jumped into her lap. She automatically stroked the orange cat, but her motions were subconscious. Slowly she lifted her head. "All day I've been thinking about how my assumptions drove everything in my life."

"You mean as far as singing?"

"As far as everything." She pulled Cheddar to her chest. "Going to Nashville. Which auditions I chose. The type of music I sang. R&B was his thing. I avoided Rhythm and Blues even though I love the insistent beat and the raw grit of the music. I love how R&B songwriters write about triumphs and failures and a little of everything in between. There are no limitations. Yet I refused to try out for any of those bands or a lead singing position."

"Yet you're auditioning for a band in LA."

"Yes, to be a backup singer and a songwriter."

An understanding floated in the air like little bubbles that suddenly connected, and made him smile. Maybe he really wasn't alone. "I get not wanting to follow a parent's footsteps."

"I thought he was the world's biggest jerk." She rubbed at her temple. "I believed he'd gotten drunk after finding out mom was pregnant, then got on his motorcycle. Riding drunk is a death certificate waiting to be signed."

"Did you think your dad didn't want you?"

"Yeah. Guess I was wrong."

He folded his arms and leaned against the counter. "Sounds like you've been sabotaging your own dreams. What are you going to do about it?"

"My dream of being a songwriter hasn't changed. And I've made a commitment to my friend, so I need to see this audition through. Depending on the outcome, I guess I'll figure out what comes next."

He'd like to help her decide what came next, but he needed to stay out of her life. She needed to decide what was best for her, and obviously she had much bigger plans than Elkridge.

"First things first. Don't you need to write a few songs? Maybe you can tap into your R&B roots."

"Don't remind me. Jade called again this morning, demanding to know where the song sheets were." She heaved out a long, frustrated breath, then an idea grabbed hold and her body vibrated with excitement. "There's a box in mom's garage with a whole bunch of music in it. It was my dad's. I bet if I plow through some of the old stuff, I can get a few new ideas."

Her enthusiasm was infectious. "That's the way to go after it."

She hopped off the counter and went to pass him. With no idea what he was doing, he snagged her wrist. Questions filled her eyes.

If he was going to lose her, he wanted to hold on to the few days they had left. "I'm truly happy for you." He loosened his grip.

"I know. I can see it in your face." The tension from seconds earlier eased. "This may sound odd, but I wonder if maybe fate pushed me into that snowbank. I needed this time to reflect. I feel so alone sometimes, and tend to second-guess whether I can do this singing thing."

"You can do anything you set your mind to. You are an amazing woman, Noelle." He spoke with a soft caress, hoping she'd open to him. "You are never alone. There is a whole town here to support you. Plus you have me."

She lifted her fingers to touch his face. She took her time, trailing her fingertips over his morning stubble. "I wish you could let go of the past." Her eyes searched his. "You have so much to offer this world with your brilliant, beautiful mind."

"We're taught in medical school to keep our emotional distance, yet hold onto the empathy. It's the best way to serve our patients' needs."

She placed her hand over his heart. "I get that, but not everyone is your patient. You don't have to keep everyone out. You can let a few of us in."

"I don't know how."

She lifted onto her toes and brushed her lips across his, then added a kiss to his cheek, then forehead, then nose, finally resting her cheek against his. "Yes you do. You just have to stop working so hard to keep the world out."

He closed his eyes against the emotions battering him and causing him to shrink inward. "Noelle. Do you know what you're asking of me?"

She lifted his hand and kissed his palm. "Yes. I'm asking you to face your past. I'm asking you to embrace it so you can let it go. I want you to find a new happy place."

He opened his eyes to see her. There was her gentle, hopeful, kindness. He wanted to hold onto her goodness, but felt the past pulling him back. He fought off the crushing hurt.

"I'll need some time."

"I know." She squeezed his hand, telling him she'd be there. Loaning him her gentle strength.

"Then let's do this. Let's work on changing our lives together."

She turned his hand over and started doodling invisible circles on his palm. "When do you want to start?"

"Now. You've only got two days to prepare a song."

She leaned forward and kissed the corners of his mouth.

"What was that for?"

"For showing me what brave looks like."

He wondered how she did it. She made him feel strong and vulnerable at the same time. He pulled her in between his legs, needing her close. He urged her to lean into him. When they were chest to chest, he caressed her back and pressed his nose to the crook of her neck to take in her essence, his lips resting against her hot skin.

She tilted her head back, pulling her hair away from her neck. He nipped and sucked her skin. Her soft mewling encouraged him. He threaded his fingers through her hair and tugged.

"You're so beautiful." He blew on her shoulder and watched chill bumps cascade down her neck and shoulders and back.

"Please." He understood her plea.

She wanted him, his touch, but he hesitated. He made a promise. He needed to keep it. For her sake. He placed his hands on her hips and pushed. Her urgent whimpers made him pause. He groaned.

"Ethan, take your first step forward." She rested her hand on his crotch. "You want to let me in, I can feel it."

"Noelle, I don't want to—"

"Hurt me? I won't let you." She pulled on his arm, forcing him to stand, then placing a hesitant hand on the waist of his sweatpants.

"Are you sure?"

She stepped back and slid her jeans down her legs.

He closed his eyes, but he still saw her standing in front of him, asking him to trust her—want her. He didn't need to see her to know she wouldn't hurt him, not intentionally.

She wouldn't be the type of woman who would hide a pregnancy from him, or take a lover because her husband was working too many hours.

Sweet Noelle wouldn't hurt another person that way.

He tightened his grip. "Noelle. My sweet Noelle."

He lifted her, and she wrapped her legs around his waist. She kissed his neck as he climbed the stairs. When he set her in the middle of his bed, she crawled backwards, then held out her hand.

"Let's make each other feel better," she said, her voice lush with need.

"I'll make you feel more than just better." He yanked off his sweatshirt and stepped out of his track pants.

She gasped. His heart leaped with pride when her appreciating gaze swept the length of him. She made him feel extraordinary. So extraordinary, he could almost burst with joy, something he hadn't felt in years. Maybe ever.

"Ethan?"

"Hmm?" He nipped her calf, then thigh, working his way up her body.

"About that sweet thing?"

"What about it?"

"I'm not in the mood for sweet. How about salty, maybe sweaty?"

Oh, God. He'd definitely needed to go to confession after this. He leaned in and blew hot air through the fabric of her panties. She shivered and fisted his hair, pulling him higher, attacking his mouth as soon as it was within range. She nipped his lip, then his cheek.

He sucked in a breath and then laughed at her bold actions. "Do that again."

She wrapped her arms around his back, and dug her nails in, scraping along his spine. He pulled her panties aside and thrust with one swift plunge. She gasped as her wet core accepted him with ease. He paused. "I need to get a condom."

"I'm still on the pill."

He trusted her. And the fact he did meant more than she'd ever know. She was leaving.

How was he supposed to keep this casual when she unraveled his knotted heart? He respected her. Believed in her.

How was he supposed to feel nothing when his world exploded with a confetti celebration every time she walked through his front door?

She leaned up and sank her teeth into his shoulder.

"Holy mother of mercy." His voice thickened.

He pulled back and thrust forward. She wrapped her legs around his hips and pulled upward, matching his tempo. She tugged. He pushed. She moaned. He groaned. He tried to slow the pace, but she wouldn't let him. Her thrusts became frantic. Holy mother. He lifted higher on his forearms. He wanted to watch her take her pleasure. Take what she needed. And it thrilled him to be the one to give her paradise.

With each thrust, she opened, wanting more. She was close. So close. He could feel her muscles contract. He grabbed her ass and lifted to push deeper.

That's it. You're going to remember me. Remember this. This is our moment.

She tilted her head back and screamed his name, flying higher and higher until she coasted off the edge. He tried to hold on, but the way her hair spread across his pillow, the way her mouth hung open, the pure bliss on her face, made him forget to hold back. He gave her what he had, and yet he wanted to give her more.

More of everything.

His hopes.

His dreams.

He'd played it safe for so long. He collapsed on top of her, rolled, and tucked her to his side. As terrifying as it was, he wanted —no, needed—Noelle in his life.

CHAPTER TWENTY

Noelle walked down the stairs quietly and met Trapper at the bottom. "Hey, big boy. Want to go out?"

The old man enjoyed her caress, then lumbered his way to the back door.

"Looks like you need another rub." She scratched Trapper's hind end. She noticed the white of his cataracts was more pronounced today, and her heart squeezed. "You're a good boy." She encouraged him to go outside.

The morning sky had barely turned the corner from nighttime. Pink and purple pushed back the black night sky. She waited in Ethan's snow boots on the back porch for Trapper. His familiar routine of walking to the edge of the cement surface and doing his business didn't take long before he made a beeline back inside.

She bent over to retrieve the dog bowl and paused halfway down while her muscles announced their impromptu strike for indulging in last night's gymnastic events. She pulled the collar of Ethan's sweatshirt closer to smell his musk.

"I was wondering where my favorite shirt went."

He hovered in the doorway, his track pants riding low on his hips, his chest naked. His abs were ripped and looked like a three-tiered layer cake, perfect for spreading with frosting. She gulped back the saliva pooling in her mouth.

"You mean my sweatshirt?" She quirked a brow, challenging him to object. She wanted to have something of his, even if his heart wasn't available. Last night in his sleep, he reached for her, and when she settled into his arms, he whispered the name Brigitte.

In those few beats of her heart he'd shattered her hopes for any kind of relationship.

He was in love. Just not with her.

He stared at her a long time, then nodded his acceptance. "It is Christmas, after all. If all you want is a used sweatshirt, you can have it."

"I asked Santa for a singing contract, but he said I'd been naughty."

"He must have been misinformed. You were awfully nice last night."

The temperature rose in the kitchen by several degrees. She needed to change the subject, and fast. She grabbed for the refrigerator door. "Omelet?"

He pushed open the laundry room door and grabbed a long-sleeved T-shirt out of the basket. "With cheese?"

"For you, I will fix it any way you like." She forced the chipper back into her voice to disguise the heartache and reached for a skillet. "What's on your agenda today?"

"I thought I was helping you with your song."

Her core quivered at the thought of spending the entire day in the presence of the scrumptious doctor who reminded her of rich, dark chocolate frosting. She sighed. "I'm thinking I just need quiet time. I'm sure something will come to me. It usually does."

He looked at her for a long moment, the corners of his mouth turning down. "Then I'll catch up on my reading. We can have a quiet day together." His eyes softened. "You're remarkable. Do you know that?"

She stared at him, stunned. "Why would you say that? You're the one who's remarkable. You're brilliant at what you do, and have dedicated your life to saving people." *Just not yourself.*

"Every doctor I've ever met is dedicated to making a name for themselves...well, except Brigitte."

There she was again. His wife. Blocking the doorway leading to the rest of his life.

"In retrospect, I see Brigitte was a taker. She needed people to need her."

Noelle set the orange juice on the counter. "Everyone needs to be needed."

"Yes, but she needed more."

She cracked several eggs in a bowl, then picked up a fork to whip the yolks and whites. "Is focusing on your work why you felt so guilty after she died. Do you believe you didn't give her enough of your time?"

He pulled the coffee pot off the maker and poured himself a mug. "I gave her what I could."

You didn't answer the question.

He tipped his coffee cup back for a good, long swallow. She studied him out of the corner of her eye, her chest aching. Even though she hadn't intended to, she'd fallen— fallen hard. She didn't want to admit to loving him. After all, she wasn't a good judge of people. But her heart refused to let go.

"Do you believe you'll ever find that kind

of love again?" As soon as the question slipped off her tongue, regret slid into place.

He choked on his coffee and wiped the dribble from his chin. "No, I don't. But, there are different kinds of love."

"Being a doctor takes focus." She folded and then flipped the eggs with the spatula. "And you're the responsible type."

He stared at her. "It's a good trait to have if you're doctor."

But he had missed her point. He was the type to marry for life, and he would carry the burden of his wife and child's deaths to his grave. Which was one of the reasons Noelle loved him. She cherished knowing he could love so deeply. The kind of love she craved.

"Yes. Responsibility is a good trait to have."

She plated the omelet and set it on the counter beside him. He caught her arm before she could escape. He brushed the hair off her face and ran his knuckles along her jawline.

"You're beautiful."

And so was your wife. The thought slipped so quickly and easily into her mind.

In the early morning hours, she'd slipped out of his bed. A quick internet search produced pictures of Brigitte, and several pictures of their daughter. Both beautiful. There was no way she could compete with such a memory. What a shame their lives were cut short.

She met his direct stare. "I want to thank you."

"For?"

She studied his face, long and hard. In a few days she wouldn't see him again. She sucked in a breath of courage. "For proving to me that not all men are jerks."

"You deserve the best."

You are picture-perfect. "I think I'll take a shower, then work for awhile. I need to see if I can write a song or two." She forced that stage smile into place. She needed to perform, at least for a few more days.

"What about breakfast?"

"I'm not hungry." *Unless you're volunteering to be my three-layer cake.* She blew out a breath and stepped back. "Hopefully by lunchtime I'll have something halfway decent for you to hear."

"Noelle? After our conversation about your dad, I started thinking…"

Her gut clenched, wondering where he was going. "About?"

"You, and your career." He scratched at his chest. "People have different motivations. Is singing a part of who you are, or are you singing just to prove that you can? I mean…" He looked down, as if searching for the perfect words to continue.

She needed to rescue him. "I've asked myself that a number of times over the years. I've come to the conclusion that singing and writing songs are as much a part of me as breathing. I can't separate the two. Even if I never get a contract, I would still sing and write songs."

"Then you'd better stop procrastinating and get those songs done." A brief flash of emotion touched his face, but he shut it down before she could get a good read.

"You're right. If I have any chance of being selected, I need to get working."

Not wanting to see the sympathy in his eyes, or the doubt, or any of the things she expected to see, she headed down the hallway, swooping Cheddar into her arms.

When she got back to the room, she sank down onto her bed.

What the hell am I doing? She needed to stop trying to connect with a man who didn't know how to let people in.

She needed to leave, make something happen in her life, not wait for an unhappy guy to figure out his own.

Maybe she should leave on Saturday. There would be less traffic on the weekend. Between the café and bakery, she had enough to pay for gas. She just needed a little more for an apartment. Relying on money to come from singing at Jack's wasn't smart. She'd been there and gotten burned in the past. Drawing in a gulp of courage, she glanced at her cell.

Could she do it? Should she? She'd resisted before.

She was out of options. She dialed, noting the time, ten past seven. It was too early, and she wouldn't leave a message. Not that type of message. She'd have to go into town. She was about to hang up when her mom's voice boomed through the speaker.

"You answered the phone."

"Of course I picked up. I got one of those answer thingies, and Ted programmed you kids' numbers in."

Nice to know. "Listen, Mom. I've had a change of plans. I need to get to LA sooner than expected. I hate to ask, but do you have a couple of hundred dollars you can loan me?"

"Does this have anything to do with sleeping with Ethan? "

Her jaw went slack. "How did—"

"Do you love him?" Her mother pushed, the way she always did. There wasn't anywhere she could hide. Mom would suss her out like a mouse in the kitchen, trap her, then tuck her in a safe spot outside and send her on her way.

"It doesn't matter."

"Sure it does. Don't do like I did and waste a whole bunch of time pretending it isn't true."

Noelle let out a slow, cheerless laugh. "Even if I told him, there's nothing here for me. Like you, he's still in love with the love of his life."

"Now you listen here, Miss. Just because you love one person doesn't mean there isn't also room for someone else. The love may be different, but it's still possible. Ethan Brennan is a good man."

Her mother didn't need to tell her that. There wasn't anyone more honorable and protective than Ethan. If she ever got the chance, she'd nominate him for the noblest bachelor of the year award.

"Ethan is content being alone. He refuses to let people into his life."

"Do you have wax in those ears? No one's

happy alone. Not really. Those of us who are just fake it well."

A blast of agitation rolled through her. "So, what about it? Will you loan me the money?"

"You are so darn stubborn. Why are you really going to LA? I know Nashville was a spur-of-the-moment type thing, and you stayed there just to prove a point. But LA? What's in LA you can't get in Denver? And don't say recording studios, or I'll get out the yellow pages."

"You were the one who raised us to follow through on our commitments. I told Jade I was going to meet her in LA, so that's what I'm going to do."

"Even if it might be the wrong choice? How far down that mountain road are you willing to walk when you know you're going in the wrong direction?"

"I've got to try something. I can't just give up..."

"Who said anything about giving up?" Her mother's huff sounded like a tornado coming through the speaker. "You've got a great voice. Let's get you some good recording equipment and get your stuff up on YouTube."

"YouTube. You know about YouTube?"

"I may not know how to work a computer very well, but I've got ears."

"That all sounds great, Mom, but recording and mixing equipment takes a lot more money than it will take to get to LA. So how about it? Will you loan me the money?"

"No, I won't give you a loan. When I had that garage sale last summer, I sold some stuff you didn't want. That money is yours. It's sitting in the bank collecting interest, so just let me know if you want cash or check."

"Seriously?"

"On one condition. You talk to Ethan. I don't want you leaving town without talking to him. You'll always regret it if you do."

She sighed. "You're right. I'll talk to him."

"What. No pushback? No pouting? No hanging up on me?"

"I'm not twelve."

A puff of laughter danced through the

phone line. "No, baby. You're a beautiful woman."

She picked at a spot on the bedspread. There were days when she wished she wasn't grown up, so she could curl into her mother's arms again, and have her mother rock her to sleep. Her heart ached.

"Thanks, Mom."

"Any time." Her mom paused. "I was going to the bank tomorrow anyway. The money will be here when you want to pick it up. Love you, baby girl."

She tucked the warm sentiment into her heart for safekeeping—she might need the comforting words to hold onto in a few days. "Love you too."

Noelle pressed the phone to her heart. By the time she lifted it back up to her ear, her mom had already hung up.

She made her way to the shower and flipped the shower nozzle over to hot and let the water warm. She pressed her hand to the wall to keep her wobbly knees from collapsing and sending her face-first to the floor, in an emotional pile of mush.

If only she could wash away her love for Ethan.

If only she was brave enough to tell him she was leaving in two days.

CHAPTER TWENTY-ONE

Ethan poured himself a cup of coffee and leaned back against the counter. Noelle had taken a shift at the café, which left him on his own for the day, and alone with his thoughts.

Noelle made a good point. He didn't need to let everyone he met or treated behind his walls, just the people who mattered. He should learn from Trapper. His dog didn't have trouble adjusting.

"Look at you two." Both dog and cat cracked open an eye but didn't budge. "All cuddled together. Trapper, I think you found a buddy."

The dog ignored the envious sentiment, stretched out a leg, giving him the doggy-finger, then settled back in for a snooze. The cat lifted his head and propped his chin on the dog's forearm.

The room fell silent.

Lonely.

Maybe he should call Tom, see if he wanted to meet for lunch. He sipped his coffee and looked out at the mountain meadow. The skies were blue. The hillside had a spread of white with spots of green. He was wondering where his cross-country skis were stored when the front doorbell rang.

Trapper didn't stir. "You're not a very good guard dog. You know that?"

The dog's tail thumped twice, but he didn't look a bit guilty.

Ethan put his mug on the counter, then headed down the hall.

Opening the front door, he paused. "Tom? I was just thinking about calling to see if you want to go for lunch."

"Good morning." Tom scanned the room

behind him. "I brought blueberry muffins. I thought we could have that breakfast we talked about. Is Noelle home?"

Home? Odd? "She's not here. She said something about a shift at the café, and helping Jenna at the bakery."

"Oh, good."

Good? The conversation was getting weirder by the minute. "Would you like to come in?"

"I can smell you've got Peaberry brewing."

"How do you always know when I get a new shipment of coffee?"

The delicious, flavorsome brew grown on Kilimanjaro emanated an aroma like no other in the world. The coffee also had a unique taste, with citrus, pineapple, and coconut layers of flavor. "Just a lucky guess."

"Come in. Take a seat. I'll pour you a cup."

Tom settled onto the brown leather sofa. "Your place is looking mighty...festive."

"That's Noelle's doing. She wanted to decorate for the holidays."

"There's nothing like the smell of a fresh

tree."

Ethan handed Tom a mug, which said, *doctor powered by coffee.*

"Mmm. This stuff is terrific." Tom leaned back and crossed his legs, studying the tree.

Ethan had known Tom long enough to know his uncle only spoke when he was ready, so he sat in the recliner next to the fireplace to wait.

"I met Dr. Handel at the café last night for coffee and to catch up on local news. While I was there I heard something that might interest you."

Ethan couldn't fathom what the local dentist—Tom's hunting buddy—would have to say that would be of any interest to him. "No surprise there. This town is always full of gossip." Ethan prompted, but Tom didn't seem in a rush.

His uncle studied the tree intently, but Ethan got the impression he didn't see the tree at all.

"I'm thinking there's more fact than fiction to what I heard," Tom tapped his fingers on the armrest, then re-crossed his legs in the opposite direction. "I overheard Maggie tell Ted that Noelle was leaving on Saturday."

Panic made Ethan sit up straighter. "Saturday? I thought she wasn't leaving until the new year."

"I guess she decided to leave early." Tom's eyes narrowed, and his mouth flattened into a straight line. "Any idea why?"

"If you think I…"

Tom waved a hand like he was waving away a fart. "Don't get your briefs in a bunch. I was just asking a question."

Ethan eased back into the chair, his gaze fixed on Tom. "This isn't just a social call, is it? There's a reason you stopped by."

Tom's fingers tapped the armchair like he was playing one of his jazz pieces on the piano. "I've never been one to mess in your business."

Ethan forced out a skeptical breath. "You messed in my business plenty when you decided to close the office without even talking to me first."

"I did it for your own good." Tom gave him the stern don't-argue eye, then leaned forward and placed the coffee cup on the table. "You know Noelle's in love with you, right?"

Love? Wow. "You don't know what you're talking about."

"You're in love too," Tom pointed at him, "You're just too focused on the wrong things to see what's in front of your face."

"She's been in town only a few days." *Seven, to be exact.*

"People can meet on a plane or at a conference and fall in love. It's instant. You've been in each other's company constantly for close to a week. You've had plenty of time to kick the tires and get rid of that new car smell."

"How would you know about love? You've never been married."

"Oh, I know plenty about love, and making sacrifices."

Ethan paused and studied the hurt in Tom's eyes. He'd seen that expression. It was similar to the one staring back at him in the bathroom mirror every day. "Looks to me like you're still in love."

How did I not know this? I've been too busy feeling sorry for myself, that's why.

Tom dropped his head and folded his hands in his lap. "I think she'd be surprised at how much I still love her."

"Still? As in the present tense?"

Tom's eyes flicked to him, then away. "Some loves can cage a man, trap him in a place and time, and won't let him go. Consuming love is like going on a hunger strike that lasts for decades. It's an excruciating way to die. I would never wish it on any man."

"I've known you all these years, and I never suspected."

"Why do you think I've been encouraging you to move on? Live your life?" Tom drew in a heavy breath. "Don't get trapped the way I did, Ethan. Brigitte is no longer alive. You need to let her go."

"Are you in love with Viola?"

"Viola?" Tom choked out a surprise. "Our office manager? Heavens, no. There was a time she wanted a relationship, but she's happy raising her grandkids."

"Who is this mystery woman?"

Tom grabbed his thighs like he was bracing for an impact. "Haven't you ever wondered why your dad and I never speak to each other?"

"I assumed it was to do with grandpa cutting you out of the will."

Tom laughed, but the sound lacked substance. "I guess you're partially correct. My father, your grandfather, was an ambitious man. He wanted his sons to carry on the tradition. Your father was just like him. I couldn't stomach the idea of building a bank account balance. I wanted to become a doctor, not to generate a good salary, but to give back rather than take."

"Is that why grandpa cut you out of the will?"

"There was a stipulation that we were to earn our first million by age twenty-five. Your father was determined to make it happen, but he didn't have the grades or smarts. He liked to take shortcuts." Tom's expression saddened. "In college, I met a lovely girl. She was smart, funny, beautiful. In my eyes, she was my perfection. We became close after her father died."

"But you never married."

"No. As a pre-med student, I had an uncertain future—student loans, a residency to get through, years of building a practice—money would be tight. I had already made the decision not to accept a dime from my father, and I questioned what I could offer her."

Tom braced his elbows on his knees, with hands wringing in time with the emotions crisscrossing his face. "She was raised with money, had a fancy education and a place in society. Her father left her a substantial amount of money, and a share in his company. We could have lived on the interest from the investments, except I couldn't accept money I hadn't earned. That was the whole point of refusing my father's trust. Back then,

I was an idealist," Tom said with disgust, and ran a hand over the back of his head.

"I wanted to provide for my family myself. I was willing to make the sacrifice. She wasn't. Halfway through the college semester, her mother became ill. Concerned she'd lose her mother so soon after her father died, she left for South Carolina. I was such a fool. I waited and waited, certain she'd come back, but she never did."

"What happened?" Ethan scooted to the edge of his seat.

"She had gotten pregnant and decided to marry for protection. She chose a man who could give her the life she'd become accustomed to rather than marry for love." Tom's eyes met his. "She met a man who was to inherit his father's fortune."

Ethan sucked in air. His chest tightened. "You're not... Are you? It's Mom you're talking about, isn't it?"

Tom gazed at him for a long silent moment. "Your father was always jealous of Eve's relationship with me. When she went home to help her mother, William discovered she was the necessary piece to execute his plan. She had money, and he needed money to fulfill the requirements of our father's will. If he married well, he'd inherit."

What an asswipe. The hurt in Tom's eyes made Ethan's anger quadruple.

"So my dad married your girlfriend."

"Yes."

If his dad had been standing in front of him, he just might have clobbered him. The fraud. He already knew his father had cheated to get at the trust money, and yet he had the balls to push Ethan to try harder, study more, get better grades in order to succeed— succeed when he himself cut corners. The sneaky bastard.

Oh, God. He studied Tom's face as his mind latched onto a single question. "But you said she was pregnant."

"Yes."

No wonder my father didn't love me. I wasn't his to love.

The many conversations with his mom

rewound and played. She'd always called his father William, never referred to him as "your dad."

His parents were always formal. The first name practice was odd, but not too off-base. Then again, his father had always treated him differently. He figured it was the firstborn thing, since his brothers always got away with far more—poor grades, staying out late. His youngest brother had even been arrested for drunk driving. Then there was his mother's wish for him to become a doctor. All these years, Ethan had thought she was just supporting his dad's ultimatums.

His gut churned into a nauseous ball of puss.

Ethan's gaze returned Tom's intense stare. "You're my dad, aren't you?"

Tom reached out a hand to touch him, but Ethan recoiled.

"Answer my question. Are you my dad?"

Tom's arm dropped to the armrest. "I don't know."

Ethan's heart raced. "We need to do a DNA test."

"No."

"What do you mean, no?"

"As far as I'm concerned, William is your father. And I'd appreciate it if you don't mention this conversation to your mother."

That's bull. "I have the right to know."

"At what cost? Either way, it would destroy your mother."

Yet she and my father destroyed me. "You're just trying to protect the woman you love." The accusation spewed across the room.

Tom's face paled as if he'd been sliced with a knife. "Is that so difficult for you to understand? Aren't you still in love with Brigitte? Haven't you spent the last three years mourning her loss? Stuck in a cage?"

"I was married to Brigitte. That was different."

"Why? Just because you had a marriage license? I loved your mother with everything in me. She was my world. She was, and is, the love of my life. Nothing will change that. But my life has been lonely. And I know I've been a fool to wait. I hoped one day she would find her way back to me." Tom stood and paced the length of the sofa, then sat back down. He leaned forward. His eyes were intense. Almost pleading. "I don't wish such an unfulfilling kind of life for you. Not when you have a choice. Noelle loves you. Unlock your cage. Live your life, Ethan."

"Noelle may love me, but she has plans that don't include me. She wants to be a songwriter, and I'm not going to stand in her way."

"But—"

"No. No buts." Ethan raked his fingers through his hair. "However, that's not to say I can't stop her from making a big mistake. I researched that band in LA. It's backed by a rapper who's spent most of his life in and out of jail. Noelle can do better."

"So what are you going to do about it?"

"I'd hate to see her waste her talent, or get sucked into another scam. I have an idea, but it will mean pulling in a few favors."

"You know someone in the music industry?" Tom's brows flattened into a skeptical line.

"Maybe."

"Then make the calls. It would be a damn shame if you let her go. Her friends miss her, and so does Maggie. And Noelle has such a big heart."

Ethan brushed his palms down his jeans while releasing a long, slow breath. "You know you pissed me off the other day when you said I didn't want to hear about Brigitte being pregnant."

"I figured as much. It was the only way I knew how to get through to you."

Great. The whole family's manipulative—why not you, too? He forced the resentment to settle. Tom had tried to manipulate him, yes, but he was a fair and ethical man. Always had been.

Tom was right. "I loved Brigitte. I did, but I never really allowed her into my life. I hurt her. I never believed a woman like her could love a guy like me. I think you're right. She didn't tell me she was pregnant because she wasn't sure I wanted another child. She had no idea she and Callie were my whole universe."

"That conclusion must have been hard to accept."

"I've been lying to myself. My marriage wasn't perfect, and I played a big part in that. My dad... William, always wanted more from me, and when I couldn't give him more, I felt unworthy. Unlovable."

"Ethan, you are loved. I love you."

Ethan held out his hands, not quite ready to accept Tom's declaration. "Please don't. Not yet. You've given me a lot to think about."

"Okay," Tom scratched at his head, then smoothed what hair he had remaining. "But are you just going to sit there? Noelle is leaving. If you're going to do anything to stop her, you need to do it fast."

Ethan sighed. "Did anyone ever tell you you're a pain?"

"Take two aspirins and get over it." Tom grinned as he pushed up off the sofa. "Ethan.

You're a good man. When you're ready, let's talk more. In the meantime, I'm sure you'll figure this out."

Ethan slowly stood and held out his hand. Tom looked at his hand, then held his arms wide. Ethan took a step forward with no hesitation. "I've always thought I look like you," he whispered.

"And I've always wondered," Tom murmured, and squeezed him tighter.

"You're right. There's no need for a test. All these years, I thought I had to prove myself to my dad. Now I know I'm free. Free to make my own choices, knowing you and Mom will always be there to support me."

Tom sniffed, his eyes turning red, and he stepped back. "I've always been proud of you."

Son. Ethan heard the endearment, even if it was left unsaid.

"Now go do something about keeping your woman in town."

"I'll try, but you're right, she's a stubborn one."

Tom walked toward the door, Ethan following.

"The best kind. The stubborn ones are ornery enough to stick." Tom hesitated when he got to the entryway. "If you want, we can talk about opening the practice back up. You were right when you said I should have discussed closing the office with you first. I thought I was doing the right thing...for the staff, but mostly for you."

Yeah, I see that now. "I'll see you after New Year's. I have a lot of thinking to do."

A smile touched Tom's eyes. "Don't take too much time thinking. The clock's ticking."

The door closed quietly behind him.

Ethan leaned his forehead against the cold wood. "I won't."

His chest felt like he'd just survived a triple bypass. Then again, maybe Tom had given him a new heart. His future looked different. Changed. He felt free. Free to choose. He'd already chosen Tom, but he also wanted to choose Noelle.

He pulled his phone out of his pocket and

scrolled through his contacts. "Phil, hey, it's Ethan."

"Ethan, it's been a long time. You aren't calling to nag me again, are you?"

Ethan's hand shook as he held the phone to his ear. "No. I've been following you on the internet. Seems you're doing fine. Hey, you said if I ever needed a favor to call. I swore I'd never collect, but..."

A hearty laugh came through the phone. "What can I do for you, Doc?"

"A beer."

"Excuse me? My doctor's telling me to drink beer?"

"Not exactly. I was hoping one of your managers might be available tomorrow to listen to a friend sing at a bar here in Elkridge."

"Is she any good?"

Ethan's chest tightened. "How do you know it's a woman?"

"My leg might be held together with rods and pins, but my head is still completely intact."

"She's better than what I hear on the radio."

"I've heard that a time or two, but I'm willing to have a listen. You're in luck. I'm in Aspen skiing with my family. How about I drive down tomorrow for that beer?"

A thrill of victory shot through his veins. "It'd be appreciated."

"What time?"

"The doors open at 7:30 at Mad Jack's Pub. How about I meet you there at eight? I'll text you the address. I'll even buy."

"You better add a burger and fries then, Doc, and I don't want to hear a word about my cholesterol."

Ethan released a satisfied chuckle. "You got it. Call if you can't make it."

"I'll be there."

"I'm counting on it." *Big time.*

Because if he didn't figure out how to get Noelle to stay, he might end up like Tom—a workaholic with no life who was pretending life was grand.

CHAPTER TWENTY-TWO

The last strum of Noelle's guitar filled the bedroom. A thrill zipped up her arm. "That's it! I did it! What do you think, Cheddar? Do you like my new song?"

She lifted the fluffy orange cat, nestled her little buddy in close, then crossed the bedroom to look out at the sunset coloring the mountain meadow. She scratched the cat's scruff. Her closed-eyes, purring cat made her chuckle. "It's perfect. If this song doesn't get me that job, nothing will."

She picked up the pad of paper with lyrics

and notes scribbled across the page. "I'd better make sure I can repeat what I just did."

She sat Cheddar on the bed, then grabbed her guitar. She closed her eyes and began to sway. "If only I had known…" Energy swelled from within, and she let the song consume her. She started softly, and the emotions built. The music walked along an emotional path to a place where love was lost.

She tapped into the feeling of having her heart ripped out of her chest. Her eyes stung with tears. She ached. She mourned. The heartfelt emotions eased into her voice until she reached the peak, then let the heartache slide down to the ending. She let the last note hang in the air. Suspended. Floating.

She didn't breathe.

She didn't move.

The clapping of hands jerked her out of her sentimental reverie.

"Wow." Ethan stood with his shoulder braced against the doorframe, arms crossed. He looked mighty scrumptious—like that LL Bean cover model—but a digital image.

He was a picture of the perfect guy. But he wasn't hers.

She scolded her stupid heart for noticing.

"Your song captures what I felt perfectly."

Yes, but the song is not about you and Brigitte. It's about me letting you go. She gulped back the hurt. "My mom sent me home with more food. I'm afraid your refrigerator is almost full. You weren't here when I got back, so I just shoved everything that wouldn't fit into the freezer out back."

"I needed gas in my car, and I wanted to check on a few patients." He paused for a moment to watch Cheddar play with the paper on the bed. "There is loads of food. Can I heat up anything for you?"

"Thank you, but I'm not really hungry." Her stomach growled. Stupid body parts. Always posting way too much information. "I think I better keep practicing."

"You need to eat. Doctor's orders."

You don't eat healthy. She drew a line in the throw carpet with her toe. "Rain check?"

Ethan pushed from the doorway and

headed her way. He stopped a foot in front of her. "You weren't going to tell me, were you?"

Her mouth dried. Oh. God. How did he know the song was about him? She tried to swallow but couldn't. "I can explain."

"How come you decided to leave so soon?"

She blinked, then blinked again to shift gears. "Who told you I was leaving?"

"Does it matter?"

"I guess not." She pulled the pages of scribbled notes into a pile. "It's a small town. I should have known some busybody would tell you sooner or later."

"But, why didn't *you* tell me?"

"I was going to tell you." *When I figured out what this push-pull thing we have going on is all about.* "I figured you'd be pleased to get your house back."

"That still doesn't answer the question. Why didn't you tell *me*?"

"I talked to my mom, and she has money I can borrow. I figured the sooner I get to LA, the sooner Jade and I can practice for tryouts."

"Tryouts. Right." He shoved his hands in

his pockets and rocked back on his heels. "Your friends will be disappointed you didn't stay around for New Year's."

Yes, my friends, but not you. "Maybe I'll come back for a few days this summer. Go rafting. If I don't get this job, I'll have a lot of spare time."

"If LA doesn't work, you can always get a job singing at Jack's."

She put the song sheets in a folder on her nightstand. "Living on tip money is hard, plus singing a couple times a week wouldn't pay the bills. I'd have to get another job, and jobs are hard to find here. Jenna and Mom are letting me pick up work as a favor, but they don't really need the help."

"The urgent care clinic is always looking to hire people."

"And what would I do in a clinic? I might be able to change bedpans or deliver flowers, but that's all, and it's not what I want to do. I want to make it singing if I can. I feel like this will be my last shot. If I can't make a go of it this time, then maybe it's time for me to explore a different career."

His frown deepened. "Don't give up, Noelle. You're good. Really good. Too good to give up."

If only she could be certain. "That's nice of you to say, but it takes more than just talent. It takes a little bit of luck, and being in the right place at the right time. At least that's what my mom says."

"Maggie is right more often than not."

"Yes, she is." *And, she was right about you. You're a good man, and probably the reason she forced the roommate thing in the first place.*

Noelle studied Ethan's face. She would've liked to run her finger along the square, scruffy jawline, and across the lips that could be both firm and soft. And the eyes, so alive with intelligence and emotion.

She had to leave, the sooner the better. For her sanity. And his.

"Tell you what, if things don't work out, you can come back here. I've been looking for a roommate. Cheddar and Trapper get along. You wouldn't have to find a place."

And see you every day, knowing we could never be together? That's emotional suicide.

"I know you're trying to help, but I can't see any way this would work. I have a better chance of finding work in LA."

"Yes, but the cost of living in California is quadruple what it is here."

She crossed her arms. "That's true, but still...once I'm there, I'll have to find a way to make it work."

He opened his mouth to say something, but her heart couldn't take any more. "I'd better get to work. I need to be ready for tomorrow night."

She grabbed her guitar and sat on the bed, hoping he would get the hint.

"What about dinner? I can bring you a plate."

Bringing up food would mean she'd have to talk to him again. He was a problem-solver. He'd do his best to solve her problem, but he couldn't—his heart wasn't available.

"I had a big lunch. Plus I have snack bars if I get hungry."

"You sure I can't get you anything?"

You could open your heart. Let me in. She shook her head. "I'm positive." She forced her mind to think of standing onstage with a crowd of thousands cheering her on, and the imagery worked. She felt her mouth curve into a smile.

Ethan backed out into the hall.

"Would you mind closing the door?"

He reached, and she waited until the latch clicked into place. Her shoulders sagged. She pulled her cat to her chest and hugged him close.

"Cheddar, how do I get myself into these messes?" She took a deep breath and let it out. "I'll figure it out, though. I always do."

But fairy tale lives only happened in storybooks.

Ethan Brennan could have been her prince, but he'd already taken a bite from the poisonous apple and was sleepwalking through life.

He was like a precious rose thorn wedged in her finger.

Their time together had been brief, but he'd dug in deep.

Pulling the splinter out would hurt, and take time to heal.

CHAPTER TWENTY-THREE

Normally an early riser, Ethan rolled over and groaned.

He threw a forearm over his eyes to block the sun streaming in through the blinds. His temples throbbed, and his mouth felt like it was stuffed with a wad of gauze. He rolled to his side and pushed into a seated position. Misery accompanied the next groan.

Trapper nudged him in the crotch, just to make sure he was awake.

"Thanks, buddy. I don't need that kind of help this morning."

He patted the dog's head and attempted to stand. He grabbed the dresser to stop the room from spinning. "Why didn't you stop me?"

Trapper gave him a disgusted look.

"Yeah, okay. I knew opening the bottle of whiskey wasn't a good idea."

A loud crash in the living room below had him holding his head. When he didn't hear screaming or crying, he headed for the bathroom first before working his way down the stairs. He held the railing to make sure he wouldn't be the next thing to crash into the living room.

"You're up." Noelle's perky cheer was a bit too loud. "I mean really up."

He glanced down. "Sorry. My sweats are still in the wash."

"Do you want me to get them for you?"

"Please?"

She moved too fast for his mind to catch up. He closed his eyes and waited for the room to stop spinning. "Here." She shoved the wad of black fabric in his direction. He cracked one eye open and held the fabric to his middle.

The scent of coffee permeated his nose, and he took an extra deep breath. "There is a God."

She giggled at his expense. "I made extra coffee after I saw the half-empty whiskey bottle. I figured you'd need a bit of help this morning."

He'd spent the night reliving his life with Brigitte and Callie so he could store their memories in a beautiful, safe place and make a commitment to get unstuck.

As much as he loved Tom, he didn't want to end up like his uncle, spending every spare moment in their urgent care clinic just to keep busy. And if Tom was his father, he wanted to learn how to be a proper son. Not the studious student, or the intelligent doctor, but a son who remembered birthdays, and met his dad for an early morning jog, and on Sundays went fishing with him.

"Would you mind setting it on the coffee

table? I'm afraid if I let go I'll embarrass myself."

Tubs and boxes lined the wall, and the tree once sparkling and crowded with tiny mementos was bare. "What are you doing?" he whimpered, gripping the handrail harder.

"I wanted to get this stuff packed up before I left."

He stumbled down the last few steps, pleased with himself for being able to maintain his dignity. "Would you mind?" He lifted his hand and twirled his index finger in a small circle.

"You mean you want me to turn around?"

He managed a nod.

"Nope. I want to see if you can actually balance in your condition."

His lip managed a sneer. "Fine." He shuffled over behind the couch and leaned over—carefully—to slide on his sport pants.

"You're no fun."

He regretted the underperforming smile on her face. He was being moody, sullen, not the person he wanted to be. Not with her, anyway.

She was wearing jeans and a red sweater. She looked like a nicely wrapped Christmas present. If only she'd put a bow on her chest. He'd love to lay her on the couch and open her package.

"You don't need to clean up. Leave it. I'll pack the decorations later and get the stuff over to your mom's." He sank down to the couch and reached for his coffee mug. "I was thinking about going out for a hike later on. Do you want to come?"

She shifted, looking around the room like she couldn't decide what to do. "I can't. Sorry. I promised Ashley and Mara we would do lunch. Then I'm going to head over to the salon to sing carols to Mrs. Talbott. She wasn't feeling well yesterday, and the singalong was postponed until today. I'm already late."

He gulped the coffee, hoping the caffeine would produce more ideas for ways to get her to stay. The bowl of pinecones, the Christmas stockings, and the wreath on the front door had already disappeared. It almost felt like she was already gone. He pulled in a long whiff of her perfume, knowing the memory of the scent would fade with time.

His breath caught. He didn't want the scent to disappear. In fact, he wanted to smell her every day.

She placed a lid on the box. "Well, I better get my car loaded."

"Stay." He blurted out. "Stay with me."

She paused. "Are you talking to Trapper? 'Cause he's in the kitchen."

"No, I'm talking to you."

She looked like he'd just given her an injection.

"I mean…stay, here, with me. Don't go to LA."

She took a step closer. "Why, Ethan? Why do you want me to stay?"

She wanted a reason. *Dear, Lord.* He urged his dehydrated brain to function. Think of something. *Anything.* Please, he begged. He grabbed onto the only forming thought. "You have friends here." The excuse deflated as soon as it was out of his mouth.

Disgust poked at his temples, and he winced. *Great job, Ethan. Award-winning.*

She walked to the front door to set the tub by her purse. "I have a friend in LA, too. That's not a good enough reason for me to stay."

He released a quick breath filled with an aching regret. He needed to try harder. "But I'm not in LA. I'm here, and I want you to stay —here, with me."

"As your roommate?"

"Yes. You don't need to pay rent. I've got that covered."

"So…you need someone to watch Trapper while you work."

"If you could do that, I would appreciate it."

"Would you like me to make the meals?"

"I love your cooking."

Suddenly her face and neck had become red and splotchy. "Noelle," he pointed. "Do you have a rash? It looks like you might be allergic to something."

"The only thing I'm allergic to is you, Ethan. You don't want a roommate—remember? And if you need a dog walker, a cook, and a maid, I suggest you post an ad on Craigslist. Don't forget to mention you're a doctor, and I'm sure you'll get plenty of responses."

Before he could figure out what she meant, rather than said, she had her hand on the front doorknob and her purse over her shoulder. "Wait."

"For what, Ethan? I want to be a songwriter. I'm good at it, and I can't imagine not singing. And you...well, you need to figure out if you'll ever be able to let another person into your life. Love is messy, and complicated, and amazing when it's right. But the only way it can be right is if two people are open and honest with each other."

"I'm being honest."

"You may think you're being honest, but you're not. I read your letters to Brigitte. She loved you, but you never felt you deserved her love. Why is that Ethan? Why?"

"I don't know."

"I think you do know, and until you figure it out, I need to do my thing. I refuse to be part of a one-sided relationship again. I deserve better, and in the end, so do you."

He swore there was a wobble in her voice as she opened the front door.

"I'll be back to get Cheddar later, and pack my things. Have a nice day, Ethan."

The door clicked shut behind her, but all he heard was Noelle saying goodbye.

The feeling of being unlovable again tightened the chain around his throat.

He leaned back against the couch. The silence of the house expanded into a deafening roar. He never realized how empty his life had become. He thought of Noelle. The few days they shared. He didn't want a roommate.

He wanted Noelle. As messy and loud and unpredictable as she was, he wanted *her*. Her and no one else.

The throbbing of his head doubled, and he closed his eyes to think of a new plan, only he drifted into a fitful sleep. Several hours later he woke up again. The sun streamed through the window, and he felt a bit more sober. He pulled his hands down his face. He needed to get it together. He replayed the earlier conversation with Noelle in his head frame by frame.

He'd blown it.

Big time.

But that didn't mean he wouldn't do a better job the next time. By his calculations, he had only one more shot. He had to hit the vein. Otherwise, he'd lose her forever.

He only had one option.

He shuffled to the kitchen to retrieve his cell phone, pulled up the keypad, and dialed from memory.

"Hello?"

"Mom? It's Ethan."

"Ethan. What a surprise."

No, it's not Sunday, no need to check the calendar. "I need your advice." Ethan rested his hip against the counter. "You're a woman."

"Glad you noticed, son," she replied, with a chuckle tacked on.

"Okay, that was stupid." He pressed the pressure points near the corner of his eyes. "You must have dated before dad, right?"

She hesitated. "Yes. There was a boy I cared for quite a lot, actually." Her voice had become soft. Cautious.

"Obviously you broke up, or you wouldn't be with dad." He chose his words carefully. "But right before you broke up, if he could have said one thing that would have convinced you to stay, what would it have been?"

"What's this all about?"

He tightened his grip on the phone. "I met this woman. Her name's Noelle."

"Oh," her voice lifted and lightened. "You've met someone. Someone special."

"Yes. She's amazing, Mom." Ethan poked at a pinecone she'd selected from the yard, rolling it across the counter. "I think you would like her, but she's leaving for LA."

"And you're staying in Elkridge."

He looked at his feet. "I love it here."

"Have you asked her to stay?"

"I did, but she insists on going, even though deep down I don't think it's what she wants."

"Have you told her how you feel?"

Ethan pressed a hand against his forehead and rubbed. "I just met her."

He could almost hear his mother's smile through the phone. "But you love her. I can hear it in your voice."

"It's different this time, Mom. She's nothing like Brigitte. Wait, that's not true. She's giving and kind, but so much more."

"Then tell her what's in your heart."

"I love her. But, what if she doesn't believe me?"

"If I had let my first boyfriend know how I felt about him, I think my life would have been different." The words sounded jammed together, like she had difficulty getting them out.

"Why didn't you tell him?" The quiver in her voice was doubly odd since he'd never known his mother to show emotion. "William offered me security"—she coughed to cover the emotion—"...and I accepted it. As foolish as that sounds, now."

Foolish for not believing in Tom, you mean. "I bet your boyfriend regrets not telling you he loved you."

"Maybe. Maybe I should have told him. But there's no going back. We made our choices."

The stubborn strength he'd grown up with had returned. But, now and forevermore, he'd know it was only a façade.

I will not hurt your mother. His uncle's words trudged through his mind. "Then I had better make the right choice. Otherwise, I'll have to live for the rest of my life with what-ifs and never knowing what might have been."

"There is one thing I will never regret." His mother's voice strengthened.

"What's that, Mom?"

"You. You were my first. When you came into my life, I needed you. You filled my life with joy back then, and you still do today. I know I shouldn't say this, but you've always been my favorite."

"Yours, but not Dad's." *And now I know why.*

"William has always been a complicated man, just like your grandfather. Both married for money, position, never love."

She didn't need to tell him the truth, if she even knew the whole truth. It didn't matter anymore. He loved his mother, and he didn't care if he lived up to his father's expectations. He'd accomplished what he set out to do. He healed people. That's what he was good at. Now it was time to heal himself.

"You *are* loved, Mom." Ethan switched the phone to his other ear. "I love you."

"Don't waste those words on me. Go tell them to your Noelle." By the tone is his mother's voice he could tell not one syllable of his previous statement had gone to waste.

"I will. Take care, Mom."

A voice bellowed in the background. "William is calling. I'd better go."

"I'll call next week."

"That would be nice, dear."

Ethan's smile faded as he placed the phone on the counter. His gut churned. "Love." He said the word out loud. It felt right. Felt good. Felt real.

"Now I just need to find a way to convince Noelle."

But would she believe he'd fallen for her so quickly? After all these years?

She'd have to believe him, or he'd end up stuck in a cage, alone again.

CHAPTER TWENTY-FOUR

Ethan opened the door to Mad Jack's bar. The local pub had a way of taking him back in time. License plates covered the walls. Crushed peanut shells were scattered across the old wood floor by customers encouraged to toss the remnants. Large, flat-screen televisions hung from the corners with professional sports games or sports highlights playing.

The small stage set at the far end was still dark, but he recognized the guitar case sitting next to the speakers as Noelle's. He scanned the crowd, and his heart did a little A-fib when he saw her talking to Ashley. He needed to reserve a seat for Phil, but his feet had other plans. He shuffled toward Noelle like a conveyor belt straight into a melting pot.

"Lookie who's here." Ashley tapped Noelle's arm.

Noelle had poured herself into a pair of faded, frayed jeans. Three-inch loops dangled past her shoulders. She had pulled her hair back into a ponytail, wavy curls drifting down her back. He couldn't help staring at the black leather vest. It was cinched and laced to perfection. Noelle looked professional. She could easily have been walking onto the stage at Madison Square Gardens, or an awards show. Too bad there wasn't a backstage at Jack's, or else he might have dragged her behind the curtain to smudge off the sparkling lip gloss.

Noelle's eyes met his. They went smoky, matching the darker shades of her eye shadow. He had no idea what Ashley was wearing. He hadn't taken the time to look.

"Ladies," Ethan said, loud enough to be heard over the bar's white noise.

"You're here early." Noelle's surprise didn't go unnoticed.

"I wanted to wish you luck before you go on."

Noelle glanced around at the nearby tables. "Ashley is saving a seat for my mom, Jenna, Chase, and Grant. Kym and Zach already flew back to California, so there's more room. We can squeeze in an extra chair if you'd like."

He might have told her about Phil's visit, but she already looked like she'd just swallowed a wad of gum. Besides, Phil might not show—not that he wasn't dependable—but things came up.

"Thanks for the offer. My uncle and Viola are coming. I'll sit with them." *Because I don't want you to get nervous if you recognize Phil.* The lull in the conversation became uncomfortable.

"You're looking mighty handsome tonight, Doctor." Ashley's grin widened. "Hoping to get lucky?" Her body jerked as if she'd just been kicked.

Noelle glared at her friend.

Ethan would have chuckled if Noelle wasn't the target of Ashley's ploy. "I'm just here to support Noelle." He hadn't come expecting to get lucky, but right now he was keeping his options open. "Would either of you like a drink?"

"I don't drink alcohol before my sets, but I'll take water with lemon if it wouldn't be any trouble."

"No trouble. Ashley? What would you like?"

"I'm good."

Ethan's gaze locked on Noelle. "You sure you don't want anything else?" *A hug? A kiss? A quickie to calm your nerves?*

Her face lit up like a Christmas wreath with sparkling lights. "Maybe later."

Then my vote's making love until the sun comes up. "I'll be back in a minute."

He forced himself to turn away, and made his way to the nearest open spot at the bar.

"Hey, Doc." Jack nodded while pouring a beer. "Figured you'd show."

"And why is that?"

"Isn't Noelle living with you?"

Ethan placed an elbow on the counter and leaned in. "Isn't there a saying about doctors, bartenders, and priests?"

"I've known you a good part of two years, and I've never had anything to give you a hard time about. Indulge me, okay?"

Jack took his role as the local search and rescue captain seriously. Only when they'd celebrated at their annual picnic did Ethan find out the group's leader had a wicked sense of humor and loved to play practical jokes.

"Go ahead, take your swings. We'll see how funny you are next month. Your annual prostate screening is coming up."

Jack's face went sullen. "You doctors sure do like to stick things where they don't belong. You have no sense of humor."

"I've got plenty, but not when it comes to Noelle."

"It's good to see you're returning to the

land of the living." Jack winked, then wiped the counter and tossed down a coaster.

"Funny, but I don't ever remember my heart stopping."

"You sure about that? For the past couple years, I'd started to wonder if you were a zombie."

He couldn't argue with that. Noelle had certainly stirred his endorphins and eased his pain. "Remind me to tell you about my trip to the wilds of Africa."

"Deal." Jack slid a laminated list of beers across the counter. "What'll it be?"

Ethan requested Noelle's water with lemon and added a lager to the list. "I've got a friend coming from out of town to hear Noelle sing. Do you mind if I reserve one of those small tables next to the booths? Noelle might recognize him, and I don't want her to get nervous."

Jack reached below the bar and slid a plastic reserved sign across the wooden bar top. "Help yourself. But you'll have to watch to make sure no one takes your spot. I swear people don't take the time to read."

"Will do." He loaded the drinks in his hand and grabbed the sign to drop on the table before heading back to Noelle. Ashley had disappeared, leaving Noelle by herself.

Her hand brushed his when she reached for the glass. A spark sizzled up his arm and across his chest to the other side.

She amazed him.

Only a few days before, he dreaded the thought of Christmas, and couldn't wait for the year to be over. Now, he wanted time to slow down—even stop—to give him time to convince Noelle to stay. It was passing way too fast.

"You look nervous." He sat, and placed a hand on her arm. "You've got this."

"I'm not really nervous, so much as anxious. I want to get on with the show. Thank you for believing in me."

He leaned closer to her ear. "Believe in yourself."

"That's easier said than done some days."

Catching sight of Phil out of the corner of his eye, he grabbed his beer and scooted the chair back. He pressed his lips to her forehead, infusing her with every ounce of courage he could spare. "I'll let you get ready."

Her eyes followed him as he stood. "I appreciate all you've done for me. You've been so kind."

She spoke as if knowing their time was ending, and he hated it. The clock was ticking, and he hadn't found a way to get her to stay. Not yet. He hoped Phil would come through. Otherwise, her boat would sail, and he'd be left struggling in the wake.

"Don't thank me yet. I might have a surprise for you."

"Oh? What is it?" She reached behind her and pulled her ponytail over her shoulder.

"You'll just have to wait and see."

"Sounds intriguing, Doc."

I hope you find it life-changing. "Have fun tonight. Give it your best."

"I always do."

That's what I'm counting on. He took a step

back, then another, then checked his reserved table and found it still empty.

"Phil. You made it."

The tall, thin man extended his hand. Phil had dressed to blend. His casual jeans and Lumineers band T-shirt didn't look out of place. But Ethan knew different.

"How's the leg?"

"Healing, thanks to you. If you hadn't found me, I don't think I'd be walking."

Or alive. "Trapper's the one who found you. I just followed behind." Ethan slid next to him at the bar. "I hope you're not skiing the back country. There are a ton of avalanche warnings."

The older man placed a hand on Ethan's shoulder. "Nope. Not anymore. I learned my lesson. I stay strictly in bounds, and I always have a ski partner with me."

"I can't believe you were in town and didn't call."

"I meant to, but we've been doing interesting work in my Aspen studio. I think I've signed the next superstar, and I'm excited.

I can't wait to get the single out." Phil pointed. "Is that the lady friend you want me to hear?"

Ethan glanced over his shoulder toward the stage. "Yes. Noelle Conroy. She's been in Nashville for a while, and is heading to LA soon to try out for a band. Between you and me, the band gig thing smells. That's why I called you. I think she needs a second opinion."

"Just so you know, I always give it straight up."

"That's all I ask."

Phil held up his beer glass. "Thanks for saving my life, Doc."

"Thanks for doing your exercises so I didn't have to listen to you cuss me out every week."

Phil placed a hand on his shoulder and squeezed while the laughter rolled on. Skiing, family, and sports propped up their conversation while they waited for their food. Phil was a diehard Raiders fan, but could easily be a Bears, Cowboys, Broncos, or Jets fan, since he had recording studios in all his homes. The guy was worth millions, but you'd never know it.

The crowd noise quieted when Mara walked to the stage. She fumbled for the microphone just as Noelle lifted Mara's hand and placed it on the mic. Mara laughed and faced the audience.

"Hey, folks."

"Hi Mara," someone up front hollered.

Mara pulled the mic closer, and let the crowd continue to heckle her as only friends could. When the noise died back, she continued. "A friend of mine's in town, and I talked her into singing for us tonight. She's amazingly talented, and homegrown. Many of you know her. Please give a special welcome to my friend, the amazing singer-songwriter, Noelle Conroy."

Cheers and hoots filled the bar. Ethan looked at the faces of the people he'd come to know, all admiring the woman who'd changed his life.

"Thank you. Thank you. What a warm welcome." Noelle settled on the stool and adjusted the guitar in her lap. "Normally, I play with a band, but it's only me tonight, so I'm going to switch it up a little."

"We love you, Noelle," Ashley shouted.

Noelle blushed. "Love you too," she laughed, although Ethan could still see the tension in her shoulders, tension he hadn't expected to see there. "Let's get this evening started, shall we?"

Noelle started the set with a toe-tapping tune. Ethan's garlic fries arrived along with Phil's burger, allowing them to settle at the reserved table, which sat off to the side of the room with a good view of the stage area.

Noelle finished one song and went straight into another, then another, and another. Ethan ordered another round of drinks. And Noelle continued to play.

Well? Ethan glanced at Phil, but his friend remained focused on the stage, not saying much. Ethan fought to remain still, but apprehension buzzed through his body.

When he couldn't stand the tension any

longer, Ethan casually leaned over to Phil. "Well, what do you think?"

"She's good."

Ethan did a virtual, hell-yeah fist pump.

"But..."

His gut clenched, his hell-yeah deflating.

"I've heard a thousand artists just like her. Her arrangements are unique, that's about it. I get the impression she's just going through the motions. There's no star quality there. I'm sorry."

Ethan wanted to defend Noelle, but what Phil said was true. He'd heard her sing in the shower, in her room, downstairs. The underlying passion wasn't there—not like it was before.

Phil tipped his watch. "I should start heading back."

"Wait." Ethan implored. "She just wrote a new song, and I think you'll like it. I'll ask her to play it."

Phil looked skeptical but nodded.

Ethan swerved through the tables like he was rushing toward the emergency room.

Although it wasn't life or death, the situation had become critical. He shifted side to side, his hands clenching again and again, waiting for her to finish.

He checked the back table. Yep, Phil was still there.

The clapping started, then she started strumming to start another song.

No, no, no. Stop.

He waved his hands and rushed to the front of the stage. "Noelle. Noelle."

"Ethan?" She covered the microphone to keep her irritation from broadcasting into the room. "What are you doing?"

"You need to play the song you wrote."

"No. It's not ready." Her wide-eyed refusal amplified her intense, hushed whisper. "I haven't had time to perfect it."

Crap. Don't start self-doubting now. "It's perfect the way it is." Ethan placed a hand on her knee. "Play it for me. Please?"

He held his breath.

"I'm not—"

"Where's that incredibly talented and

confident woman I've come to know?"

The pressure in his chest expanded.

"Okay. But if I mess it up, I'm going to blame it on you."

"Fine." A sizzle of expectation spread from his fingers to his toes.

"I'll sing it, but you need to sit there." She pointed to an empty seat at a table in the front row.

He squeezed her knee. "You'll do fine." He gave her two thumbs up.

She nodded, and he took a seat.

"What's going on?" Maggie asked.

"I'm trying to make your daughter's dreams come true."

Maggie gave him one of her familiar gruff glares. "Looks to me like you already have." Maggie placed a hand on his arm. "Welcome back, Doc."

Ethan felt the warmth but didn't hear what Maggie said. Noelle had captured his attention with her sweet lips and amazing green eyes. She didn't know it, but this was her lucky chance, and he hoped he was her lucky charm.

"This is a song I wrote a few days ago, and I'm still working out the kinks, so bear with me. I hope you like it. It's about saying goodbye to someone you love."

Noelle bowed her head and cleared her throat. The song began softly with just the guitar, then the humming started. The passion poured from every cell. She closed her eyes and swayed. When she opened her eyes, she looked directly at him.

Shock made him pause.

She'd changed the words.

The song wasn't about Brigitte.

It was about her. She was the one saying goodbye. She was saying goodbye to him.

He couldn't worry about that now. He'd convince her to change her mind...later. Right now, all that mattered was for her to sing her heart out.

When the last cord drifted into the audience, the crowd was stunned into silence. For a heartbeat no one made a sound. No one breathed. Then the applause started slowly while people wiped away their tears. The cheers expanded and escalated until several people were on their feet. She'd done it. She did what she needed to do. He searched for Phil. The music producer was giving him two thumbs up. A river of relief flooded his heart.

"Thank you." She gulped back the emotion. "After that, I think I need a quick break."

She was up and off the stage before Ethan could stand.

Maggie brushed by him. "I'd better go check on my girl."

Ethan took a step to follow Maggie, but decided Noelle's best option would be to hear what Phil thought. He walked around the edge of the crowded room. "Well?"

Phil handed him a card. "Here's the phone number of my manager in Aspen. Have her give him a call. I want to see what she can do in the studio. If she can write more songs like that, I'll offer her a contract."

"Seriously?" Excitement exploded up his arms and down his legs. He should have played it cool. Professionally. But this was for Noelle. "Thanks, man. I appreciate this."

Phil laughed. "There are no guarantees, Doc."

"Are you throwing my words back at me?"

"When I asked you if I'd walk again, I wanted you to lie your ass off and tell me everything would be fine."

"But you had a lot of rehabilitation and hard work in front of you. I promised I'd be there for you. I remember there were a few times I had to threaten to drive down to the rehabilitation center, but you did okay."

"I appreciated the phone calls." Phil gripped his shoulder. "Tell your friend she's got voice lessons and hard work in front of her, but we'll get her there, especially if she can write songs like that one."

"Phil." Ethan held out his hand. "I appreciate you coming tonight."

"Next time I'm in town, I'll invite you up to the cabin. We'll watch a game, and I'll throw a couple of steaks on the grill."

Phil's so-called cabin sat on sixty-three

acres. The home, surrounded by aspen and pine trees, had a view from the upper deck of the continental divide that could take your breath away. Plus the ten-thousand-square-foot home boasted a sound studio like no other. "You got it."

Ethan glanced at Phil's card, with a name and phone number written in bold black letters. His fingers tightened around the precious piece of paper. Then he extended his hand. "Thanks, Phil."

"I hope she appreciates you."

He stared at the hallway where Noelle had disappeared.

"She does." *I hope.*

Phil made his way to the door, and Ethan made his way toward Noelle.

Now all he had to do was get the stubborn woman to change her mind.

CHAPTER TWENTY-FIVE

Noelle loved the thrill of being center stage. Feeling the energy in the room. The applause for a job well done. But now the adrenaline rush was over, exhaustion seeped into every cell. Her fingers ached and her throat was scratchy.

Performing two sets was a lot to do on her own, and unlike Nashville, where people ate dinner, chatted, and ignored the band, tonight everyone was looking at her.

"Very impressive." The sensual, masculine voice set off a wave of tingles.

There Ethan stood, looking more

delicious than Doc B's cherry lollipops. She wanted him to touch her, hold her, promise her forever, but he couldn't—and he was too honorable to lie. "Thanks, but I wish you hadn't requested that new song."

"Why? It was fantastic."

"Don't you think folks will figure out it's about…" …*about us.*

She wanted to bash him over the head till he figured out the song was about them. Every line had pricked her heart full of holes. Didn't he get she was bleeding, standing right there in front of him, asking him to love her? Yet he didn't see her as anything other than a roommate and friend.

"What's most important is you have an opportunity to record it." He oozed with excitement, and looked like a kid who'd found the missing piece of his prized game.

"I'll record it eventually, when I get the money to purchase studio time."

"You get to record it now, in a professional studio."

She reached for her guitar case. "Ethan,

you're not making any sense. How many beers did you have tonight?"

He pulled a piece of paper from his pocket and thrust it at her midsection. "This is for you."

She stared at the black and gold card, too exhausted to figure out what game he was playing.

He lifted her hand and placed the card in her palm. "It's your golden ticket."

She lifted the black and gold card toward the light. Phillip T. Sutton, Music and Audio Productions, Las Vegas, NV. Sutton. Sutton. There must be a million Suttons in the world, but why did the name sound so familiar? "Where did you get this card?"

"He's a friend. He came to hear you sing tonight."

She couldn't help but trip over her skepticism. She extended her arm to give him the card back, but he pushed her hand back.

"Phil owed me a favor. I called, and he was able to meet for a beer. He wants you to call the number on the back, and talk to one of his managers. He said something about laying down tracks."

I bet he did. In his car or his couch or in his bed.

No, no, no. Ethan would never have a friend like that. Stop being so negative. "Look, Ethan, I know you mean well, but I've spent too much time calling and making appointments with people who didn't have the connections I need."

He shoved his hands in his pockets. "Trust me. This guy is the real deal."

"Sure. Maybe he works for someone, who knows someone, who knows someone else." The way Ethan was looking at her, he could have been gnawing Buffalo jerky his jaws were clenched so tight. She threw up her hand, and added on a state-of-the-art eye-roll. "Fine. I'll take the card."

"And you will call, right?"

"Sure. I'll call." She slipped the card into her purse just as Ashley arrived.

"Are you coming?" Ashley handed Noelle her coat.

"I'll just be a minute," Noelle confirmed.

"Hurry up, it's cold outside, and the hot wings are getting cold. Dad's holding dinner for us."

"You're not coming back to the house?" Ethan's brows drew together, scoring lines of confusion on his face.

"I haven't spent much time with Ash. She invited me to spend the night."

"You can come too," Ashley offered, "but I can't promise you won't get your toenails painted."

Ethan's face shaded the dearest tint of pink. "No thanks."

"I hope you don't mind if I leave Cheddar at the house. He's fed and shouldn't be a problem."

"Go ahead. He'll be fine. I'll see you in the morning. We can talk more then."

Disappointment and frustration wrestled to see which one could beat up her heart the best. Hadn't she promised herself not to allow men to hurt her anymore? In less than a month she'd done it again.

Noelle took a deep breath, shoved her arms through her coat sleeves, then lifted her guitar. She should just leave. Never look back, but her heart betrayed her again.

"Ethan?"

He spun around like a football player spinning off a tackle. "Thanks for coming tonight. It meant a lot to have you here."

"You're welcome."

His intense stare made her pulse race. Her breath became shallow He looked like he'd like to remove every piece of her clothing with his teeth. She could imagine the scrape of his jaw against her inner thigh. His warm hands on her skin.

"Noelle. Are you coming? Jenna's waiting at the house. Grant decided to stay home with Kyle, so it's girls' night."

Noelle blinked the sensation away. "Yes. I'm coming."

But not in the way she wanted to be, with Ethan on the bottom, her on top, riding him into the sunset.

She stopped just outside the bar's front

428 | LYZ KELLEY

door to let the cool air chill the vision. Ashley pulled up in a massive pickup truck. Noelle stored her guitar behind the seat, then heaved herself into the passenger seat of the four-by-four's cab.

door to let the cool air chill the vision. Ashley pulled up in a massive pickup truck. Noelle stored her guitar behind the seat, then heaved herself into the passenger seat of the four-by-four's cab.

"You sure you don't want to go back to the cabin with Hotness Honey?"

"Hotness...what? How do you come up with this stuff?"

"Let me know when you're visiting next, and I'll make sure Jenna throws one of her Sin Sugar parties. I blushed so hard at the last one, my toenails turned red for a week."

Sorrow dissolved the oxygen in her lungs.

She wouldn't be back. At least not for a long time. By then Jenna might have thought up a whole new line of products.

Once she arrived in LA, she'd have to hit the streets, find a job, and figure out how to make her life work. She studied Ashley's profile.

"Ash, are you happy here? I mean, in Elkridge?"

Her friend stared ahead, the headlights

reflecting off the icy roads. "There was a time I wanted nothing to do with this place. I planned to go to college in San Diego, get my teaching certificate, and make my mark on the world. At the time, all I could think about was college boys, the beach, getting a tan, being around people who had the same interests, and leaving all the Elkridge baggage behind. Then my mom got sick and I had to come home."

"But that was a couple of years ago. What about now?"

"I'm married to the most amazing man. I have a couple of kids who are the joy of my life. Plus, I'm finding out my dad is quite the comedian, particularly when he's in love."

"Love? Wait. I thought you and your dad had problems."

"It's funny how when you fall in love, life takes on a different shade of honesty, with a little bit of forgiveness mixed in."

"Sounds like you found the perfect life."

"Oh, trust me. Six people plus a dog under one roof is far from perfect, but it's my life, and I adore it." Ashley drove up her long driveway. "What are you going to do about Ethan?"

The question nudged her out of her melancholy. "Nothing. Ethan's just a friend."

"Please tell me you're not going blind like Mara. She can't see, and even Mara knows the cute doctor would love to give you a thorough physical."

"How do you know he hasn't already?"

"Oh, my. Do tell."

Noelle's face flushed. "I thought...I hoped...I wanted to help him. He's so broken, but he's also such a great guy. He deserves so much more."

"And what about you? What do you deserve?"

Her thoughts got stuck in a pile of emotional junk. What a doozy of a question. What did she deserve? She deserved to fall in love with a guy who wasn't emotionally stuck in the past, and who had enough patience to support her while she figured a few things out.

Noelle folded her hands in her lap. "I need to take a little time and figure out what I really want."

"Are you sure LA is what you want?"

"What choice do I have? It's not like jobs fall out of the sky here—not my type of jobs, anyway." Noelle waggled her finger at Ashley. "And don't you dare mention the doctor. He's already done enough interfering in my life."

"By giving you a place to stay." The incredulity came along with an attitude.

"No, by inviting one of his buddies to hear me sing tonight. He gave Ethan some story about being a record producer. I thought Ethan was a better judge of character."

"Why do you assume Ethan's not telling you the truth?"

"Come on. What are the odds of Ethan knowing a guy at a production company who happens to be in town, and takes the night off, during Christmas no less, to hear me sing? The guy even had this bogus card. Like I haven't run into that ploy before. "

Ashley pulled the truck into her family's

three-car garage. "Give me the card." She wiggled her fingers.

"Why?" A choking sensation shimmied up Noelle's spine.

"I want to call his 'so-called friend' and check him out."

"It's late."

"He was just in the bar an hour ago. He can't be asleep already. Hand it over."

Noelle grabbed her phone and the business card. "Fine, but I'll call. When this guy turns out to be a total fraud—and he will, guaranteed—you owe me a bowl of mint chocolate chip ice cream, and I mean the whole bowl, not a wimpy-dimpy scoop."

"You're on. I'll even add hot fudge."

"Fine. Be ready to pay up, sistah."

Noelle retrieved the card and held it up to the light. "All right, Mr. Phillip T. Sutton. Here I come."

The phone rang, then rang again. She pulled the phone away from her ear, but Ashley was speaking in her phone to leave a message.

Just as she was anticipating the call to roll over to voicemail, a man's voice boomed over the line.

"This better be good."

The masculine barking tone tuned up the 'A' in her attitude. "Is Mr. Phillips T. Sutton available?" She emphasized the 'T' to highlight the idiotic. Who used their middle name on business cards anymore?

"Who is this?"

A bear coming out of hibernation might have been more pleasant. Noelle nearly hung up on the fraud, but curiosity and Ashley's stare got the better of her.

"Noelle Conroy. I'd like to tell Mr. Phillip T. Sutton playing games isn't honorable. Artists work hard at their craft and spend years studying and practicing and putting their heart and soul into their work. They deserve to be treated with…"

"Respect," Ashley whispered.

"…treated with respect," Noelle finished. Pride for putting this jerk into the trash can where he belonged slipped into place.

"Ethan didn't tell you who I am, did he, Miss Conroy?"

"No." She leaned back in the car seat, and crossed her legs, letting her foot bounce. "He gave me your card."

"Yes, I gave him my personal card. I didn't have any studio cards with me. Usually I let my business managers take care of contacting talent, but when I hear talent, I take an interest."

I bet you do. "So what will your interest cost me?"

"Nothing but your time, Miss Conroy. At professional studios, we pay the artist, not the other way around, and at my studio, we only make stars."

Stars...right? "Like who?"

"Have you heard of Sara Linen, or the band called Mismatched Shoes?"

The cogs churned the pieces of information over and over and over and her chest tightened. A thread of information floated to the surface, and she gasped. "Tell me you're not PT Sutton, the visionary behind crossing over pop and country sounds. The three-time Grammy winner and mixing master."

The other end of the line was silent. She closed her eyes and dropped her forehead to the dashboard. "Mr. Sutton. I'm afraid there's been a misunderstanding."

"I believe you are correct, Miss Conroy. However, if you can continue producing original work like you sang tonight, I see a promising future for you. But Miss Conroy?"

"Yes, sir?" Her voice sounded tiny to her own ears.

"If you work for me, you'll need to put everything you got into every song—leave nothing on the table. Understand?"

"Yes, sir. I understand."

"Good. Then call my manager. He'll send me the audio files, and we can discuss next steps."

Excitement choked off her air.

"Miss Conroy, are you still there?"

"Yes. I'll make the call. First thing in the morning." Since it would take months before an appointment would be available. Studios were booked months in advance, and rarely had any openings.

The phone call ended, and Noelle stared at her phone.

"Well?" Ashley asked.

Noelle sat back in the seat and stared at the garage wall. "Ethan wasn't lying when he said he was connected. I owe you a bunch of ice cream. Though right now I could eat the entire gallon."

"Well, duh. He doesn't strike me as the kind who would lie."

"I'll have to apologize to Ethan." Shame shimmied up her skin. "What will I say?"

Ashley dropped the keys in her purse and grabbed the to-go bag. "Ice cream and fudge?"

"Huh?"

"You need ice cream, hot fudge, and a bubble bath first. The solution to the world's problems will have to wait."

"Does that actually work?"

"No, but while you're indulging in carb heaven, life seems grand until reality sets in.

Besides, why do today what you can put off until tomorrow?"

"You're right. I'll tell Ethan I'm excited about the opportunity and thank him for making the connection first thing in the morning."

"There. Problem solved, and you didn't even need hot fudge."

"Oh, no, you don't. You're not getting out of sharing ice cream."

"Then we better hurry up. Jenna and my Dad are inside. We might be out of luck."

Noelle slid out of the truck and followed Ashley inside.

The house smelled like home.

She set her purse on the counter. In that instant, she figured out what she'd been missing—a sense of home, a place to write songs, play her guitar, but more importantly, waking up beside the person she loved. Ethan instantly came to mind, and she understood why.

She really did love him. Loved him with her whole heart, and she was certain, if she were patient enough, someday he would be able to love her in return.

She had decisions to make to avoid the regret of saying, "if I'd only known today would be the last day, I would have..."

CHAPTER TWENTY-SIX

Noelle sat at the breakfast island in the Bryants' oversized kitchen, thumbing through her phone.

"You're up early." Dale Bryant, Ashley's father, headed straight for the coffee maker to pop in a pod. He inspected her over his shoulder. "Do you want anything? Let's see. We have dark roast, hazelnut, vanilla bean, hot chocolate, and it looks like...apple cider."

"I'm good, thanks. I'm sorry if I woke you. I was trying to be quiet."

"You're good. I can be sound asleep, but

when my brain hears an unusual noise, I wake up. It's my Marine training kicking in."

"Do you miss it, I mean, being in the military?"

"Once in a while. The Corps was family, but I missed Ashley more."

"She's glad you came home."

"No more than I am."

Ashley's dad didn't fit her image of a highly decorated war hero who received important calls from senators and presidents.

If he'd been in uniform, he might have conveyed a different image, but his well-loved jeans and paint-splattered sweatshirt didn't look important or highly decorated. She didn't know him, but he had intelligent eyes, and his casual manner was very soothing. He felt safe, as a father should be. "May I ask you something?"

He hesitated, looked around as if to say, who, me? He settled back against the counter while the tang of coffee filled the kitchen. "Sure."

"It's a rather personal question, and you don't have to answer if you don't want."

"Go on, ask your question, and I'll decide if it's one I can answer."

She picked up an apple and twisted the stem clockwise. "You lost your wife." She cranked the stem again. "Hank over at the gas station lost his wife." She cranked the stem again, and again. "Ethan Brennan lost his wife." She concentrated on forming the right question. "How does a man know when it's time to let go of his wife's memory and move on?"

Dale crossed his arms and assessed her. "That's a tough one."

The apple stem broke from the core, and she set it on the place mat, rolling it back and forth. She almost gave up on waiting for Mr. Bryant to answer her question, then his head tilted to the side.

"I didn't realize I was ready until one day my heart found someone new. You might say Gwen sneaked up on me."

"So you're saying you didn't know you were in love?"

"Guys tend to be a little slow about those kinds of things. There are times we need to be smacked over the head."

With a two-by-four. "How did you know you were ready?"

"To move on?" He slid his mug out of the coffee maker. "I think it's different for each person."

That's no help. Noelle played with the fringe on the place mat. "It's a miracle anyone falls in love."

Dale's chuckle was low and soft. "True." He observed her with a critical eye, although not judgmental. "Ashley most likely will not be up for awhile. Can I give you a lift?"

The purples and pinks of the sunrise were starting to spread over the ridge. "If you wouldn't mind dropping me in town, I'd like to get my car since I'm leaving for LA today. I can always call Ashley from the road to say goodbye."

"You better get started before the traffic

on I-70 gets bad. Do you have gas in your car?"

Her stomach muscles eased. "Full tank."

"Tires and battery checked?"

"Hank checked my car over when I arrived."

"Good." Dale selected a travel mug from one of the many cabinets in the ginormous kitchen and transferred the steaming liquid into the metal container. "Give me a couple of minutes to put on my shoes. I'll meet you in the garage."

She must have been distracted, because it took no time for Dale to drop her off in town, pick up her car and drive to Ethan's cabin. The weird thing was, the house was dark, and his car was missing.

An unsettled need choked off her air. She struggled to breathe as she walked up the front steps. The door was locked. *How odd.* She lifted the flower pot and, just as Ethan told her, the house key was taped to the porch.

After entering, she tripped over a large

object. Ouch, that hurt, she reached for her shin and hall light with opposite hands. Ethan had brought down her luggage and stacked the cases next to the door. The kennel, cooler, a litter box, and a bag of cat food were also there. She picked up the handwritten note that had fallen to the floor.

NOELLE,

I thought you might want to get an early start. Bagged ice is in the freezer. You should find your favorites in the cooler. Have a safe trip. Be well.

Love, Ethan.

LOVE. He wrote love. Did he mean love...like, real love? She felt nauseous. Hearing the commotion, Trapper appeared in the doorway of the kitchen. "Hey, buddy."

With his head down, he walked slowly toward her. Her heart stung. Trapper somehow knew she was leaving. Animals always knew. They could sense it...but should she go? Should she stay? The LA gig wouldn't wait, and who knew how long before she could get booked in the studio? She had to go with LA—that's what she knew for the moment.

She bent to give the dog a good rub. "You're stiff today. I can feel the knots in your legs."

He sat and handed her his paw.

Tears stung the back of her eyes. "I know, buddy. I don't want to go, but I made a promise to my friend." She gently released Trapper's leg.

In the pre-dawn hours, she had lain on the couch and texted her contact information to the number on the back of the card. She received an automated message. Experience had told her "I'll get back to you," could take weeks, or even months. She'd learned not to wait.

The stacked luggage by the door twisted and pulled on her emotions. He loved her, but he'd packed her things. Why?

Ethan must want her to go.

It was obvious...wasn't it?

Otherwise he wouldn't have put her luggage by the door. Or would he?

She scratched under Trapper's chin. "I made a promise to meet Jade in LA, so that's what I'll do." The bold conviction was so thin, it could have disappeared with one swipe of the eraser.

Trapper whined. "Oh, please, please don't do that. You'll break my heart." She walked around the perimeter of the living room, then meandered into the kitchen, touching each surface, reliving each conversation. Her fingers flexed, remembering Ethan. His warmth beneath her hands. The way he made her feel. The curve of his mouth when he smiled.

Her heart ached with a longing so strong she fought to take a breath. She fisted her hands holding back tears.

She wouldn't cry.

Not over a man.

She'd promised herself. Never again.

Cheddar came sauntering toward her.

"There you are." The cat wrapped around her ankles and nudged between her legs. "Hey, fluff." She picked up her fur-baby. "I missed you last night."

Cheddar rubbed his chin against Noelle's face.

"Well, I guess it's time to go." She opened the kennel and placed Cheddar inside. "It's just until we get on the road. Then I'll let you out. Okay?"

Loading her stuff didn't take much time. By now she had the system down. She let Trapper out for a quick break, stalling for time, hoping Ethan would return from wherever he'd gone. She let the minute hand of her watch roll in a circle, even though her heart was telling her time had run out.

Locking the door, she rested her hand on the handle. The wind had chilled the metal, but she would only remember the warmth inside. She pressed her hand against the glass. "Goodbye, Ethan Brennan. I hope you have a good life."

The car keys dangled from her fingers as she walked down the steps.

She didn't look back.

She couldn't.

"Hey, Mom." Noelle called. "I just stopped in to say goodbye."

Maggie shoved a pen behind her ear. "So soon? It's not even a decent hour. You sure you can't stay for breakfast?"

"I need to hit the road, Mom."

Maggie opened her arms, and Noelle walked into the embrace.

"I love you, baby girl."

"Love you too, Mom."

"Let me get your money." Maggie retrieved an envelope from under the cash register drawer.

Noelle shook her head. "Keep it. The couple of hundred dollars I earned from singing at Jack's will get me to LA."

"But, honey, this money is yours."

"We both know it's not. My CD collection and stuffed bears couldn't possibly have been sold for much. I've never asked you for money." Noelle took a deep breath. "I've got a good track record going. If you don't mind, I don't want to break it now. It's a pride thing. You raised me to budget, save, and plan. I'd like to think you taught me well."

"I hope you also learned it's okay to ask for help sometimes."

The soft sentiment coming from her ball-busting mother was too hard to take. She took a step back.

"Did you have your talk with Ethan?"

"I was going to, but he wasn't home, and he's not answering his phone, so I'll have to call later."

"Not home? That's odd."

Ted's face appeared through the grill window. He didn't appear to be his usual peppy self. And he looked sad. "Heard on the radio there's a big accident just outside of town. A head-on collision with a couple of fatalities. One car rolled down into the river. It will take…"

Oh, God, no.

Noelle's heart thrashed against her rib cage.

She ran toward the front door.

Fear blocked Noelle's ears until everything sounded distant, tinny.

She jumped in her car to start the engine. "Please, please, please let him be okay." The old Ford pickup in front of her slowed. "Come on, come *on!* Move, people."

She thumped the palms of her hands against the steering wheel. Her foot pressed the accelerator, then the brake, then the accelerator, getting as close to the truck's bumper as possible. She must get to the accident.

"Move. Move. Move. Come on. Turn at the light."

A held breath whooshed out, and she tapped the brake to put space between the cars in front of her.

"No, no, noooo." The truck continued straight.

Ethan's face the night he appeared at her window came to mind. She didn't realize then how concerned he'd been for her safety.

Her safety.

He did everything he could to make sure she was safe. That's what doctors do. They take care of people. Like he'd taken care of her. Helped her learn what being protected felt like. Shown her sex could be about giving and receiving.

It wasn't sex. He'd made love to her. She was sure of it.

He loved her.

He did.

He showed her in so many different ways. Why hadn't she seen it?

"I've been such an idiot." Her knee bounced a mile a minute with her foot on the brake. Cheddar protested the jerky stop-and-go. "I know. You're okay." *Please let Ethan be okay.*

Painful inch by painful inch, she crept toward the red and blue flashing lights.

"Please let him be okay."

Several hundred yards from the accident, she couldn't wait. She pulled to the side of the road, jumped out of the car, closed it to keep Cheddar warm, and ran.

Emergency crew vehicles were scattered everywhere. The accident ahead was blocked from view by fire trucks and a sheriff's department SUV. Just as she got close enough to see, an ambulance blared, and pulled onto the highway.

"Wait. Wait."

She waved frantically at the emergency vehicle.

An arm wrapped around her waist. Tears blurred vision. She fought to get free.

"Noelle. Easy. It's me."

The familiar voice broke through her panic.

"Ethan?" She jumped, and strong arms caught her. "Thank God you're safe."

She tightened her arms around his

shoulders. *Feeling him against her allowed her to breathe again.* She took a deep, savoring breath, filling her lungs with his earthy scent. After the adrenaline stopped hammering through her veins, she slowly opened her eyes to find several deputies and volunteer emergency responders standing in a circle around them.

"Hey." She waved as the heat of embarrassment brushed up her cheeks.

Jack stepped forward. "Well, boys, what do you think? I'm not sure the jaws-of-life will be able to extract this woman from that man. She seems pretty stuck."

Ernie adjusted his campaign hat. "I agree, sir. She's jammed in there pretty tight."

Ethan's arms tightened around Noelle, then set her on the ground. "Don't you gentlemen have traffic to direct, or a couple of cars to get hauled out of here?" He glared at Jack. "My job here is done. The emergency room staff are waiting and can handle things once the ambulance arrives."

Ethan was protecting her again.

Soft chuckles faded away as Ethan guided her around to the other side of the fire truck, out of sight.

"I thought you were leaving."

"I was, but…"

His hand pressed into her back. "…but?"

"I met this nice guy. He's smart, and handsome, and he's not a jerk."

He leaned in, a smile recreating those facial curves she'd come to adore. "Is this guy someone I know?"

Before she could answer, her phone rang. About to hit ignore, she hesitated, then looked at Ethan.

"I think it's your friend's manager." She bit her lip, unsure whether to talk to him, or answer her phone. "I should have trusted you more. I'm—"

"We'll talk about that later. Answer the call."

"Hello?"

"Is this Noelle Conroy?" A distracted male asked.

"Yes." She held her breath.

"My name is Kurt Morgan." His voice became clearer, his attention more engaged. "I just talked to Phil Sutton. He'd like to schedule you for studio time." Kurt paused. "I've rearranged my calendar. It looks like I now have an opening on Tuesday from one to four at our studio in Aspen. Does the time work for you?"

Tuesday? As in this Tuesday?

She looked at Ethan, a thrilled tsunami swelling and swamping her entire system. "Yes. Yes, the time works." *I'll make it work.*

"Good. Make sure to bring your music. Phil wants me to look over the songs you've written. Oh, and do you mind if a couple of studio musicians sit in? I'd like to get their opinion of the arrangements."

"No, I don't mind." *In fact I'm so excited I'm about to pee my pants.*

"Good. I'll see you Tuesday."

"Tuesday." She breathed the word as if it had wings.

Ethan looked at her and waited while she gathered her thoughts. "That was the manager from a studio in Aspen. He wants to look over my portfolio of music."

"I wondered if you had called." His face lit up like a neon sign.

"I did call." She laid a hand on his chest. "I don't know how to thank you."

"You were the one who did the hard work."

"And just think. He liked our song."

Ethan shook his head. "You mean your song. The one where you were telling me goodbye." Ethan leaned down to eye level. "It wasn't until after I got home that I figured out you were saying goodbye. That's why you got so upset after you finished the song. You were saying goodbye to me."

She bit her lip. *So that's why you put my things by the door.* "I kept thinking about how I would feel if suddenly you were gone. What I would say? What I would do? And there it was. The song practically wrote itself."

"If I'm not mistaken, there's a line in there...I'd tell her I loved her."

"Him. I'd tell him I loved him."

Ethan's eyes glazed over, and he looked like a man who'd been clubbed over the head. Dale was right. Men were a bit slow.

Urgent lips captured her mouth. She squeaked with surprise, then in a microsecond settled in to enjoy the bliss. His kiss was insistent. Demanding. He tongued and nibbled her lower lip until one of the guys on the crew whistled. She bowed her head, and let her forehead rest on his chest.

"Noelle, I love you."

Her heart stopped for just a second before the staccato beat started again, this time at a steady pace.

"Ethan—"

"But I want you to follow your dreams. You need to sing and write songs. I wouldn't want you to have any regrets. If you decide you need to go to LA, then you need to go."

"What if LA isn't my dream? I have a

pretty good deal here, and I think Jade will understand. Phil Sutton has been known to make things happen. Plus, you aren't in LA."

He kissed her forehead, the corner of her eye, her nose, then drew back. "Why don't we go back to my place? We can talk there."

"But I need to find a place to stay and a job and..." He tugged on her arm to get her attention.

"Stay with me." The words weren't demanding or controlling, and he wasn't talking about spending the next few days with him. His eyes spoke of forever—as in 'til death do us part.

"I'll stay with you on one condition."

He pulled back to look into her eyes. "I've always found the word *condition* rather unsettling."

She smiled. "You know conditions won't kill you. Right?"

His mouth twitched with a touch of humor. "What is your condition?"

"I need you to hear me. When I tell you I

love you, I'm not just telling you I love the brilliant doctor or the guy who checks on his patients, I'm telling you I love the guy who goes out of his way to fix me a birthday dinner, and shares his bathroom, and hangs Christmas ornaments just to please a girl. I love you, Ethan. Just you. If I keep telling you that every day, maybe, just maybe, you can find a way to let me in—maybe just a little."

Ethan kissed her nose, then pressed his forehead against hers. "As long as you promise me you'll nag me about eating right and exercising, and be patient when I don't get things just right, then I'll promise I'll try."

"Deal!" Her heart jumped and leapt, then did a pom-pom shuffle. "Okay. Now we have that settled." She flung her arms in the air, and he caught her in a hug.

She eventually leaned back. "What's next?"

"We talk. We laugh. We live a good life."

"Are you sure?" She gave him a stern eye.

"In the past few days, you've taught me a thing or two."

"Like how to smile?"

"And, more." He nipped at her chin before setting her on the ground. "My mother and Tom gave me insights into what it's like to live life wishing circumstances were different. I want to get married again."

"You do?" Shock waves reverberated through her system.

"Yep, and I want to have kids, plant a vegetable garden, and cook you dinners. And no more protein shakes...well, maybe a few. I can't wait for you to write a lullaby for our first child. You do want kids, right?"

She wanted to wipe the worry off his face. "I've always wanted to have a little girl, but I'd take a houseful of boys, as long as you're their father."

"Thanks to you," He stroked her cheek. "I'm not afraid of being a father anymore."

"Afraid? What were you afraid of?"

"Of never being enough. Never being able to protect the ones I love. Then you showed up, and you challenged my sanitized life by plowing into a snowbank, always losing your keys, and dribbling flour everywhere when you bake. You've changed my life. You made me want to be in love again. Believe that I can be enough for the person I love."

She wrapped her arms around his waist. "You're the kindest and most generous man I've ever met. It would be a waste if you never loved again. You have so much to give."

"And I want to give my love to you."

"Stop. You're making me cry." She reached for him again, her heart filled to overflowing.

One of the firefighters walked around to the side of the truck. "Don't mean to interrupt, but we got another call."

Ethan stiffened. "Do you need me on this one?"

"It's Lizzy Cranston again. She said there's an elk stuck in her backyard."

"I'll let you deal with Mrs. Cranston this time. I'm sure she'll call again next week."

"You sure you don't want to take this one?" The volunteer firefighter winked, then lifted into the passenger seat. "Just kidding. Thanks, Doc. Appreciate your help."

Ethan wrapped an arm around her waist and pulled her back a safe distance as the truck drove away. "Ready to go home?"

She touched his cheek. "Before we go, we need to talk about Brigitte and Callie. They were special people in your life. I hope you know it's okay to still love them. I will never take their place in your heart, nor do I want to. They helped shape the man you are today."

"You're right. Part of me will always miss them, but you've taught me there is more than enough room for others. Loving you will be different, but no less special. I'll protect you, support you, help you make your dreams come true."

She sucked in a breath. "What about your dreams? You were going to save the world."

"I realized a long time ago, I never wanted to save the world. Tom was right. I just wanted to heal one person at a time."

"Well, Doc, it seems we have a plan."

He kissed her forehead, and then walked her to her car. "One day at a time?"

"Definitely. My plans never seem to work the way I expect them to, anyway."

He walked along several steps in silence, his feet kicking at the gravel on the side of the road.

Ethan reached to open her car door, but she put a hand on his. "Did I say something wrong?"

He squinted into the sunlight, then studied her face. "I'd better tell you now."

Trepidation jammed in her throat, and she swallowed hard. "Tell me what? This sounds serious."

"I think Tom's my dad."

Without thinking her hand swung, and she swatted at his arm. "Is that all? You scared the heck out of me."

"Is that all?" He choked.

"You two look alike. Act alike. Think alike. It's so obvious you're related. If he is your dad, it makes sense. At least you have a father...or two." She lifted up on her toes to kiss his cheek and whisper in his ear. "This is a small town, remember? No one gets to keep secrets."

"Then we had better plan a wedding quickly, before the town plans one for us."

She sputtered. "How about an engagement party? Then we can plan a wedding." She kissed his cheek again, then slid behind the wheel. "Will Cheddar and Trapper get to be in the wedding?"

"You can have any type of wedding you want, as long as you're mine and happy."

He leaned in through the window and captured her mouth, taking his time. "I love you, Noelle Conroy," he said against her mouth.

She savored the slow, gentle warmth. "I love you, too, Ethan Brennan." A thought crossed her mind and her core heated. "Let's go home. I've got an itch I need you to examine."

"I hope you didn't get into the poison oak behind the house. Let me see."

She started the engine. "I guess no one ever taught you the right way to play doctor,

Doctor." She giggled at his heated expression. "See you at home."

She adored the look on the face she once thought was devoid of expression.

Home. She pointed the car toward Elkridge.

The place where she grew up.

The place she had rediscovered.

The place where Ethan and love lived.

I'm so glad you could join Noelle and Ethan on their journey to their happily ever after.

Those of you who have read my books or been part of my newsletter have heard my explanation for why Authors never see their Star Ratings requested by Amazon, so thank you for allowing me to share the information once again.

When Amazon asks a reader to "Rate this

book" on their Kindle, Amazon is the only one to see these ratings.

I'm left clueless about how you feel about this book. Your input matters.

Book reviews help me decide what kind of books I write. Plus, the more people who leave a review, the more likely Amazon is to move a book up in the rankings? Written reviews help other readers find and love a series.

Please continue to rate the book on your Kindle or reader as this helps Amazon, but take an extra moment to pop over to the review section and leave a few words!

Seriously, a few words like, "great story," is enough.

If you have not read my Elkridge Series or the Lonely Ridge Collection, and have no idea why authors keep asking you as a reader to take a few minutes to leave even a couple of word reviews, here's the break down of how reviews work in this crazy business.

Reviews (not ratings) help authors qualify for advertising opportunities. Without triple digit reviews, an author may miss out on these valuable opportunities. And with only a "star rating" the author has little chance of participating in specific promotions, which means authors continue to struggle, and many talented writers give up writing altogether.

Readers aren't the only ones who use reviews to help make purchasing decisions. Producers and directors use your reviews when looking for new projects.

This is why I'm asking for your help.

A few kind words make such a massive difference to me. Your words give me the encouragement I need to continue writing because honestly, I write my books for you, and I'd like to keep delivering the types of stories you want to read.

And, yes, every book in a series needs reviews, not just the first book. Even if a book has been out for awhile, a fresh review can breathe new life into a book.

So, please take a few minutes to leave a short review. Even a couple of words will brighten my day.

Lastly. Thank you for reading this book. I hope to see you again soon. Cheers!

I wish you all the best the day offers, and I hope you enjoy reading the next book in the Elkridge Series.

DEDICATION

*When the world condemns, there is nothing more
soothing than a mother's love.
Thanks mom, for being my shelter from the storm.*

AUTHOR NOTES

Dear Reader,

When I retired from pursuing my sport, I returned home to Denver. However, my future plans were already set. Two weeks later, I packed up again and headed off to finish my education.

However during those two weeks at home, I met an interesting man line-dancing at a local club. He was intelligent, funny, and studying to be a physician. But when it came time to leave, I didn't think twice. I was young and determined and focused on executing my pre-designed plan.

This book is about revisiting the questions: What if I had fallen in love? What if he had asked me to stay?

Looking back, I'm happy I stuck with my plan. If I had stayed, I wouldn't be married to the wonderful man in my life today.

Do you have a "what if" in your life? I'd love to hear your story.

Wishing you all the best life has to offer.

~Lyz

More Books By
Lyz Kelley

SILVER FOX RESORT
SILVER SPOON
SILVER DOLLAR
SILVER BELLS

SECRETS
BILLIONAIRE'S SECRET
DOCTOR'S SECRET

THE ELKRIDGE SERIES
BLINDED
ABANDONED
ORPHANED
RESCUED
UNMISTAKEN
ATONEMENT
BITTERSWEET

THANK YOU FOR READING:
UNMISTAKEN

Award-winning author Lyz Kelley mixes a little bit of heart, healing, humanity, happiness, honor, hope, and honor in all her books that are written especially for you.

She's is a total disaster in the kitchen, a compulsive neat freak, a tea snob, and adores writing about and falling in love with everyday heroes.

Please also consider leaving a review on Amazon Goodreads and/or BookBub. Reviews help readers find new books to read, and authors find their footing.

You can also find Lyz on Facebook and Instagram for news, contests, giveaways, and more exciting stuff!

COPYRIGHT

 Belvitri
Services

www.ingramcontent.com/pod-product-compliance
Lightning Source LLC
Chambersburg PA
CBHW030543020726
47494CB00005B/1458